EAST OF
LINCOLN

D1714551

Also by

Harlin Hailey

*The Downsizing
of Hudson Foster*

EAST OF LINCOLN

A NOVEL

HARLIN HAILEY

To My Mother

ONE HAS TO believe in what one is doing, one has to commit oneself inwardly, in order to do painting. Once obsessed, one ultimately carries it to the point of believing that one might change human beings through painting. But if one lacks passionate commitment, there is nothing left to do. Then it is best to leave it alone. For basically painting is total idiocy.

—GERHARD RICHTER

ONCE, IF MY memory serves me well, my life was a banquet where every heart revealed itself, where every wine flowed.

—ARTHUR RIMBAUD, *A SEASON IN HELL*

EAST OF
LINCOLN

The Late Boomers

IT WAS BALES who came up with the plan.

We'd stage the Artist's death, watch his paintings soar in value, then sell at the peak. It was brilliant, actually. The Artist would get famous, go viral, and we'd all get a cut. Except for the Artist, of course. Or so they'd all think.

But it didn't work out that way. We never executed the plan, but I know now it seeded something nasty inside that troubled mind of Bales's. And even to this day, I'm still trying to work through it all. Let alone comprehend it. It's not easy writing about the death of a loved one. But you do the best you can.

So forgive me, I'm still raw.

My real name is Richard Jenkins. But you won't hear it much in this tale. Most of the time they call me Clean. My father is a retired high school principal, my mother a State Farm agent. I grew up in Van Nuys, California, in a nice ranch house in a leafy suburb, and graduated from San Diego State University with a business degree that time rendered moot. Along with silly dreams, girls I've loved before, and old tarnished trophies. I'm fifty-three years old now, and I was once a "successful" real estate agent in the San Fernando Valley.

Now I'm not.

And that's all you need to know about me. Because for all intents and purposes, I'm invisible.

So what do you do when you find yourself on the wrong side of history for the first time in your life? How do you survive? Well, you make decisions. Moral decisions. And then you live with the consequences. That's what you do. That's all you can do. Because for so many years, you had it so good. So good you slept through wars, had sex without condoms, raped the land, and hogged the dream. And then suddenly—*bang!*—you find yourself at odds with the day at hand. What used to work just doesn't anymore. So you take a hard look at yourself in the mirror and ask that mediocre reflection, *Who the fuck am I? Where do I go from here?* And then you realize who you are, where you came from.

We were the late boomers, born between 1956 and 1965: three-channel kids, told what to watch, how to live, and what to think.

We drank the Jim Jones punch. Mastered the fine art of consumption. And now America has left us for dead, our distended bellies rotting on the side of the road, forever jonesing.

We were going to film the Artist's death on my iPhone. Dark and grainy, like that Pollock documentary. Have him rant into the camera about how his life had become unmanageable and that the best thing to do would be to kill himself. I suggested a handgun. The Artist had intimated a fondness for pills. But it was Bales who brought the plan down to its base. Suicide was too conventional, he said, too clichéd, and what the public needed was a murder. That's when he pulled the samurai sword off the mantelpiece. He unsheathed it from the red leather scabbard, dropped down on one knee, and studied its polished blade by the soft glow of firelight. The Artist thought he was joking, but I knew he was serious.

The sad thing was, I didn't do a damn thing about it.

I don't blame myself for what happened to the Artist on the night of December 21, but it still haunts me. These days, I blame the Great Recession. That horrible time of crippling stagnation that left us feeling weightless and hollowed out. I mean, what can I say? It stole our lives, then broke our hearts.

All you had to do was look around. The sign-posts of our demise were plain as day. The Artist had become increasingly distant, withdrawn. Some said emotionally unhinged. And then there was Bales, dredging the abyss of cheap alcohol and drugs, an entitled punk looking to save his own ass. He didn't know it then, but he was mining for table scraps from a bygone era—a fruit fly darting from one scheme to another. And me, nothing more than a bald, fragile shell of my former self, philosophically at odds with the decline of the empire. *Give me liberty or give me death!*

Those were just words now.

I guarantee you this: you take away a man's rice bowl and you'll watch him turn into a savage. Watch him descend into hell.

The story I'm going to tell you is the same story I told the cops. I wasn't there the night of the murder. But I wish I had been. I would've killed the fuck. That's the cold sound truth. Maybe I should have seen it coming, but it wouldn't have mattered anyway. There wasn't a damn thing I could have done about it. End-of-the-world forces were working beyond my control—beyond everyone's control.

So what follows here is only a fragmented recollection of my own personal fog of war, a hazy recounting of unaccommodated men gone mad. It is often harsh, sometimes brutal, but always honest.

My father once said, "Everybody's got a story in Los Angeles."

This is mine.

Bales Meets
Mr. Clean

THE NIGHT I met Bales, he was screaming at his wife in the courtyard about the sorry state of their financial affairs. The first thing I noticed about him was his sharp, mean nose. I remember the evening clearly because I was watching the third presidential debate with the Artist, the famous "horses and bayonets" beatdown. The night Obama sank Romney's battleship and cruised into history. It was Monday, October 22, 2012. The debate had just wrapped when the shouting started next door.

"Who the hell is that?" I said.

"It's my neighbor," said the Artist. "He's getting a divorce."

We leaned in, listening through the thin apartment walls: two voyeurs of misery.

He: You're dead to me! Don't ever talk to me again, you whore!

She: Why is it me? Why is it always me? Look at yourself! Drunk and broke. Drunk and broke.

He: Get out! Get the fuck out, you bitch!

There was a loud crash, and something thumped against the wall. I cringed and looked at the Artist. He shrugged his shoulders. We heard a door open and then slam shut, voices spilling outside.

The Artist got up off the couch and peeked through the miniblinds. He motioned me over. I looked through the large picture window and watched an all-too-familiar scene go down in the grassy courtyard. A husband and wife fighting over money. Divorce, American style.

He: You know I'm outta work. I don't have that kind of cash.

She: No shit. Drinking thirty beers a day tends to drain a bank account.

He: That's not fair. I've given you everything you've ever wanted. And you're still not happy!

"All hands on deck," I said, peering out through the blinds. "He looks like a Nantucket Prep. Blue button-down. Red club pants. Those ridiculous Top-Siders."

"Don't let the plaid boat shoes fool you," the Artist said. "He was an all-city QB for Cate."

"Remotely interesting. How old is he?"

"He said he was fifty-one."

I scratched my chin. "Huh. Looks older with that gray hair. That gaunt jaw."

"He's in top shape, though," said the Artist. "I mean, look at him. Tall, lean, and cut. The cold stare of a Burmese python. I wouldn't want to mess with the guy. He said he's competing in the Cross-Fit Games."

"At fifty-one?" I said. "Yeah, right. And I'm starting for the Chargers on Sunday. How long have you known him?"

"He moved in four months ago. But we just started hanging out. His name's Bales. John Bales. He calls me A instead of the Artist."

"How sweet," I said. "You're on nickname terms."

The shouting match continued in the dimly lit courtyard. Two humans circling each other like cage fighters under a sliced moon.

She: Get your shit together. Be a fucking man!

He: Bye. I'm leaving you now. Bye.

She: That's it. Run away, little man. Just like you always do.

It was at that moment that a Talking Heads song swam into my brain. "Once in a Lifetime." A distressed David Byrne wailing about the trappings of modern life. Staring out at the silver-haired man being flogged and stripped of his dignity, his dark raccoon eyes filled with resignation and futility, I sensed that he too was hearing the same song inside his head.

I felt sorry for the guy. Even if he was the loser that she proclaimed him to be, I'd lived long enough to know that it took two to tango. His wife, bless her heart, could have starred in any number of reality shows, her face stretched and pulled into something that might sneak up on you in the dark. A skinny, middle-aged, frozen-faced creature with short, dry hair the color of Nebraska straw. I'd often wondered what these plastic surgery mavens saw in the mirror that I didn't. Whatever it was, it cost money, and lots of it. And it was clear that she was taking him for all he had.

"Shit," the Artist said. "He's coming over. Quick."

I glanced out into the night and saw the guy race-walking toward the Artist's apartment, head down, arms swinging like pendulums.

We dropped out of sight and dove for the sofa.

The door banged open and Bales entered like a bull. "My daughter wants an Icelandic pony for Christmas," he said. "*An Icelandic pony.*" He threw his arms up. "Un-fucking-believable!"

He ranted for another full minute before he noticed me.

"Who the fuck's this?"

"This is Richard," the Artist said. "A buddy of mine from work."

"Richard," he said, rolling the *R* like he was revving an engine. "What are you, a fuckin' fighter pilot?"

He pointed at my bald head.

"Believe me," I said, "a naked scalp wouldn't be my first choice."

"No, no. You're rockin' the shaved look. I get that. But from now on, your nickname is Mr. Clean. Not Laurence Fishburne Clean, but Mr. Clean. You know, the bald guy that cleans things."

I slumped back on the couch. "Whatever makes you happy," I said. "You seem to be the fraternity president. The big man on campus."

He laughed a low, savage laugh. "I'll call you Norwood if you like," he said. "Or how about Male Pattern Baldness? Or just MPB for short. How's that grab ya? Hey, MBP, what's happenin'? Need a lift over to your Bosley appointment?"

I knew he was having a go at my expense, but my skin was bunker-thick by now. One of the many perks of living in L.A.

"Mr. Clean is fine," I said. "And you? What do I call you?"

He raised a hand. "That's a great question, Clean. And one that I mulled over in this large brain of mine for more than a few nights." He paced the living room, tapping his temple with a slim forefinger. "I've narrowed it down to three options."

"Drumroll, please."

He shot me a cold stare, then punched his words. "*Stop Me Before I Fuck Up Again, Fuckface*, or just plain ol' *Fucko*."

The Artist laughed, but the dude was serious.

"So which one did you choose?" I said.

Bales rested his forehead against the front door. "You can now address me as Fucko. Just plain ol' Fucko."

"Is that *Just* Fucko?" I said. "Or *Plain Ol'* Fucko?"

He advanced with clenched fists. "It's Fucko," he said. "Just Fucko. What part of that don't you understand, bald man?"

The sound of his voice felt like a hot knife at my throat.

"Okay," I said, backing off. "Life's about choice. Flavors. It's your call."

He took a deep breath, then ran a furious hand through his spiky gray hair. "Until I produce an income again...*I'm Fucko.* That's because I'm a *loooser* who can't buy his daughter a *fucking Icelandic pony!*"

Bales kicked over a zebra-skin chair, jarring a nearby painting. "I got nothing! Fucking nothing!"

"Easy," the Artist said, rising from the couch. "That's a work in progress."

The Artist, clearly rattled, picked the canvas up off the floor and carefully leaned it against the wall.

"Sorry, A," Bales said, massaging the back of his neck.

The Artist tried to lighten the mood. "Hey," he said, grinning, "did you watch the debate? Obama made Romney look like a jackass when he started talking shit about the Navy."

"No," Bales said softly. "I didn't see it."

"You missed it. Obama spanked him. Had Romney backpedaling like a little bitch. Here, watch this. It's epic."

I watched Bales roll his eyes and throw his head back in exasperation, as if nothing could be more painful at the moment. The Artist rewound the DVR and played a clip from the debate. Obama was on-screen, chopping the air with his right hand, armed with a quiver of barbs. "*We also have fewer horses and bayonets, because the nature of our military has changed. We have these things called aircraft carriers, where planes land on them. We have these ships that go underwater, nuclear submarines. And so the question is not a game of Battleship, where we are counting ships…*"

The Artist laughed and froze the screen. "It was great, man. Verbal judo. One zinger after another."

"Congratulations," Bales said. "I hope he wins the election."

There was a fatalistic air about him, I thought, the stench of baronial rot. Somewhere along the way he'd given up, or someone had beaten the up out of him. You could see that he didn't give a damn. And it was clear the White House would be of no help.

Bales managed a strained smile. "Look…I gotta go."

He turned to me with an underlying sense of sadness, head down, eyes locked on the floor. "Sorry for the drama, man. The name's Bales. John Bales. Nice to meet you, Clean."

"Yeah, you too," I said.

We fist-bumped in the glimmering light of the TV, and then he was gone.

And I remember thinking that night he was just like Hurricane Sandy. Blowing in with no rhyme or reason, and no clue about the destruction that lay ahead.

The Artist of
Santa Monica

THE ARTIST'S REAL name was Jimmy Miller. He lived in Santa Monica on Ninth Street, south of Wilshire, in a one-bedroom apartment. It was just like all the other low-rent structures on the Westside. Tired and run-down, several years of deferred maintenance sagging its bones. The two-story, fifteen-unit U-shaped building, typical of Southern California, was a stucco shitbox with a smooth facade of institutional beige. I should know, I lived in one across town. Beach-weathered front doors opened out to a small grassy courtyard that offered just enough space to trick its inhabitants into thinking they were living the high life in vintage luxury. This was common in these parts.

Fooling yourself is an L.A. pastime.

Nothing much happened in the courtyard except for the occasional semi-hostile neighborly exchange—who parked in whose spot, and who was over-the-top loud last night. Sound was of the utmost importance because the walls were so thin. You knew every neighbor by the shows they watched, the music they listened to, the company they kept, and what they said on the phone.

Common courtesy walked a thin line.

The name of this rathole was the Wilshire Arms Apartments. It said so in olive-green script right above the stucco entrance—a gap between two palms. Once a proud testament to boosterism, the featureless building now rotted under the pressure of a bleached-out subtropical sun.

If the wrecking ball didn't find its way here soon, most of the people would die here. It was what they wanted anyway. Most lived in constant fear that the building would be sold out from under them—torn down to erect playgrounds for the rich—and they would lose their treasured rent-controlled units. Which was a valid concern. The one-bedrooms now fetched close to three thousand dollars a month on the open market. Most of the residents were middle-aged and low-income, with nowhere else to go.

And they were all acutely aware that once you lost your apartment, you lost your community. No one likes change, *but*…it was in the atmosphere. And in these troubled times, if you weren't moving forward, you were just hanging on.

A new fish restaurant had opened next door, and depending on when you arrived, you could smell the pungent catch of the day assaulting the stale courtyard air. We used to joke about what dish we were going to eat that night. I would start with the clam chowder and crackers, and finish with the albacore tuna melt. The Artist, oysters on the half shell, followed by the swordfish sliders. But it was only a fantasy. Neither of us had much money. It never failed to make us laugh, though. And a laugh was something we desperately needed at the time.

I'd met the Artist fifteen years earlier at a ranch house in Westwood. I'd had the real estate listing and he was a painter with the house-staging crew. We were in the kitchen one day when the hardballing owner came in and shouted, "Who the fuck's the brilliant artist that painted the foyer shit brown?" There was dead silence for a moment, and then the Artist stood up and stepped forward, legs shaking. The Mexican workers held their breaths.

"I am the artist," he'd said.

And he'd said it like he was standing up there in front of the great and powerful Oz. Legs quaking, body shivering, and I remember saying to myself, *Jesus Christ, the guy needs help.*

So I helped him.

"I'll fix it this afternoon," I'd said. "My bad."

"See that you do," the owner had said. "Goddamn realtors. Earn your fucking pay."

The Artist never got used to the ugly L.A. attitude or the arrogant my-shit-don't-stink crowd. He still clung to his refined, well-mannered upbringing like a Southern gentleman clutching a shotgun.

"Thanks, dude," he'd said.

"Don't sweat it. The guy's an asshole."

We became good friends after that. I'd often call him up and tease him. "Is this the Artist formerly known as Shit Brown?" We'd both laugh. But after a while the joke ran its course, and I took to calling him the Artist all the time. Everyone else did, too. Like most artists, he was passionate but gentle. Born in Natchez, Mississippi, from hearty working-class stock, he possessed a soft, smooth Southern drawl that women wanted to swallow and men wanted to trust. He said his lazy delivery came from many warm summer days of playing on the banks of the Mississippi River.

32

He dropped out of college and moved to L.A. in '82, headed west to pursue his dream of becoming a contemporary painter. It was the same year I graduated from State. For a while he'd been a legend in the emerging downtown arts scene, but eventually he tired of the posers and pop painters and moved to Venice Beach (when it was still cool). He was mentored for a spell by Billy Al Bengston, met his heroes Ed Moses and Laddie John Dill, then rented his own studio on Fourth Street in Santa Monica— when such things were still affordable. For a few years he supported his work by painting buildings and house interiors, and later on made big money staging mansions for Hollywood stars. But then, just like everything else during the Great Recession, it all dried up. People no longer needed his services, and nobody was buying his paintings. He'd lost his studio and was now painting in the alley behind his building.

That's where I found him on the evening after the debate, bent over a canvas like Jackson Pollock, paintbrush in hand.

"What's up?" he said, glancing sideways at my approach.

He was a midsized man, slender and tan, with a signature blond flattop. He wore a white V-neck

T-shirt, paint-splattered Levi's, and a worn-out pair of black rubber flip-flops. Though he was approaching fifty, he looked ten years younger.

The last beach boy.

"Just checkin' in, man," I said. "What's up with you? You seem far away. Still stinging from the Cardinals loss?"

He shrugged. I could tell that something was wrong.

"You know what?" he said. "I'm broke, man. I'm in deep, deep, deep trouble. And I'm scared to death. I'm short rent—that's it. I'm homeless."

"You'll sell something soon," I said.

The Artist sighed. "Have you ever just kept waiting for something that never came?"

"Yeah, and so has everyone else in town. It's slow for everybody."

He shook his head. "Nobody's buying anything. They'll let their insurance lapse, they'll screw over the painter, but damn if they won't spend three hundred dollars on a sushi dinner. It's insane."

I stood silent in the gloaming.

"It's these rich people," he said. "Waiting for the election. Waiting for the fiscal cliff. Waiting for the world to end. It's driving me nuts."

"I know," I said. "They're gutting the middle class. Me included."

"Look, I'm sorry," he said. "I don't want to bore you with my problems. It's just these last few years, I've been living like a dog. I don't know how much longer I can take it."

The economic times had broken us down. And some of us had been dancing on the edge for so long, we were approaching a breaking point.

"I understand," I said.

He pointed across the street to a building on Wilshire Boulevard.

"You see that flower shop?"

"Yeah."

"Ten years ago I did a job for the owner and he paid me twenty grand. And at that time it was a bargain. Well, you know what? The owner's son calls me yesterday and says he wants to repaint the inside."

"That sounds promising."

"That's what I thought. But immediately he leads with 'we don't have much money' and says the budget is fifteen hundred dollars." He looked at me in disbelief. "*Fifteen hundred dollars?* That won't even cover the cost of materials. I had to turn it down. I walked."

"And then *he* goes out for sushi?"

The Artist smiled. "Yes! That dick."

I pointed down at the painting on the ground, dominated by an autumnal-red Ferris wheel, striking in its refusal to yield. "Is that from the Santa Monica Pier?"

"Yeah," he said. "The amusement park."

"Very cool. The red pops. Almost like it's breathing. And I love the stick people on the roller coaster. Hands up, screaming."

A homeless old black man pushing a shopping cart wheeled up. He wore a floral shower curtain like a toga.

"Hey, Willie," the Artist said. "Looking good in embossed fabric."

"My man," Willie said. He shook hands street style with the Artist. "If it ain't the alley master. Van Gogh behind the Dumpster." He looked down at the bold painting, contemplating the riot of color before him. "Whoa! That's some explosive shit. Like somebody dropped a crack pipe. That's beautiful, man."

"Thanks," the Artist said. "Hey, Willie, did you see Obama last night? He was on fire."

"I sure did," Willie said. "Watched it at the VA. He's gonna be in town tomorrow, you know. Gotta defend them accusations from that Trump fellow."

"Yeah, I heard. Gonna be on *The Tonight Show*."

"Uh-huh. I'll be watching." Willie adjusted the blue plastic tarp on his shopping cart, securing his belongings, all the belongings he had on earth. He said, "But right now I gotta bounce. Brother got work to do. You take care of yourself."

"Yeah, you too," said the Artist.

Willie rolled through the alley, checking the trash cans for golden nuggets. Something we were all doing at the time, scrounging for the almighty, elusive buck.

"Hey, man," I said. "How's your neighbor, Bales? I mean that dude was seriously close to imploding last night. I thought his neck muscles were going to snap."

The Artist managed a laugh. "He kept insisting I call him Fucko, but I refused. He's a fascinating guy. Really smart. And I guess he used to be rich." He paused. "I heard him say on the phone he didn't know how much longer he could keep slumming it here. Saying anything east of Lincoln is the ghetto."

My eyes panned the Artist's shabby apartment building, the cockroach cluster at the base of the stairs. "AWOL," I said. "Always west of Lincoln."

Lincoln Boulevard, I thought. The main vein between Santa Monica and LAX. "Cash for Gold" to the east, ocean views to the west. Back in the day, the mean street had represented nothing more than a parking lot of metal gumbo, an endless slog through mind-numbing beach traffic. But it was more than just a clogged artery now. To some it was a state of mind, an acronym, their Alamo. The dividing line between the rich and the rest of us.

AWOL. *Always west of Lincoln.*

"Yeah, that's the vibe I got," the Artist said. "You know what he told me once?"

"What?"

"He said he used to work for one of the big tech companies, making over eight hundred grand a year."

"Geez," I said. "That's serious coin. What happened?"

The Artist shook his head, looking grim.

"He got fired."

"Huh. Did he say why?"

"He told me not to tell anyone."

"Sure he did."

The Artist grabbed a can of paint from the garage. He gave me a look. "You gotta promise me, dude."

People told the Artist things in the alley they wouldn't tell family. He was just that guy.

"Like I'm gonna blog it on the blog I don't fucking have," I said. "Seriously, who am I going to tell?"

The Artist swiveled his head, inspecting the alley, then whispered, "He said he got fired for *sexual assault*. Kind of hinted at *rape*."

I thought for a moment, stood there with my arms crossed under a blazing sunset. "Wow. Kinda makes sense, though," I said. "I mean, the way he went off last night. The dude's aggressive. Clear anger-management issues."

"He said he didn't do it. Said he got railroaded by some new hire."

"Maybe so. But he's definitely got that *bang the secretary* look. Was he married at the time?"

The Artist wiped his hands on the front of his jeans. "I don't know."

"Did he give you any details?"

"He didn't volunteer any, and I didn't ask."

"No, I guess you wouldn't have. The bigger question is, do you believe him?"

The Artist looked away, weighing the gravity of the question. "Yeah. We had a heart-to-heart. I've got no reason not to."

I took off my shades in the low October sun. "Well, one thing we know for sure. He's a pretty jumpy guy."

"You'd be too if you'd lost it all. He said he'll never get another job like that again."

"I believe that," I said. "Times are tough. We all have to reinvent ourselves now."

I stared off into the California twilight, hands in my pockets. Palm trees clicking in the wind.

"Hey," the Artist said, "why don't you meet us for happy hour? He wants to buy me a beer at Barney's. I think he feels bad about last night."

"You scared he'll go off again?"

The Artist shrugged. "Maybe."

"What the hell," I said. "I'll be your bodyguard. Fuck it."

· · · · · · · · · · · · · · · · · ·

I MET BALES and the Artist at Barney's Beanery on the Third Street Promenade. They were sitting at the bar watching the Lakers game on the big screen. The Artist had changed into a fresh white T-shirt and a clean pair of 501s, a Cardinals baseball hat cocked atop his head. Bales looked breezy in a yellow Lacoste polo and a slim pair of chinos, like he'd just played eighteen at Wilshire.

"Mr. Clean, so good of you to join us," Bales said, looking up from his barstool. "Whoa, you're fucking tall. I didn't notice last night."

"Six-four," I said. "And that's because I was sitting last night."

Bales turned to the Artist. "Jesus, A. Look at this guy. He's a beast."

"All-state wrestler junior year," the Artist told Bales proudly.

"Right on," Bales said, looking back at me. "You play any ball?"

"Just wrestled at Van Nuys High. Until I blew my knee out."

"Sorry to hear that," Bales said. "Did you do an intense rehab?"

"What for?" I said. "I healed and moved on."

Bales smiled. "So what have you *moved on* to now? I mean, when you're not out in the alley watching the Artist paint."

I looked away. "I'm not sure."

And I wasn't, not anymore. If I'd known how deep I was in financially at this point, I would've done something about it. But even now, I couldn't tell you what that might have been.

"Ah," Bales said. "Floating untethered like the rest of us."

I shrugged. "I was in real estate for over twenty years, before it all tanked."

Bales nodded and slid out a barstool. "Have a seat, big man."

I sat down and Bales motioned to the bartender, then looked at me. "What are you drinking?"

"Sam Adams."

Bales ordered and said, "So how long you gone without a deal?"

"A year."

"Really? I heard it was picking up."

"It is," I said. "The Westside's on fire."

"So what's your problem?"

"No clients. Most of them were middle income— wiped out in the recession. They either can't afford a house now or can't get a loan."

"Then who's buying all the real estate?" asked the Artist.

"All cash buyers," I said. "Middle East investors, private equity, and the Chinese. And let's not forget the teenage billionaires." I grabbed an olive from the bar caddy and popped it into my mouth. "The tech boom rolls on."

"So how are you eating?" Bales asked.

"Savings, mostly. I was selling stuff on Craigslist and eBay for a while. Buying at thrift stores and eking out a small profit."

"Sounds like hard work."

I stared at him, trancelike. "Yeah," I said finally. "It's dead. The Goodwill's jacking prices. Margins have shrunk. So I'm looking for a job."

Bales poked me in the shoulder. "Welcome to the club, big boy." He studied me for a moment, head tilted. "Look," he said. "I've got some shit to sell on eBay if you're interested. It might make us a few bucks."

"I'd be happy to look at what you've got," I said.

He winked. "I'd be happy to show you."

I nodded and sipped my beer, watched Kobe jack a three ball.

"The Lakers suck this year," I said, returning the conversation back to the neutral zone.

"They shoulda got Phil Jackson," the Artist said.

"Forget Phil Jackson," Bales said. "You know who the true Zen master is?"

"Who?" I said.

"The handsome Artist here."

The Artist looked surprised. "How so?"

"You're the only one who really knows who they are anymore," Bales said. "You get up every morning with a sense of purpose and passion. I mean, every day I see you holding court in the alley with garbage soldiers, Saudi princes, and hot chicks with Chihuahuas. And they're all out there just to watch you turn that canvas into something beautiful. It's amazing. Not many of us can bring people together like that. It's a gift."

"Yeah, but I'm not making any money. They're not buying anything."

"You don't need money," Bales said. "Just let the universe do its work." He turned to me. "I mean, Clean, look at that face." He pointed at the Artist. "He looks like Tab Hunter. The 'Sigh Guy.' Am I wrong?"

I examined the Artist. More of a Mickey Mantle type, I thought—blond flattop, tanned face, clear blue eyes. He was the only guy I ever knew who had not been online to find a date. He didn't need to. He was that good-looking. All he had to do was show up. It was something that most men would never understand.

"No," I said. "You're not wrong. The guy's getting more action out in the alley than anybody I know. He tapped a homeless girl the other day."

"She was a freegan," said the Artist. "And she wasn't homeless. She was from Seattle."

"A freegan?" I said.

"Dumpster diver," Bales said. "Part of the anti-consumerist movement. Likes to eat reclaimed food. That kind of shit."

"I bet she had a nose ring," I said.

"She did have a nose ring." The Artist's face lit up. "And a small bluebird tattoo above her left breast. It was hot."

"See?" Bales said. "That's what I'm talking about. Ask any middle-aged doofus in America if he's fucked a woman with a bluebird tattoo in the last year, and only one person will raise their hand." Bales pointed at the Artist. "That'd be you, my friend. That's why you don't need money."

"Yeah, well," the Artist said, staring down into a pint of pale ale, "it sure comes in handy when the rent's due."

"So what are you going to do about it?" I said. "The economy's changed. You're getting older. You've got to try something different."

I shouldn't have said it, but I did. It frustrated me to listen to the Artist moan. I mean, we all had to adjust. And I knew that if he walked up and down the boutiques of Montana Avenue, the owners would be falling all over themselves to display his paintings. But he felt that would cheapen the work. Said he'd burn it all before he'd let those hacks take a piece of him.

The Artist did what he always did in uncomfortable situations: changed the subject, or avoided it. "I need to use the bathroom," he said, rising abruptly from his barstool.

"Whatever," I said.

I watched the Artist shuffle through the sawdust on the floor, and Bales said, "What was that all about?"

"The Artist is afraid of success," I said. "He's got paintings worth thousands of dollars. He won't sell them. He doesn't even try."

I'm no art snob. But like my father I have a good eye. I instinctively know what is good and what is bad. I'd been to my fair share of fine museums and galleries, and I'd never seen anything like the Artist. There was a reason everyone loved his work. The only problem was the people who wanted to pay for it couldn't, and those who could wanted it for free. It was what most artists eventually discovered in L.A.

A raucous chorus of "Happy Birthday" caught our attention. Bales and I glanced over and saw a group of young women with preternaturally bright teeth and mallrat fashion singing to a pretty Asian.

Bales sang along under his breath. "...*dear, blah blah, happy fuckin' blah blah to you.*"

"A few cuties," I said.

Bales fingered an empty shot glass and said with a tinge of regret in his voice, "Pass-through chicks."

"What's that?"

"Los Angeles is a turnstile city," he said. "It thrives on turnover. Most people pass through here to go somewhere else they don't want to go. A few will become enchanted with the lie. But it's just a matter of time before they run out of money. Just a matter of time before they realize they fucked up coming out here."

"How do you know they're just passing through?"

"You can tell by the laughter. It reeks of discovery. Not jaundiced or jaded like the locals."

"I'm a local," I said. "I don't have a jaded laugh."

Bales cracked a pretentious smile and sipped his beer.

"That's because you're from the Valley."

I'd given him a pass last night, written off his bizarre behavior as that of a victim of divorce. But now he was treating me like I was one generation removed from steerage. Which I was. That one arrogant comment told me all I needed to know about Bales. He was a pompous asshole. Someone who viewed me as culturally inferior. A heathen content with a two-year-old Beaujolais. He was making it quite clear that we would never be friends, just two people who might tolerate each other.

One of the young women tied a huge balloon bouquet around the table leg. The colorful, festive balloons mushroomed out into the bar area.

Bales looked over and fished out a small pocket-knife from his pants. "I'm gonna pop one of those bitches," he said.

The menacing tone in his voice distressed me, and the second the Artist returned and sat down at the bar, Bales tackled him from behind. Beers spilled as the Artist tried to wrestle himself free from Bales's bear hug.

"Oh, boo-hoo. *Boo-fucking-hoo*," Bales said, mocking the Artist. "Mommy, I don't have any money. I'm broke. *Boo-hoo*."

The hefty, bearded bartender moved quickly toward the fracas. "Hey, sport," he said. "Take it outside."

The Artist laughed, dodged the soft rabbit punches that Bales was throwing.

"He's cool," I told the bartender, not knowing why I was covering for Bales.

"Fuck it," Bales said, releasing the Artist. "Let's get out of this hellhole. Fuck everybody." He stumbled back, then spread his hands and said, "Let's smoke some weed. Get fucked up!"

As the Artist and I exited, I heard a sound, like two gunshots.

POP!

POP!

Then I heard a young woman yell, "*You motherfucker!*"

Fire and Rain

THE NEXT MORNING I was on the phone with the Artist, rummaging through my sock drawer.

He said, "Popping balloons? Seriously. Who does that?"

"It was disturbing on many levels," I said.

"I can see the fifth-grade bully doing something like that, but a fifty-one-year-old man? That's crazy."

"I didn't see it," I said. "But I heard it. I thought somebody got shot."

I didn't tell the Artist that Bales had a knife. That would have freaked him out. It was only a pocketknife, but that was still big enough to get you expelled from polite society.

"You know, that girl had to feel bad," the Artist said. "One minute she's enjoying her birthday, then some drunk pops her balloons."

"I told you. The guy's a provocateur. He's *screaming* red flags."

A mindful pause.

"You know," the Artist said, his lazy drawl thick with worry. "He told me earlier that he didn't even remember doing it. That he blacked out."

"I don't know what's worse," I said. "If it were me, I'd quietly lose the guy."

"Maybe. But he's still reeling from the divorce. Annnd—"

"You want to be a good neighbor."

"Kinda," the Artist said. "It's his Blue Period."

"He is somber, I'll give you that. But he's no Picasso. Just be careful. He makes me uncomfortable."

"No, I hear ya."

"Look," I said, smelling my cleanest pair of dirty socks. "Let's talk this afternoon. I've got one of those video job interviews coming up on Skype."

"That all sounds very George Jetson."

"Yeah," I said. "It's some new high-tech online real estate company."

"What do you wear for that?"

"I don't have a clue."

He laughed. "I'm glad I'm not doing it. Good luck."

"Thanks, dude," I said. "It should be fun. I'll keep you posted."

I hung up the phone. I hadn't really thought about what I was going to wear. It was something that never occurred to me. It used to be that in American business you wore a suit and tie, or at least a sport coat. Now only service people or low-level employees wore a suit.

I walked across the bedroom and slid open my closet door. There wasn't much in there. It was a wardrobe from a different time. Ralph Lauren pin-stripe suits with wide lapels that had cost eight hundred dollars once but now suited up the mannequin at the Salvation Army. Big stuffy dress shirts that doubled as slipcovers, fat ties that could strangle an elephant, and baggy pleated slacks that shouted, "*Who ya gonna call?…Ghostbusters!*"

I was so far out of the game I didn't know it, like an old typewriter still hanging around. But I had to pick something.

What to choose? What to choose?

My blue eyes scanned my rather limited options. I reached inside the closet, fingering the clothes as I searched for something in style.

A black T-shirt?

No, I hadn't earned the right to wear a black T-shirt during an interview—yet. Besides, I wasn't sure I could pull it off.

A hoodie?

I'd look like a drunk monk.

How about one of those Brooks Brothers suits?

Sure, if you're into time travel. Cough a dust ball.

Khakis and a polo?

I don't work at Walmart.

I finally settled on a white Adidas track jacket. I thought it looked good. But what did I know?

Thirty minutes later I was gawking at my image on the computer screen. I looked like a convict. My bald head shone like a cut diamond. I'd never done a video interview before. Hell, it'd been more than twenty years since I'd done a résumé. But I wasn't lying when I said I needed a job. Money was tight. And it wasn't like I was sitting on my ass. I was trying in real estate. I just didn't have the cash for marketing anymore, much less the MLS dues. It was as if twenty years of my work life had suddenly vanished into cyberspace.

I took the last few minutes to prepare. I closed the windows to muffle the sound of the wind outside, placed a white T-shirt over my desk lamp to soften the harsh light, and cleared a few dirty wineglasses from the background. Then I checked the Internet connection, grabbed the headset, and plugged in.

Let's do this, I thought.

The call came in right on time.

"Hello," I said, still fiddling with my headset.

"Hi, Richard. My name is Carol Anderson, I'm the senior vice president here at Land Grab Real Estate."

I guessed the woman staring at me on the computer screen to be in her early twenties. She was casually beautiful in a bohemian way, with flowing amber hair, pale skin, and modern art eyeglasses.

"First off, I'd like to thank you for being available for an interview today on Skype," she said.

I smiled. "Thank you for the opportunity."

"Great," she said. "Right now I'm going to ask you a couple of preliminary questions, just to get a feel for you as a candidate."

"Sounds good."

"Okay," she said, her image slightly jerky on-screen. "Pick two celebrities to be your parents."

That one caught me off guard. My eyes rolled back like digits on a pinball machine. "Uh, what?"

"Did you not hear the question, Mr. Jenkins?"

WTF?

"No, I heard it. It just threw me for a loop. I was expecting something about my background, or where I want to be in ten years. Which, frankly, dead could be a legitimate reply."

"Time is short, sir," she said. "Answer the question, please."

Time is short, she's got that right.

"Uh. Ward Bond and June Cleaver?" I said, rubbing my bald skull like Brando in the jungle.

"Who?"

"Ward Bond. You know, *The Searchers*, *Wagon Train*?"

She looked at me like I was an old couch, something discarded on the side of the road. "Next question."

"Please."

"What's your favorite song?"

"Easy," I said. "'Fire and Rain.'"

"Never heard of it."

James Taylor? Really?!

"Tell me why you picked this particular song," she said, all business.

I said, "Because every time I hear it, I think of the people I love or have ever loved."

I didn't tell her that it was the last song my cousin heard right before he blew his head off.

"Fine," she said. "Perform it for me."

Now I'd been out of the job market for over thirty years. So you can imagine how shocked I was to process an interview such as this. It was during these trying moments that I realized how much technology had separated the generations. But what most people don't know about me is that I love music. From Adele to Zeppelin. Bluegrass to classical. I'm also a pretty decent guitar player. So this was my wheelhouse. I just needed to make sure I understood the question.

"You mean, you want me to sing it?"

She made an exasperated grunt and looked up. "Yes."

I nodded. "Okay, okay. Here goes nothing."

Just then I saw the neighbor's black cat Herbert jump up onto my dresser and into view. Oops. Forgot about him. He didn't do me any favors when he started licking his balls on camera. I tried to keep it together, staring straight into the lens.

"Uh, do you want me to play guitar, too?" I asked.

By the look on her tormented face I could see that she hadn't been asked that question before. And hopefully never would again.

"Whatever feels right," she said.

Ah, yes. Whatever feels right. The millennial default.

In hindsight, I probably wouldn't have requested the instrument. Because when I got up I remembered I was still wearing my pajama bottoms. Anyway,

I plucked my steel-string acoustic guitar from the closet and sat back down.

"You ready?" I said.

She pushed her trendy rectangular glasses up on her nose. "Anytime you are."

"All right," I said. "It's showtime." I slapped my guitar three times and counted down, "One, two, three." And then I launched into J.T. My voice was moody and introspective, my fingers nimble and free, nailing the chords and hitting the notes. The amazing thing was, she listened to the entire song. And when I finally finished, she sat in silence for a long moment, then said, "Wow. I wasn't expecting that. That was *really* good."

"Thanks," I said. "It was either that or 'Comfortably Numb.'"

That went over her head, too. I know this because she peered at me as if maggots were crawling out of my eyes.

"Well," she said. "That completes our first round. I'll pass this info along to my superiors, and if you're a match, we'll be in touch. Thank you so much."

"Thank you."

Her image disappeared, and that was it.

I turned off the computer. Then I chucked a Nerf ball at that pesky cat.

Chasing the Sun

SANTA MONICA IS a city where the absurd meets the sea. A stark contrast between the haves and have-nots. And if you can see past the palm trees and the bright blue ocean sparkle, then you soon realize it's all a wet dream, a thirsty face hidden behind sunglasses and lies. It's home to insane wealth, sun-kissed dreamers (the few who are still left), street urchins, teenage wastrels, goggle-eyed tourists, and international sleazeballs of every stripe. For several decades it had been one of the coolest, edgiest beach towns on the West Coast, but that was over thirty years ago—before the high priests of big business moved in and killed its charm. And its affordability. Dreaming is over now. But if this sounds like your kind of place, bring your bathing suit. And don't forget your checkbook.

Personally, I hate Santa Monica (can you tell?), and I'm not a hater. It's famous for overpromising and underdelivering, and for fleecing its residents for cash any way it can get it. But it was the Artist's home and he loved it. So for the time being, I had to love it, too.

On this particularly warm October evening I was cutting through the alley on foot to see him, something I'd often done due to the lack of parking on Wilshire or Ninth. Tonight I'd gotten lucky and scored a spot on Arizona. It didn't take long for one of the living dead to jump out from behind a Dumpster. I heard the voice first, a woman with a thick accent.

"Where you go?"

I spun around and saw this Asian chick pitching out from the soft blue dark.

"Who, me?" I said, tapping my chest.

She got up close, face-to-face. "Yeah, you," she said. "Where you go?"

I pointed north. "Over there."

"Oh. You go see Ahh-tist?"

"Yeah," I said. "You know him?"

She nodded. "He come to my home sometime. I see you watch him painting. Him work good."

Her kimchi breath announced her Korean roots. I pegged her around thirty-five, but she was dressed much younger. Short black shorts, pink-and-black-striped tights, and a wool tweed fisherman's hat. Her face was hooker hard, but that didn't mean she was one.

"You tell him come see me," she said. "I make good banana bread for him. You come too. O-kay?"

"All right. I'll tell him."

She lit a cigarette and studied me, her head tilted sideways.

"You sure? Because he like my banana bread. It make him laugh. You know what I say?" She let out a smoker's hack, shaking her cigarette at me. "You tell him Jae make more. You tell him that."

A balmy gust blew through the narrow lane, shuddering the palm fronds and splashing my face with warm, dry air.

"I'll tell him."

I turned and started walking.

"You do that," she said, my back fading against her voice.

THE DOOR TO the Artist's first-floor apartment was open, and I walked in. Bales was sitting on the couch watching TV and smoking a joint. He wore a fencer's mask on his head, flipped up, the way an NFL player rests his helmet during a time-out.

"What's up?" I said.

Bales smiled like a truant, twinkling his fingers at me.

"Just chasing the sun, bro."

I watched him take a drag, then said, "Where's the Artist?"

"He's takin' a dump."

I heard the toilet flush and the Artist emerged from his Old Hollywood black-and-white-tiled bathroom. "Hey," he said, smiling.

We fist-bumped.

"Hey, I just ran into this Korean gal out in the alley," I said. "She said you like her banana bread."

Bales chimed in. "I bet she did."

"Is she a neighbor?"

"No," the Artist said. "Her name's Jae. She works across the street in the nail salon. She cuts my hair for free."

"What a shock," I said. "Did you do her?"

The Artist looked down. "Yeah, I hit it a few weeks ago. But I won't be back. Her place smells of ox bone soup and Marlboro Lights."

"A classic case of horizontal regret," Bales said.

"What about the banana bread?" I asked.

"She bakes it with pot, sometimes hash. Last time I was there it was so strong, I almost freaked out. I couldn't feel my legs. And she talks nonstop. Droning on about how bad the Vietnamese women are she works with, saying they all talk like quacking ducks." The Artist plopped down on a leather club chair. "Plus she bugs me. She takes long cigarette breaks and watches me paint. Always asking, *Whut dat? Whut dat?* I can't understand her half the time with that accent."

Bales said, "Clean, you want a hit?"

He pushed the joint hard to my face.

"I haven't done that since college," I said.

"This ain't college."

For most of the country this was a time of extremes. We were so divided as a nation on how to move forward that some people threw caution to the wind.

Others just froze. I chose the former.

"Sure," I said. "Why not."

I grabbed the joint and put it to my lips as if it were the first time in my neighbor's garage. I gingerly inhaled, then inspected the joint like it was a cockroach to be eaten before inhaling again. I coughed.

Bales said, "Yeah, Clean. Get it up in there. That's some good medicine."

I passed the joint to the Artist, then sat down in the other club chair and leaned back, already light-headed.

Bales said, "So, I hear you had an interview. How'd it go?"

I tried to focus, staring down at Bales's purple velvet slippers tapping the floor like *My Three Sons*. Through my foggy lens I recognized the embroidered gold crown emblem on the high-end footwear, the Church's logo.

"I had one of those Skype interviews," I said.

I watched the Artist change the channel. He wanted to watch *Dancing with the Stars*. Said that blond gymnast had a nice ass.

"Was it a tech company?" Bales asked.

"Yeah," I said, floating out of my body now.

I had forgotten how relaxed marijuana made me feel. I almost brought up the balloon-popping incident but decided to let it go.

"Did they ask you some off-the-wall questions?"

"Two," I said, drifting. "What was my favorite song. Which I ended up performing. And…"

I spaced, not being able to remember the other question. I just stared at the Artist's swank digs, soaking it all in, my mouth open, slack and dry. The exterior of the building had been battered by the damp, salty nights, but inside he had transformed the mundane into the sublime. Cool and classic, like a Roy Orbison song. The rustic space was modern and cozy, with farmhouse-white walls and wide-planked pine flooring. The Artist was fond of saying that a woman will forgive the outside of your apartment, but never the inside. It must be neat and clean, and it must have game.

I glanced up at the exposed wood beams, tracking them to an ornate white fireplace mantel. On the mantel rested a Japanese samurai sword, which I uncomfortably imagined had gutted a few Americans. An antique silver picture frame sat nearby, its interior displaying a slogan in silver cursive:

I'm not moody, paranoid, or self-absorbed. I'm artistic.

The sleek brown leather couch, the "workbench" as he called it, the reclaimed wood coffee table, and two leather club chairs were fenced in by several works of abstract art: stacked three deep, white wall to white wall. Only one picture hung above the sofa, a framed black-and-white photograph of his late father's '56 Chevy truck. The only blight, the only thing wildly at odds with the rest of the room, was an old, big-backed Sony TV.

"When you gonna lose the TV?" I said, not recognizing my own voice.

"When I can afford a new one," he said. "Which may be never. I know it de-games me."

"Not only is it zero game," Bales said, "it dates you back to the Paleolithic Age. Just don't show anybody the stone tools in your kitchen."

The Artist laughed, then said, "Before I forget, my friend Mary is having a Halloween party. We're all invited. Costumes optional."

"Mary-with-the-hair-in-her-face?" said Bales.

"Yes. She's a pretty girl."

"Yeah," Bales said, "when you can see her face. She looks like Cousin It with all that hair. All you can see is her nose. It peeks out like a clit boner."

I was so stoned I forgot to laugh, or couldn't.

The Artist asked me, "What was the song?"

"Uh…what? Oh…'Fire and Rain,'" I finally said.

"Great song," the Artist said.

"You're aware," Bales said, "that when they ask you that question, you're already cooked. That's how they weed out the old and ugly. I'll leave it for you to decide which category you fall into."

Fuckin' Bales. Already bumming my high.

"That's blatant ageism," I said.

"In its purest form. How old was the interviewer?"

"She was young."

Bales laughed, then hopped up off the sofa and went into the kitchen and fetched us each a Miller Lite tall boy. He seemed to know just what we needed at that moment.

He handed me a beer, and I cracked the pull tab and chugged half the can. The liquid gold flowed easy and cold down my parched throat, soothing my cottonmouth.

"I conducted many of those Skype interviews," Bales said. "And all were done in less than five minutes. The instant I saw the applicant, I'd made my decision. It saves the corporations time and money. It's a way around ageism. And future health claims from old fucks like us."

"Brutal," said the Artist.

"It's paint by numbers," Bales said. "Pretty soon photos, height and weight charts will be required. Just like in Asia."

"She liked my song, though," I said proudly.

"Oh, come off it, man," Bales said. "She was just entertaining herself. I mean, you looked like a fucking Medicare patient to that girl. Some old fart in a sweat suit in Marina del Rey."

I thought a second. "Maybe it was my neighbor's cat. It jumped up into view. Maybe that put her off."

Bales said, "Dude! You could've had naked midgets dancing around in the background. It wouldn't have mattered. Face it, you're old. She was just happy you didn't invite her to a John Tesh concert."

"I don't believe that," I said.

Bales lit the roach and sucked a hit. "Welcome to *Silicon Beach*," he said. "I mean, if you're older than twenty-five in this town, you're toast. The sooner you accept that, the sooner you'll move forward. Entrepreneurship is all we've got left."

I digested this unwanted information for a moment. Then a man's voice rose up from outside—high and tight, like my buzz.

"*Hey! Move your car, man! Move your fuckin' car!*"

"Fuck. It's Foreskin," Bales said, sitting up on the couch.

"Did you park in his spot?" the Artist asked.

"Of course I did. You're in my spot."

I shook my head and said, "How can you guys live here?"

"Where?" Bales said. "The People's Republic of Santa Monica, or the opulent Wilshire Arms?"

"Santa Monica," I said. "All this parking lot drama. Always shuffling cars, and for what? No space? Another jaywalking ticket?"

"*Move your fuckin' car, man!*"

Bales hopped off the sofa and shouted out the door, "Coming!" Then he muttered under his breath, "Fucking Foreskin."

Bales had a nickname for us all. Big Salad. Hashtag. Clean. Foreskin. Bobby Homegrown (who would later become my dealer, and even later one name: Homegrown.) And Mary-with-the-hair-in-her-face. Foreskin lived in number 12. He earned his dubious moniker for the shiny full-length black leather jacket that he was fond of prancing around in. Bales said he looked like a big black cock.

Bales exited, and I got really stoned and watched the rest of *Dancing with the Stars* with the Artist. Watched the blond gymnast shake her moneymaker.

Later Bales returned with In-N-Out double-double cheeseburgers and French fries, and we all smoked and drank and ate the rest of the night away watching the late edition of *SportsCenter*.

The last thing I remember saying was, "Do you know where I can score some of this pot?"

The End of Bling

I SPENT THE entire weekend stoned. It's not something that I'm proud of at the age of fifty-three, but there it is.

On Saturday I walked to the cleaners on Washington, and the Armenian owner said, "I haven't seen you around in a while."

I was so high I could see the curvature of the earth.

Then I mumbled something inaudible to the effect of, "I've been around."

He looked surprised. "Okay. Well, it's good to see you." His viney hand gestured toward the help, two young Mexican women with wide brown eyes. "Lupe and Ana will take good care of you," he said.

I forgot I was stoned. *Was I around? Had I ever been around?*

I managed to pull some slacks from my backpack and place them on the counter. "Is Jorge in? I just need to get these hemmed."

The Mexican women looked nervously at each other, brown eyes blinking. I immediately knew that something was wrong. And I don't know why I suspected it, but I did.

"Is he dead?" I asked.

The bigger and wider of the two women nodded. "*Si, señor.*"

"How?"

"A heart attack."

I shook my head. "How old?"

"Fifty-seven."

"Damn. He was a good guy."

"*Si, señor.*"

I looked off into the busy street, watching the flow of frantic, misguided traffic. "I'm going to miss him," I said. "My condolences to the family."

I picked up my dress shirts and walked across the street to El Pollo Loco. My high had been doused but not my hunger. I must have looked like an old fool as I sauntered up to the drive-through window and ordered a chicken burrito. I was in such a spaced-out state that I failed to comprehend my surroundings.

A guy in a black truck honked when I unwrapped my food and started eating in the middle of the drive-through. I looked up, avocado salsa caked on my lips, and mumbled with my mouth full, "*Sorry, bro.*"

I slung the dry cleaning over my shoulder and walked leisurely toward home. I thought about what Bales had said about my job prospects—about my age. I decided to take him up on his eBay offer. See what he had to sell.

IT WAS AROUND three in the afternoon on Monday, October 29, when I knocked on Bales's weather-beaten front door. It was one of those gray beach days with little or no light. After a moment of staring at the brass number 4, I concluded that the loud music I heard was coming from inside his unit. I leaned in and recognized Mott the Hoople's "All the Young Dudes." At least he had good taste in music. He could've left me standing out here wagging my head to Rascal Flatts.

I waited on the paint-peeling stoop a long minute, mouthing the words to the classic rock song. When no one answered, I twisted the knob, opened the door, and stuck my head inside. "Bales?" I called. "Bales?"

It smelled like a meth lab in there, a sulfurous stink of rotten eggs and cat urine. The modest room was dark, but when my eyes came into sharp focus, I glimpsed a white modular sofa and a glass-topped coffee table piled high with orange plastic pill bottles and empty aluminum beer cans. Twenty-five talls at least, standing proud and erect like used artillery shells.

I called again, louder this time. "Bales!"

Still no answer. Then I remembered what he'd said: "*My door's always open, bro. Just come on in.*"

So I did. I walked slowly through the cluttered living room, following the sound of music, and almost tripped over a surfboard. I stopped to regain my balance and stared at the dark seventy-two-inch flat-screen mounted on the wall. My pale reflection stared back.

When I turned into the master bedroom, I found him balled up on the floor, crying. The space around him was a pathetic mess. It looked like a suicide bomber had hit—clothes and shoes everywhere, scattered like projectiles shot from a cannon. The bed was unmade, moving boxes served as furniture, and the air was stale and dense. The instant the music stopped, I spotted a vintage turntable on the wooden Danish dresser. Along with an orange-colored glass water pipe.

I bent down and touched his shoulder. "You okay, man?"

"Fuck it, Clean, I can't take it anymore. I want my life back…my kids."

"I know it must be hard," I said.

"I can't get a job." His chest heaved and shuddered. "And I can't afford my medication…I might as well shoot myself."

I'd lived long enough to know that L.A. and guns did not go together, and when someone mentioned killing themselves, however veiled, they usually meant it. Whether or not they could actually go through with it was another matter. But at this time I felt no moral obligation to quash those tendencies.

That was a big mistake.

"You need some help up?" I said.

He snorted through the tears. "Yeah."

I stepped back and extended my hand. He grabbed it and I hoisted him to his feet. He was disheveled, unshaven, wearing cargo shorts and a wild floral shirt.

"Thanks," he said, wiping his runny nose on his shirtsleeve.

I gave him a moment to collect himself.

"I'm sorry, man," he said.

"No sweat," I said. "Life happens."

Bales surveyed the messy space, scratching his gray stubble nervously. "Sorry about the room," he said. "A little wainscoting and some molding should do the trick."

"I'm a bachelor," I said. "I know the gig."

He pointed. "Look, uh. Everything's in the closet. Take a look. I need to use the bathroom."

"Cool."

I strolled into the small walk-in closet and flipped on the light. It smelled of mildew and dust. I saw shoeboxes of men's designer sneakers stacked high and deep: Lanvin. Gucci. Boss. Prada. Bally. Louis Vuitton.

A boneyard of opulence, I thought. And then I remembered what the Artist had told me. He said that Bales had once lived in a multimillion-dollar estate in Broad Beach. Said he'd grown up well-off, north of Montana in Santa Monica. Attended grade school with Charlie Sheen and Sean Penn, his summers spent tanning and swimming in Malibu with the Kecks, Tapers, and Chandlers. This, I assumed, accounted for his unapproachable air. Evidently, his father was a prominent heart surgeon at

UCLA Medical Center, and his mother championed several local charities, including her current post as president of the Junior League of Los Angeles. At one time a heart surgeon's salary was considered big money on the Westside, but now it was barely middle class. Something I'm quite sure Bales was aware of.

You could tell he was comfortable giving orders, though, and that only stems from a proper pedigree. Boarding school at the exclusive Cate Academy, where he'd lettered in three sports: football, basketball, and volleyball. Then on to Stanford Business School. I suppose I could've Googled him, dug deeper into his past, but I didn't really care at the time. I'd already seen enough to know I wasn't going to become lifelong friends with the guy. It must have been hard, though. Once living across the street from Sly Stallone and Pierce Brosnan, then finding yourself wallowing in the stench of a moldy shitbox at the age of fifty-one.

No wonder he was angry.

I was compelled back to the now when I heard a vigorous snorting sound coming from the bathroom. It could have been anything, though after what I saw on the coffee table, I assumed it was drugs. But I wasn't here to judge. I was here for the shoes.

I was counting the boxes when Bales returned.

"Fifty-one pairs," he said. "That's twenty-five thousand dollars retail. All mint condition."

His gray hair was slicked back now, his face full of tics, twitches, and eye blinks.

"I got a bunch of shirts too," he said. He picked uncomfortably at his flowery Italian shirt like it was a straitjacket. "Etro. Kiton. Hickey Freeman. Whatever. I got 'em."

"The shirts are great," I said, "but unfortunately they don't bring in the big bucks. It's the sneakers people want."

His eyes were black and beady and he got up in my face. "I don't give a shit. Just get rid of it."

I spotted a thin white film around his left nostril. Watched him grind his teeth from side to side.

"That's what I'm here for," I said, my voice even and calm.

"Where do you think I'm going to wear this shit anymore, Clean? Tell me, huh? Malibu Farmers Market? The Coffee Bean? Fucking walking around with a baby stroller in a pair of Ugg boots and skinny jeans. It's a bubble, man. A fucking bubble." He picked up one of the shearling boots and flung it hard across the room. "It's over," he yelled. "Fuckin' over!"

He slunk down against the wall, both hands over his face.

"It's the end of bling," he said softly. "The end of bling."

I knew what he meant. Not only was it the end of bling, it was the end of an era. The end of our once-comfortable lives as we knew them. And whether you'd done it to yourself or been crushed by global forces, it was painful to watch. I'd seen families rip each other apart like wolves in the desert.

And for a moment I could relate. Bales expected better—we all did. That's how we were raised. It was as if the maid was on vacation, or the nanny had been called away to Manila for a family emergency, or the valet had forgotten where he'd parked the car. It was all just a melodramatic *Downton Abbey* episode, some bad dream that never really happened. But it had. And his dealing would be our dealing.

"I'll have the Artist take pictures of the inventory," I said. "I'll have it listed in a couple of days."

He dropped his head between his knees and waved a defeated hand.

"Just sell it. Every last bit of it."

LATER THAT NIGHT I took stock of my own life. My fall wasn't as swift and hard as Bales's, but the destination was the same. From Neiman Marcus to the Jewish Council thrift shops. From Duckhorn wine to the low-end cellars of Carlo Rossi (the big jug). From Gelson's Market to Dollar General. I was even thinking about selling my car, something unthinkable in this town.

I decided to start a journal, maybe look back for clues as to how we'd all gotten here. How we'd all lost the narrative of our lives. But before I did that, I crawled up on the roof of my apartment building to smoke a joint. Bobby Homegrown had hooked me up with a gram of OG Kush. I sat in my favorite lawn chair, lit the spliff, and inhaled under a fat yellow moon. Maybe that was why Bales was so emotional today, I thought.

"You want some company?"

I tried to hide the pot when I heard the voice.

"Don't worry about me. I'm cool."

"No worries," I said. "This is just for my bad back."

"Sure it is."

It was my sixty-five-year-old neighbor, Paula. I watched her approach and pull up a folding beach chair beside me, her platinum hair shining in the moonlight like a sculpted piece of metal.

For a moment, I let the weed take me in, gazing up into the clear night sky.

"Well, Mr. Bogart," she said. "Are you gonna offer me some of that?"

I looked surprised. "I didn't know you partook."

She laughed. "I don't know what that means. But I'd like a hit."

She was an old flower child from south Boston. Straight and direct and salty—just like I like them. There wasn't anything that came from her mouth that was tainted by lies or untruths. She was a genuine free spirit with no agenda other than living life on her own terms. I'd gotten to know her late last summer when she'd helped me sublet my apartment for a month to a German lady who preferred a homestay to a motel. She was a personal trainer and was in top shape for someone her age. Hell, for any age. Ripe and strong, she looked right out of Central Casting, that perfect, healthy senior zip-lining through the jungles of Costa Rica.

I passed her the joint and watched her inhale. The evening light mapped the lines around her mouth.

"Be careful," I said. "It's some stony shit."

She raised her chin and blew out a solid body of smoke. "Did you hear the neighbors below me last night?"

"The two Portuguese chicks?"

"Yeah, the LMU students."

"No," I said. "I didn't hear anything."

"Fuck," Paula said in her thick Southie accent. "They came home fucking drunk at two in the morning with some guy who laughed like the Jolly Green Giant. And you know our walls are so thin, I heard everything."

"What were they saying?"

"It was like a porno movie in there. One girl says, 'You fuck my dog first, then I'll fuck you.'"

My building was full of women, and they all liked to talk. Mostly about each other.

"What did the dog have to say about that?" I said.

Paula laughed and brushed her hair back, the smell of lavender blooming in the wind. I could see the weed kicking in because she was staring dreamily at the moon. Her thoughts shape-shifting inside her petite skull.

"Isn't it beautiful?" she said. "And look at all the stars."

I didn't have the heart to tell her that the "stars" were actually airplanes approaching LAX.

"Yeah," I said. "It's a nice night."

She took another drag and we talked, and she told me that every one of the women in the building smoked medicinal marijuana, even eighty-year-old Marie, whom Paula said she scored from—Marie's grandson worked in a Long Beach dispensary. Paula also told me how the upstairs neighbor Norma (Ms. OCD) had started giving prostate massages for a hundred dollars a pop because her dog-walking business had dried up. I said that choking chickens was an admirable way of earning a living. Then she asked me how my business was.

"Not so good," I said. After which she started in with her end-of-the-world talk.

"That's because the shift is taking place," she said.

I cocked my head. "The shift?"

She had that look on her face, that creepy crystal-ball gaze.

"Yes," she said. "On December twenty-first, the change will happen. The dawning of the new Age of Aquarius. It won't be about money and greed anymore. The universe is telling us that this destructive path we've been on is no longer sustainable. Although the Piscean values of power and control will take time to fade. That's why all this turmoil is happening. To jolt us into a better future."

"So you don't believe the Mayan apocalypse theory, or that some cataclysmic event will disrupt earth?"

"Not at all," she said. "It's going to be a spiritual transformation. A rebalancing of the cosmos. The Mayans were misunderstood."

"So what are we supposed to do? Go full-on bare-foot Zen? Hug it out with strangers?"

"If that's the path you choose."

"What if I choose another path?"

"Let the universe guide you. Look for serendipitous encounters. Signs."

She took another toke and exhaled. The pungent odor of Northern California grass filled the cool evening air.

"Every person that comes into your life now was meant to teach you something," she said. "Then once you learn what you're supposed to, you can move forward. Or ascend."

"I think it's just marketing," I said. I picked up a small rock and hurled it into the alley. "They've found a way to monetize it."

"Trust me. You will step through that door. And by this time next year, you will be an expanded man."

She smiled warmly, her silver hair creasing in the breeze.

"Did you know the guy in apartment one is a doomsday prepper?" she said. "He believes in that shit. Thinks the world is headed for a *Mad Max* showdown."

"The dude with the pedostache and the flak jacket?"

"Yes," she said. "He showed me his bug-out bag yesterday."

I flinched. "That's disturbing."

"He calls it end-of-the-world fashion."

"I call it nuts."

"Call it what you will," she said. "But we are in the process of transitioning to the fifth dimension. Deal with it."

Pale Rider

I STOOD ON the front porch of Mary's Craftsman bungalow dressed as Clint Eastwood in *A Fistful of Dollars*. Wide-brimmed beaver hat, nub stogie, and a Mexican poncho. I could hear the roar of laughter and rap music coming from inside the modest house, and I told myself I was lucky to be here. While most of the country was out trick-or-treating, New Yorkers were busy hunting for food, water, and shelter. The power was still out on most of the East Coast, and it was clear that the aftermath of Hurricane Sandy would linger for months. But here in Santa Monica the sunset turned the sky blood orange and deep purple, and the evening air was warm and still, as if trapped in a dome.

It was a beautiful Halloween night.

Mary-with-the-hair-in-her-face answered the door wearing a naughty nurse costume.

"Welcome," she said, trying desperately to pull the long auburn strands of hair away from her pointy, upturned nose. "It's so good to see you. Come on in."

"Thanks," I said. "Love your costume."

"You, too. Listen, drinks and food are in the kitchen. Please, help yourself."

She was a cool lady. Her only flaw was that she'd ridden the horse of beauty too long. She'd been a party girl most of her life, working odd jobs for the rich and the occasional gallery or boutique gig. But now that she was touching fifty, all she could get was part-time work at Nordstrom Rack. Like so many unmarried women of a certain age, she supplemented her income with housesitting and dog walking. I'd met her at a few parties over the years and always found her attractive. I knew she preferred young pool boys, but tonight she had an older gentleman on her arm. His name was Felix, her Argentinian lover.

I slipped through the living room crowd and spotted Bales on the couch. He was wearing a military gas mask and a red velvet smoking jacket. I knew it was him by his crisp white Gucci sneakers and arrogant slouch.

When I approached he said, "Look at Clean, coming in here all good, the bad, and the ugly."

"You got the ugly part right."

"Don't give yourself too much credit," he said, standing up. "Follow me. I want to show you something."

He led me into the bedroom. Right to the bong. "Trick or treat?"

"Flame," I said, holding the glass water pipe to my lips.

Bales struck a match and lit the bowl. I did my part and inhaled.

He said, "Ever had a plate job, Clean?"

I exhaled, then blew out a smoke ring.

"What?"

"Simple question."

"No."

"I have. I picked up this hot blonde at Will Rogers State Beach about twenty years ago. I took her to the Sizzler for dinner. Stuffed her with pasta and bread— three tiramisu desserts. Then I brought her back to my place and I scooched under the glass coffee table. Had her stand naked above me, then told her to take a shit. Told her to push real hard like she was having a baby. It came out soft and slow at first, tiny squirts, then little brown veins streaked down her thighs. I didn't know what to think at the time. But I now know I should've incorporated more multi-grains. What do you think, Clean? Should I shoot for a more marbled approach next time?"

I paused.

"Some people get off on distasteful things," I said. "It's none of my business."

He smiled. "Spoken like a true Angeleno, Clean. I like that."

"I'm glad you approve."

I'd heard the Hollywood doo-doo stories. The scat freaks and the gerbil chasers. To each his own, I guess. Just not in my house.

"Hey, watch this," Bales said. "The fucking cat's a stoner."

I looked at the furry white feline lounging on the bed's plush comforter.

Bales grabbed the glass bong off the dresser and took a hit. He held the smoke in, then grabbed the cat off the bed. He cupped its face with both hands and proceeded to blow a slow, steady stream of marijuana smoke up its nose. The cat struggled, hind legs kicking, trying desperately to escape. But it was futile; his head was in a vise grip.

"Look at the scrapper," Bales said. "He's fighting now, but he'll be jelly soon."

"You're a sicko, Bales," I said. "Let it go."

Bales ignored my command, cradling the cat against his body. "You know what they say about cats," he said.

"What's that?"

"They always land on their feet."

"I wouldn't bet on Skipper," I said. "He's a pretty fat cat."

Bales cracked an off-the-reservation grin. "Why don't we find out? Test the theory. If I throw it face-first against the wall, will its legs deploy?"

"I don't want to find out. It's not cool. And it's not your cat."

"I don't give a shit."

And he didn't. He'd already given me the impression that he was the neighborhood kid who liked to torture animals. Light insects on fire.

"Here goes." Bales cocked the cat behind his head like he was about to throw a football. The feline's legs hung lifeless—big eyes blinking, its baked brain traveling the margins.

"Don't do it," I said.

Bales jerked his arm forward, then stopped abruptly. He lowered the cat, kissed its forehead, then tossed it back on the bed like he was discarding a pair of dirty underwear. "You didn't think I

was going to hurt the cat, did you? I'm a proud sup-
porter of PETA." He beamed like Chucky and back-
slapped me. "You sell my shit yet?"

In L.A. there are no likeable characters. Only those
to distrust less.

"I'm listing it all tomorrow," I said, still stunned.

"Right on."

I turned and headed for the exit.

"Hey," he said. "What did the Artist tell you about
me?"

I stopped, looked over my shoulder. "About what?"

"About anything. You know the Artist. He's a little
bitch. Loves to talk."

"Nothing much. Just said you're getting a divorce."

"Is that it?"

"Yeah, that's it," I lied.

"Okay. So how long did you say you've known
the Artist?"

"I didn't. But over fifteen years."

"All right. I get it. You guys are good friends." He
nodded. "I applaud fellowship."

"He's a good guy," I said.

I took a step toward the door.

"You want to know if I did it…don't you?"

I froze, then looked him straight in the eye.

"Excuse me?"

Bales leaned against the dresser and gave me a dark look. "You know what I'm talking about."

I did. The sexual assault charge. But I had no intention of wandering in the garden of his private life. He'd have to tend to that himself.

"I'm not sure what you're referring to, Bales," I said. "But I'm thirsty. I'm dressed as Clint Eastwood with a neck scarf…and I want a drink."

He laughed. Which was rare. The only time I ever heard him laugh was when he hurt something or someone.

"Up to you, pale rider," he said. "Up to you."

I strolled into the living room and found the Artist sitting on the couch with Mary-with-the-hair-in-her-face and some hot blond dressed as Tinkerbell. He wore a black beret and a white T-shirt, passing himself off as French painter Henri Matisse. It was a mail-in costume on all accounts.

He looked me over and said, "I was wondering where Clint was."

I squinted and gave him a *Dirty Harry* stare.

"I was talking to a chair."

I dusted off my poncho and breezed into the kitchen like a gunfighter. I opened the fridge and heard Bales shout, "Put on some fucking music, not this jungle boogie!"

I had my head in the icebox when I heard a grating, recognizable voice behind me. A voice that made you beg for a chalkboard scratch.

"How was the shit?"

Startled, I grabbed a can of original Coors and turned around. It was Bobby Homegrown wearing a cartoonish Romney mask.

"Goddammit, Homegrown," I said. "Stop scaring people."

I'd forgotten all the dealer chitchat that one had to go through to procure. I didn't need to talk to the dealer anymore. I didn't want to be his friend. I was fifty-three years old. I just wanted the dope.

"You, uh…you want some white?"

"No, Homegrown," I said. "I don't want any fucking white. It's not 1987 and we're not at The Palace." I swigged my beer. "It's a different time."

"Ease off, bro," he said, his tongue wagging inside the mouth hole of the Romney mask. "I'm no pusher. I'm just a handyman."

He was the strangest looking handyman I ever saw—a skinny, thirty-year-old, pasty-white Goth with chopped black hair and emo eyes.

He looked like a fucking geometry problem.

Bales said he looked so thin and flimsy you could punch a hole in his forehead with an index finger.

I guess he was pretty good at his job, though. He worked for several building owners in the area, including the Artist's. But he derived the bulk of his discretionary income from dealing drugs. Mainly to a growing and untapped market—seniors and baby boomers. Ever since California had "legalized" marijuana for medicinal purposes, he'd watched his part-time business explode. The boomers had been green-lighted a return to the insatiable appetites of their youth; whether out of nostalgia, pain relief, or escape was of no concern of his, because what he soon realized was that these aging Caucasians would pay just about anything for a bong hit.

And when they wanted it, they wanted it now.

Add in delivery charges and bag pinching, and he was making a fortune.

One day while I was watching TV with the Artist, I heard Bales next door saying to Homegrown, "I want the bag here by five. And every minute that you're late, I'm docking you a dollar. You will not talk to me upon arrival. There will be no small talk or brotherly love gestures. Don't even fucking feign a smile. I certainly will not shake your limp, greasy palm. I will simply hand you the money and you will give me the pot. After that I might say thank you, but I highly doubt it, and you can say whatever the fuck you want, as long as it is no longer than three words. But it will be expected that you will leave immediately, and then wait patiently in the shadows or shrubs in which you reside until I call you again. At which time, the entire cycle repeats itself. And until you are able to carry on a normal conversation, one that doesn't sound like you're a mongoloid cretin, then all that you are, and ever will be, is a freakish delivery boy. Something to be gazed upon only inside a specimen box. And just when you're exploring thoughts of going off the rails and asking this old guy what he's into—then stop. I'm not interested in hearing you talk. Not interested in hearing about how you lost your virginity at the Wilco concert. And when your mind starts to play games it thinks it can win, stop. Because in the time it takes you to form a complete sentence, I've already showered and shaved and stroked my extra-large cock into a furious orgasm. Now beat it."

And I knew how Bales felt. Homegrown's slow, affected speech attested to the fact that he smoked copious amounts of grass on a twenty-four-hour basis. And God knows what else. To be frank, I wasn't interested. But in order to turn on and tune out, I would have to endure more painful encounters with this drug-addled handyman.

I chugged my beer and tossed the empty into the trash can. "You know, Homegrown," I said, "take it for what it's worth. Sounding like a stoner at eighteen is cool, but at thirty it does not work."

He peeled off his Romney mask, his glossy black hair settling into a severe angle above the right ear. He looked confused. "So, uh…what you're sayin' is… you want some more green?"

I grabbed another beer from the fridge, disgusted.

"Leave it in the planter by the front door." I flipped back my poncho and revealed a six-shooter. "And don't mangle the roses this time."

I drifted into the living room, my cowboy boots clomping on the hardwood floor. I passed a dude in drag wearing a long purple wig. "Nice costume," I said, tipping my gunslinger hat. "Casual yet elegant."

"Oh, it's not a costume," he/she said. "I just got off work."

I admired the ensemble, a white slim-fit shirt with ripped high-end jeans and gold metallic oxfords.

"Well, you look great," I said. "Bringing the sexy back."

He/she smiled and said in a low-pitched voice, "Thanks, handsome."

If you're going to make it in L.A. today, this type of interaction should not unnerve you. If it does, you're better off back in Bumpkinville—or Russia.

I picked my way through the party crowd, saying sorry when I knocked into someone, and joined Mary-with-the-hair-in-her-face and the Artist on the couch. I sipped my beer and observed.

Mary-with-the-hair-in-her-face was telling the Artist that she needed a new wardrobe. She hadn't bought anything new in over three years, she said. Money was tight, and she couldn't afford to get her old stuff back from the cleaners. I could see the Artist nodding, but the look on his face suggested his thoughts were elsewhere. Rent was due tomorrow, and nobody locked into his fears more than the Artist.

Bales was talking with this sleepy-eyed brunette and told her that he was afflicted by a terrible disease. She said that she was very sorry to hear that, but wanted to know what it was. Bales said it was unfortunate, that what he had been diagnosed with was "large cocks disease." I don't remember if she laughed, cried, or walked away, but I think she left. The Korean woman, Jae, was there, passing around a silver tray of her famous pot-laced banana bread. She landed on me and said, "Do you want to get high?"

And I said, "You know what, Jae? It's going to be a pass. And I'm sure it's quite delicious." I patted my growing waistline. "But I'm prediabetic." Which at the time I had no idea I was.

Bales danced over by the couch, wearing his gas mask. He yelled playfully, "Fire in the hole! Fire in the hole!" He laughed strangely and danced away, swallowed up by the gyrating party crowd.

Fire in the hole, I thought.

Isn't that what they say just before the blast? Something to ready you? A heads-up to prevent a heads-off?

I wish now that I could have back this moment in time to prevent the suffering that it caused. But no human on earth could have planned for it. It was as if time stood still. Something bombing victims tell you only after they've processed the tragedy.

Certain bites of dialogue still hang in the rafters of my mind, bringing me back to the moment just before it happened:

"*If Romney wins, I'm gonna shoot myself.*" (This I distinctly heard many times that night.)

"*I made a lot of money during the Clinton era. Bush and Obama, not so much.*"

"*Did you know that two-thirds of all long-term care insurance claims are filed by women?*"

And that's when someone yelled, "He's having a heart attack!"

Mary screamed.

And when the dance floor cleared, some dude with a military crew cut was kneeling over Bales.

Bales was lying on his back on the cold hardwood floor, bug-eyed, clutching his chest. The only sound in the stunned room was his labored, asthmatic breathing.

"Call nine-one-one!" the crew cut guy shouted. "Call nine-one-one!"

AN HOUR LATER I was sitting in the emergency room of Saint John's Hospital with the Artist. It was one thirty in the morning and we were the only ones in there. It was eerily quiet except for the clicking noise made by the nervous manipulation of blue amber worry beads between the Artist's left thumb and forefinger. The beads were a gift from Bales. A souvenir from his last trip to Oman.

I tried to read a dog-eared copy of *Star Magazine*, but my mind kept racing. I thought about a book I'd read at my mother's house in Las Vegas, Joan Didion's *The Year of Magical Thinking*. It was hard to imagine the tragedies that she'd endured in such a short period of time. Losing her husband and going through all that sickness with her daughter. But one thought kept repeating itself. The same thought that kept coming back to her.

Life changes in an instant.

The doctor entered fifteen minutes later. He was tall and straight-backed, with a commanding helmet of silver hair. He looked noble, as if he'd just returned from the opera.

"Which one of you is Mr. Miller?"

The Artist stood up.

"That's me," he said. "Is he all right?"

"He's fine," the doctor said. "He's resting comfortably. His vitals are stable. But we're going to keep him here overnight. Just to be sure."

"What happened to him?"

"Hard to say. Stress, most likely." The doctor examined a clipboard. "His blood pressure was two-oh-five over one-ten. Quite high." He looked up. "Unfortunately, it's something we've seen a lot of in this economy. And the pills and alcohol don't help. Why don't you go on home? Get some sleep. I know it's been a trying night. We'll call you tomorrow, let you know what time you can pick him up."

"Thank you, Doctor," the Artist said.

"Good night."

The doctor exited through double doors, and I said, "Have you seen the meds that guy takes?"

"He told me he was taking something for depression."

"Dude," I said. "He's got a war chest of scripts in his apartment. For all I know, he's bipolar."

The Artist rushed to his defense.

"You heard what the doctor said. It was stress. He's just in a bad place right now. Like most of us."

"You believe the doctor?" I said. "He's a freaking pill roller. What the hell does he know?"

"More than us. He's seen what's happening out there. People are losing it. I mean, just the other day I saw a news story about some guy who held up a Rite Aid. He didn't want money. Just drugs for his sick wife."

I sighed. "Whatever, dude. Let's get outta here. I hate hospitals."

Hashtag and the
Purple Slippers

I WAS SITTING at my computer around two the next day, listing Bales's shoes on eBay, when the Artist called. He told me he'd picked up Bales around noon and they went to JP's for a burger and a beer. He said Bales looked fine, was in good spirits, and now was back at his apartment taking a nap. That all sounded fairly pedestrian—that is until the Artist told me he'd just gotten a call from Mary-with-the-hair-in-her-face.

I said, "Is everything okay?"

"Not really," he said.

"Why? Is she still in shock about last night?"

"Kinda," he said. "But first off, she's pissed because somebody took a shit in her bathtub."

"What? Who would do that?"

"I don't know," the Artist said, "but that's not the worst of it."

"Hard to top a fecal deposit."

"Maybe so. But she said somebody stole her grandmother's diamond brooch. She claims it's worth three thousand dollars. I just wanted to give you a heads-up, in case you see her."

I stared at my computer screen, my mind processing what I thought he was trying to tell me.

"Wait," I said. "Are you saying…she thinks *I* stole her brooch?"

"I don't know what she thinks," the Artist said, "but she said she saw you in the bedroom last night."

I raised my voice. "No shit! That's where the bathroom is. Everybody was in there."

"I know. I know."

"Look," I said. "I didn't drop a Baby Ruth in the pool. And I sure as hell didn't steal anybody's brooch. And if she accuses me of that again, I'm gonna go off on her."

"I know you didn't. She's just emotional now."

I sighed, uploading a photo of a pair of black leather Louis Vuitton high-top sneakers onto eBay.

"Did she report it to the cops?" I said.

"Yeah. This morning."

A long silence eclipsed our conversation. And now that the Artist had informed me of such things that he thought I should know, I sensed he wanted to vent about his current plight. I thought about asking him if he'd scraped up rent yet but was so damn flustered that someone would actually accuse me of stealing that I ruthlessly let him dangle high above his own worst apprehensions.

"Well, thanks for the info," I said abruptly and hung up.

. . . .

LATER THAT NIGHT Bales came to his rescue. Hashtag, the Artist, and I were binge-watching *The Sopranos* and eating Del Taco when he arrived at the door holding a new sixty-inch Samsung TV.

"Special delivery for the Artist," Bales said.

Bales powered his way through the front door, deftly maneuvering the heavy TV set around the art-cluttered living room. It was the first time I saw the athlete in him, the striated muscle on his forearms, toned and exercised, and his strong hands gripping the sides of the box like an eagle's talons clutching its prey. I'm not saying he was superhuman. But you'd be a fool not to take notice.

"What's this?" asked the Artist.

"A present from Best Buy," said Bales, leaning the large box against the wall. "I know how much you lazy mugs like to sit around and watch your programs."

"But I thought you were broke?"

"Still am," Bales said. "But I received a little four-grand kicker from the company today. The last of my settlement."

"But I can't…"

"Consider it a loan," Bales said. "I'll take it when I move out of this smelly hole. Which I'm hoping is sooner rather than later."

The stolen brooch popped into my mind. The three thousand dollars. But what did I know? I'd only met Bales ten days ago. So my intuition took a backseat, neglected like a lost art.

"That's a nice TV," I said.

Hashtag itched his ball sack through his khaki shorts and said, "You probably could have gotten it cheaper on Amazon."

"Shut the fuck up," Bales said. "And if I see you playing games on that *fucking* phone again, I swear to God, I'll toss it into the ocean. I want you present and *engaged* tonight."

"What?"

"And stop farting. Nobody gave you fart blanche to rip the room. It smells like sour cooch in here."

Bales had adopted Hashtag as his little brother to beat up. His real name was Rick Hassler and he lived upstairs in number 8. He earned his nickname because he was always on the phone texting, tweeting, Facebooking, or playing Angry Birds with some Mormon dude in Salt Lake City. It drove Bales crazy. That and his oafish body. Although Hashtag was raised in affluence, he had the look of a washed-up heavyweight boxer. Early forties—fat and balding— with curly black hair and a bulbous nose that begged for a straight right.

But he didn't give a shit about his appearance and neither did we. His entire food-stained wardrobe consisted of polo shirts and khaki shorts. And if he owned anything other than flip-flops, I never saw them. He also had the nasty habit of picking at his scrotum (which never made it easy shaking hands with him. He's why the fist bump was invented). But the main reason Bales had him tag along was the money. He was a carefree trust-fund kid from Pasadena who received six grand a month to squander as he pleased. And with most of us light in the wallet at the time, Bales made sure a large cut of the fat man's dough came our way.

Bales said, "How much you short rent, A?"

"Four hundred dollars."

"How long do you have until the landlord brings in the hounds?"

"He usually collects on the fourth of the month."

Bales shrugged. "You got a few days to come up with something." He let the Artist hang a moment, teasing him.

"I'll tell you what," Bales said. "I was just going to give you the money, but I knew you wouldn't take it. The proud Southern man that you are. So tell me, what painting can I buy for four hundred dollars?"

The Artist brightened. "Are you serious?"

"I sure am," Bales said. "I never joke about a fine art purchase."

The Artist bolted up from his chair with excitement and dashed into the bedroom. He quickly returned carrying two small canvases, each the size of a record album. Then he laid them out gently on the hardwood floor, like swatches of carpet.

"Pick one," he said.

Bales studied the textured layers of color between the two choices, his gaze finally settling on a blue-green abstracted wave. The overall feeling the piece gave was one of serenity, a kind of a prismatic green that seemed to glow despite the low-level light, a harlin hailey

deep and luminous intoxicating green, as if its color
had been scrubbed from the ocean's current.

"This will look good in the living room," Bales
said. He picked up the painting. "Soothe the savage
beast!" He swung his eyes. "What about you,
Hashtag? You're rich. Why don't you buy something
instead of jiggling your lard-loving flesh?"

Hashtag chomped down on a burrito. "I've already
bought six. I can't even fit them all on my wall."

"Fair enough," Bales said. "What about you,
Clean? Have you bought anything from the Artist?"

I shifted in my chair. "Is this an interrogation?"

"Two," the Artist said, speaking on my behalf. "He
bought two big pieces. And his dad bought one, too."

I turned to Bales. "I paid a lot more than four
hundred bucks, I'll tell you that. And I'll be happy
to buy more when I can."

Hashtag swiped a napkin across his mouth and
said to Bales, "Hey, I saw you coming out of the
Fourth Street pawn shop today. I was driving by
and honked, but you didn't see me."

Bales looked at him coldly. "What are you talking
about? I was at Best Buy. Getting the TV."

"You sure?" Hashtag said, scratching the bald spot
on his crown. "Because I noticed those purple slippers you always wear."

Bales seemed to look past him. "The silver spoon must be clouding your vision, you doughy schmuck."

Hashtag looked puzzled. "I coulda sworn it was you."

I craned my head toward the Artist. He was staring at Bales, eyes rapt, like he was some warrior poet. A fresh sale and rent paid. What more could he want?

Bales said, "Look, I'm back from the brink. I didn't die—all right? My heart's fine. It's time to celebrate." He turned to Hashtag. "Go buy us some beer, Fatty."

Hashtag spoke with his mouth full. "What do you want?"

"Stella, Beck's, or Heineken. None of that bathtub beer you bought last time. Now fly, wingnut."

Hashtag rose from the couch and fixed his Apple headset, gently placing a bud in each ear. Then he quietly walked out the door into the dark, his chubby face lit by the aqueous blue glow of his cell phone.

Bales said, "Let's ditch the fat sap and eat big at El Cholo. I'm buying."

"You gonna blow all your money in one night?" I said.

"It's only money, Clean. I used to spill more than this. Besides, I should have some shoe money coming in soon. Am I right?"

I showed him the eBay listing on my iPhone.

"Sweet," he said. "Five watchers, huh?"

"Yeah," I said. "One of them will take the bait soon."

The Way of the
Samurai

BALES'S SHOES SOLD for $8,400 to some guy in Busan, South Korea. It was a trend that I'd noticed gradually, but after this sale it struck me that I couldn't remember the last time I'd sold to an American buyer. I looked up my last five transactions on eBay and checked the shipping addresses: Shanghai, Kuala Lumpur, Moscow, Singapore, Busan. If it wasn't clear to me before, it was now.

The money was moving from west to east. So was the gold.

My cut of the deal was twenty percent—$1,680. Enough to cover a month's worth of bills and more cheap wine. It was, as my father is fond of saying, better than a sharp stick in the eye. But still not enough to halt my slide. We'd all made our November rent thanks to Bales. And despite some of his disturbing actions, or alleged actions, we were all grateful for the chance to "earn" some money.

On the morning of November 6, Election Day 2012, I walked to the Coffee Bean and Tea Leaf for my usual Earl Grey tea. The air was crisp and cool at 7:45 a.m., and the streets were abuzz with political energy. On the walk back an elderly Asian woman with a missing front tooth asked me enthusiastically if I'd voted yet.

"Soon," I said, still ripple-eyed from last night's vino. "Soon."

She cut a jagged grin. "That's good," she said. "Real good."

I had renounced all party affiliations a few years ago. I'd voted both Republican and Democrat in the past, but now I had become disillusioned with the constant acrimony that existed in American politics. My protest vote would be cast for an independent. Some said I was throwing my vote away, but then I reminded them that we lived in California. I'd voted for Obama the first go-around, but his hawkish stance on foreign policy had left me wanting change. I'd had enough of war.

I arrived at the Mar Vista polling station at 8:45, and, true to form, most of the people were old and white. The future never failed to remind me of my destiny. But I didn't need reminding; the demographics slapped me in the face every day. Bales referred to the beach communities as "the gray coasts." Where youth goes to die. At the time, I thought his dogmatic views on the subject were extreme, but the last few years of my casual observation had proved him right.

Most of the volunteers working the polls were elderly women. I was approaching the sign-in table when a bag lady in a red overcoat clutching a small mangy mutt rushed me and got up in my grill.

"You're gonna vote for Romney, aren't you, Blue Eyes?"

I pulled my face back. "Excuse me?"

"It's not too late to change your mind." Her singsong voice had a street quality about it. Lincoln and Pico cred.

"How do you know I'm voting for Romney?" I said.

"You look like that type."

"And what type is that?"

"A dog killer."

A dog killer?

Is that what I had been reduced to? Is that the look the Great Recession had bestowed upon me? How could I even respond to that? I did what I always do in those situations. I resorted to humor. "Look, ma'am," I said, quoting Romney from the campaign trail. "I'm not in this race to slow the rise of the oceans or heal the planet. Because I'm a flesh-eating zombie. And I'm here to gorge on Obama supporters." I brought my face to hers. "That includes you, *and your little dog*."

She stepped back, her dark eyes big as black cherries.

"Oh, my."

I cracked my neck. "Yes, 'oh, my.' Now if you'll excuse me, madam, it's time for me to vote."

She uttered a little snort and walked away.

LATER THAT EVENING we gathered in the Artist's living room to watch the election results. The new Samsung TV, mounted earlier by Homegrown and a couple of his Mexican workers, covered the entire western wall. On the big screen, political pundits traversed a map of the nation, placing red or blue placards on top of the states, indicating which way the vote had gone. The coasts were blue—everything else red.

"Did you vote for the dog strapper?" Bales asked, already half in the bag.

"No," I said. "But I'm all in favor of binders of women."

The Artist laughed and passed me a joint.

"So who did you vote for?"

"I wanted to write in Ron Paul," I said, "but the idiots working the polling station didn't have a pencil. So I punched Gary Johnson's card."

Bales sank into the couch and tossed back a beer. "Looks like you radically changed the course of American history."

I took a hit of weed.

"It's moot anyway," I said, holding in the smoke. "The fastest-growing voter base is the Latinos." I exhaled smoothly. "I don't count anymore."

The Artist went into the kitchen and brought back a bowl of buttered popcorn and set it down on the coffee table. He looked at me. "I thought you were voting for Obama," he said.

"No, I told you. I don't like what he's done with Afghanistan. He said he'd pull the troops out. He never did."

"We should have learned from the Russians," Bales said, grabbing a handful of popcorn. "Once you get your ass kicked, it's time to go home."

Around 10 p.m. Pacific Standard Time, Barack Hussein Obama was declared the winner of the 2012 presidential election. You could almost hear the entire state of California let out a collective sigh of relief.

The Artist jumped up from his chair and screamed, "Yes! Yes! Screw you, Boner! Screw you, teabaggers! You and all the other racist white people." He clapped his hands and chanted, "Four more years! Four more years! Four more years!"

On the TV, Romney's motorcade was seen leaving the building. Then the coverage switched to an enthusiastic college mob in Ohio. A fresh-faced kid held up a sign that read *Judge Judy 2016.*

Bales got up off the couch and brought us all a beer. "Hate to bum your high, A," he said. "But four more years of what? What's he going to do for you?"

"He's not Romney," the Artist said. "That's a start."

"Maybe so, but I doubt it." Bales walked across the room and fingered the samurai sword above the fireplace. "What's the heroic backstory on this?"

"It was my grandfather's," said the Artist. "He took it off a dead Japanese officer on Iwo Jima."

"You sure you didn't buy it on eBay?"

"You wish," the Artist said.

Bales grabbed the weapon off the mantel and ran his forefinger along the red leather scabbard. And after a moment of admiring the intricate carvings of a regal dragon on the handle, he unsheathed the curved blade.

"Be careful," the Artist said. "It's sharp, man."

"Can you imagine sticking someone with this?"

"Easy, Bales," I said. "We don't need another trip to the emergency room."

Bales admired the cold, hard steel, twisting and turning the weapon in his palm, the sword's thirty-inch blade sparkling under the pendant light.

"No chance of that," Bales said. "Did he slay the dragon? Cut the guy's head off?"

"I don't know," the Artist said. "Grandpa was part of the Silent Generation. He didn't talk much."

Bales sheathed the blade. "I hope he did. Then cut off the Jap's dick and stuffed it inside his mouth. Fuckin' slope."

I shared a look with the Artist.

"So, four more years of Obamacrap," Bales said, plopping down on the couch. "What are we going to do to improve our lives, gentlemen? How are we going to make some dough?"

"I've got another interview," I said.

Bales cracked a beer. "Yeah? Do enlighten us on your prospects."

"Property management," I said. "Ten bucks an hour…plus commission. It's something to help pay the bills. Get some marketing money."

Bales scoffed. "Really? Ten bucks an hour? You might as well hold the monkey cup."

"Yeah?" I said. "What are you doing? Besides getting blasted on a nightly basis."

Bales sat up. "You don't get it, do you?"

"Get what?" the Artist said.

"That America has already fucked you—*us*." Bales glanced at the sword on the mantel. "All we got left is revolution."

"What are you talking about?" I said.

"I'm talking about the American dream, Clean. It's over. Welcome to Slave Nation."

"I'm no slave," I said. "I work for myself."

"You did. But not anymore. With your skillset, you'll be lucky to find a cubicle farm to call home."

I felt the sudden sweat under my arms, my palms clammy. I couldn't work in a cubicle. I'd stroke out before payday.

"You don't know a damn thing about me," I said.

"I know you can't code. You're not a robot. And you're not making any money in real estate. What else do I need to know?"

The Artist listened intently—rolling a fresh joint on a Bad Company album—as Bales and I jousted over an uncertain future.

"So I'll ask again," Bales said. "How do we make money?"

Hashtag shrugged. "The stock market?"

"It's rigged," said Bales. "They're screwing you, and you, and"—he pointed at us one by one, stopping at Hashtag—"not you, you fat fuck. You got money rolling in. All you got to do is float around in orbit till you explode."

Hashtag brought his unobservant face up from a game of phone Scrabble.

"I don't float around in orbit."

"No, you don't," Bales said. "You sit around. My point is, if you follow the rules today, *you're a sucker*. Can't you see? There are no jobs. The rich have broken the social contract—cornered economic opportunity. They're laughing at us. Right in our fucking faces."

"So what do you propose we do about it?" I said.

"I don't know yet," he said. "But I know this. We can't afford shit. So sorry to say, Clean, your chicken-wage job won't even pay your health insurance. Let alone a mortgage." Bales chugged his beer with a fair amount of anger in his eyes. There was something turning over and over in his head. He had that look. That pimp-slap look. He let out a terminal sigh and finally said, "None of this is about race, or white privilege. The people have it wrong. It's about one thing, and one thing only...*money*. You either got it or you don't. That's the new divide. The color green."

"I'm not waving the white flag," I said. "We just have to adjust our expectations. Exploit the new normal."

Bales chuckled without humor. "Why don't you go shine up your spiffy wing tips, Clean. Go pound the pavement. But for what?"

"Clients, a job—that's what."

Bales knocked his skull with a balled fist. "How many times can you beat your head up against the wall? You possess *nothing* that corporations want today. You're old, white, and male. Demographics have castrated you."

I folded my arms. "I refuse to believe that."

"Oh, you do?"

I shook my head. "Yeah, I do."

"Then you're more of a fool than I thought."

Bales waited for a response, like it was my draw in poker. But when I refused to be his sparring partner, he raked back his silver hair and cast his dark eyes around the room, searching for help. There was none. He looked back at me as if he couldn't believe I had squandered his wisdom. "You know why you can't get clients?" he said.

"Why?"

"Because the prime real estate is now owned by a few wealthy corporations—the oligarchs. They've consolidated the power. The information. It's happening in all industries."

"I'm not that bearish," I said. "I'll work at McDonald's if I have to."

Bales flipped. "Christ, man! Stop chasing unicorns! You're not qualified for that job. You have to be bilingual. It just shows your ignorance."

"So what's left?" asked the Artist.

Bales leaned back on the sofa, a despondent look on his face. "Picking up dog shit for eight bucks an hour."

He was incensed, his carotid artery pulsating on his neck. I watched his shaky right hand pull out a pill bottle from his dark blue Patagonia vest. He steadied his long, trembling fingers, slowly twisted off the cap, and shook out a handful of pills into his palm. He studied them a moment, as if delighted by their kaleidoscopic presence. Then he stuffed the entire lot into the back of his throat and gulped it all down with a bottle of beer.

Seconds later, he burped half the alphabet.

Uncomfortable, I looked over at the Artist. He caught my eye, then sheepishly looked floorward. Hashtag, as always, had no read on the situation.

As midnight approached, the booze and the drugs had washed Bales into an impaired mess. He was sprawled on the couch, one arm dangling, mumbling to himself. "In Asia, the smart ones are moving to the city. Here in California, the smart ones are moving out. I gotta get out of this town…I'm dyin'. Seattle, Denver, maybe Dallas…anywhere but here… L.A. is dead."

His speech was slurred, like that of a stroke patient.

"Why don't you go to bed?" I said.

"Why don't you fuckin' go to bed? And where is that midget Big Salad? I'm hungry."

Big Salad was a short guy with a thin, sandy mullet. Played drums in the house band down at Rusty's Surf Ranch on the pier. Bales gave him his nickname because he was a vegan, always walking around the complex with one of those big plastic salad containers from Ralph's supermarket. Fresh greens piled high, bathing in an entire bottle of Newman's Own Italian dressing.

"He's not here," said the Artist. "He's got a gig."

"Figures," Bales said. "That little prick. Probably getting his fauxhawk trimmed. What's left of it, anyway." He laughed like a moonshine drunk.

"C'mon," I said. "I'll help you over to your apartment."

"I don't need anybody's help," Bales said.

Bales staggered to his feet and stumbled across the room, groping at the fireplace mantel for balance. I rose from my chair, but without warning he yanked the sword off its mount. He clumsily unsheathed its blade, like a wounded warrior making his last stand.

"Don't touch me!" he said. "Don't you fuckin' touch me."

The Artist pleaded, "Please, John. Put down the sword."

Bales started wielding the Japanese weapon, stabbing at the air. "Look at me," he said. "I'm a samurai warrior. Woo-hoo!"

His eyes were wide and crazy weird, his waxen, florid face a testament to the night's toxic ingestions.

"*John*," the Artist said, "you're gonna hurt yourself."

"Bales, put it down!" I said.

But Bales had no intention of dropping the weapon. He was playing his own game. The only game he knew: high drama.

"I know what you want," Bales said. "You want my head on a pike." He raised the sword to his neck. "Don't ever forget what you saw here tonight. Because I'm a fuckin' baller. A bone-poppin' player."

"*John, it's sharp,*" said the Artist.

Bales looked at us and laughed, a loud, drunken bellow. We watched as he stumbled back, then slowly lowered the blade from his windpipe.

I blew out a breath in relief.

"No," Bales said, unsteady on his feet. "You're not gonna get off that easy." Then he reached into my soul with hollow, vacant eyes and, while still holding my gaze, slashed the blade across the palm of his right hand. The Artist looked on in horror as blood pooled on the polished hardwood.

"John!" the Artist said, rushing over.

Bales dropped to his knees, clutching the blood-red sword. "It's just a pinprick," he said. "Just a little pinprick."

I still remember what he mumbled over and over that night right before he passed out.

"We gotta make a plan. We gotta make a plan. We gotta make a motherfuckin'..."

Twilight's Last
Gleaming

I GAVE UP the dope and booze for a few days. It was Friday, November 9, 2012, and I wanted to be straight for my interview. Wanted to prove Bales wrong about his declining-America thesis. He didn't remember cutting himself on election night. He did, however, recount having woken from a vivid dream in which people addressed him as Bales the Redeemer.

Walking into a sleek glass building at the corner of Olympic and Sawtelle, I felt strangely at ease with my surroundings. Dressed in flat-front straight-legged khaki pants and a dark blue button-down, I convinced myself that I was the modern portrait of today's new businessman.

The secretary told me to have a seat on the black leather sofa and brought me some bottled water while I waited. The lobby's chic decor gave me hope that green resided within.

The clatter of wheels on marble shifted my gaze to a scraggly long-haired kid whizzing by on a skate-board—inside the building! *Fucking degenerate*, I thought. *Show a little class.*

Moments later I was greeted by a lumbering middle-aged white man wearing an XXL Tommy Bahama silk shirt and high-waisted Wrangler jeans.

I secretly wondered how long it would be before I joined the Hawaiian Punch brigade.

"Mr. Jenkins?" he said.

I rose from the couch. "Yes."

"Garrett Spendlove."

We shook hands.

"Nice to meet you," I said.

"You too. C'mon back."

I followed him into the conference room and we both took a seat.

"Here's my résumé," I said, sliding my CV across the table.

He studied my work history and I studied him. The overhead light exposed his crude hair trans-plant, doll-head plugs jutting up like rusty rebar.

"I see you've been with RE/MAX for over twenty years," he said. "What brings you here?"

"Money."

He winced and shifted his big body in the chair.

"You'll have to excuse me," he said. "But I had a colonoscopy yesterday and I'm still on fire."

I nodded.

"The dadgum thing cost me three grand out of pocket," he said, "and I've got insurance. The doc said I took a shit during the procedure. Said my prep work was lousy."

"American health care at its finest," I said.

He smiled and pushed my résumé away. "I'm not gonna blow smoke up your ass," he said. "Or mine. We struggled just like everyone else in the down-turn. If my father hadn't owned the building, I'd be in your shoes. Out on the street. The only difference between me and you…is luck. Nothing more. So don't beat yourself up. It's the story of a lot of people. We only survived by downsizing and sub-letting space to some of these high-tech firms. It's been a brutal five years." He fell silent, folding his beefy hands on the table. "But my father is convinced now is the time to expand."

"And what do you think?"

"It doesn't matter what I think. What matters is bringing in new accounts. That's why you're here.

We need business development people to make that happen."

"I'm your man," I said.

"Okay. Here it is. The position is straight commission with no benefits until after six months. You prove yourself, we'll sweeten the pot."

My eyes narrowed. "But the ad said it was ten bucks an hour plus bonus."

"The old man called an audible…what can I say?"

"So," I said, groping for words. "What are you really offering me?"

He shrugged. "An established firm that might open a few doors."

I dropped my head. He sensed my desperation, my fall into something black. "Do you have a book of business?" he asked.

"I don't have squat."

"What about your natural market?"

"They're all dead."

"Old clients?"

"All broke."

His face showed genuine concern. "Damn. Do you speak Spanish?"

"Nada."

He pointed a finger. "Learn that language. It's the future."

I pleaded, "You're one of the biggest property management firms in the city. Surely you must have a few warm leads for me to call."

"I've got veterans struggling to make ends meet right now. They're working the database. Newbies got to cold-call. You know how it is. Things are changing. Winds are shifting. It's every man for himself out there."

"But I can work for myself for free."

He nodded in agreement. "That would be my suggestion. Keep swinging the bat. Call your old clients. Blow somebody. I mean, what can I tell you?"

He leaned back in his chair, both hands gripping the armrests, gazing out the window. "Do you own a house?"

"Why?"

"A lot of my guys are renting out rooms to get by now. Something to think about."

"Not anymore," I said. "Lost it to divorce."

He exhaled. "Rough. You're in real estate. You know what's happening out there. The Fed driving down interest rates. Thousand-foot crab shacks going for a million bucks. It's a joke. Hell, the Chinese have offered to buy the building for a boatload. It all makes about as much sense as listening to the radio on a Harley."

"So why not sell out?"

"The old man believes in America."

"And you?"

He dropped his head and twirled my résumé around with his thick forefinger on the table. Then looked up, dead serious. "I don't know anymore."

I sighed. Twilight's last gleaming.

"Look," he said. "Did you see that scrawny kid in the lobby on a skateboard?"

"Yeah."

"He works upstairs for a big data-mining company. Makes one hundred and twenty grand a year working five hours a day. Skateboards four."

I shook my head. "*Jesus*. Is that where it's going?"

"It's not where it's going," he said. "It's *where it is*." He paused. "It's a big bag of poo-poo. And we're all gonna have to do the heavy lifting."

He stood up and extended his hand.

"Good luck to ya, Mr. Jenkins. Keep your chin up. And if you come across a property management client, bring them here. I'd be happy to piece you off."

I walked out into the lobby stunned, not knowing if I even shook his hand.

Standing in the middle of the large sky-lit atrium, looking up into the vast abyss of space and time, I felt the ugly kid on the skateboard riding circles around me.

The music was faint on the building's sound system, but I recognized the Ray Charles song.

"Hit The Road, Jack."

All in the Family

THESE ARE NOT normal times.

I told myself that when I got home after the interview. After being humiliated by a gutter rat on a skateboard. It was ironic, too, because when I first saw the kid, I arrogantly dismissed him as a degenerate, a lost boy on a road to nowhere. But it appeared now that I was the lost boy. Except that I was not a boy. I was a middle-aged man lost in a city that eats people like me. Then shits them out like yesterday's courage. And to this day when I see a kid on a skateboard, I don't see a degenerate. I see a CEO in a T-shirt. And that's disturbing.

I'll give you a few tidbits about me. I'm divorced and used to have a girlfriend—up until a few months ago. We hadn't been dating long, maybe ninety days, but then I stopped calling. She gets it now. No more psychologizing. She's moved on. And that's what I wanted, because she doesn't deserve me. Not in the place I'm in at the moment.

I've got a daughter in college back east, and she's my number one priority. My pride and joy. And failing to provide for her is my worst nightmare. As I'm sure it is with most parents.

So I stand here at this historic junction in American history and try to stay positive. That's all I can do.

I turned on the TV and glimpsed the news, saw the debris from the Japanese tsunami washing up on the shores of Hawaii. And I thought, *That's me— garbage. Floating out to sea. Where I wash up is anyone's guess.*

It was around this time I started to acquire the look. The look of a wanderer, a hands-in-the-pockets gawker, someone who used to raise his voice but now doesn't. And if you've ever visited a third-world country and wondered why all the young men are just hanging around, it's because there's no work. And won't be for a long time. Which leaves you with two options. Stay or leave. Three if you want to blow your head off.

I walked into my home office (my bedroom) and saw the blinking red light on my answering machine. It's my favorite machine. Has been since 1989. It's a classic Radio Shack DuoFone model with the plastic wooden top. You remember those? How excited you got when you came home and saw that blinking red light, so full of promise, mystery, and intrigue? Your heart fluttered, and just for a moment you allowed your hopes to soar above the clouds, temporarily shelving the negativity of the day. Remember that?

Then you'd steel your mind and crack your knuckles and pray for that life-changing call. That one pregnant call that sweeps us up and carries us away. That one joyous call telling you you sold a script, got accepted to your favorite university, or in my case, closed a real estate deal. And then you'd step back and pound your chest like an orangutan in heat and shout, "*Yo, bitch! I am the man!*"

Now, over these last few years, you took a deep breath and crossed your fingers as you rewound the squealing cassette tape and heard the robotic voice say: *Message one…beeeeeep.* And then more often than not it would be from one of your struggling friends, who you loved, but you wished it was somebody bigger. You'd call them back and the conversation would go something like this: "Hey, man, just checking in."

"What's up?"

"Nothing much. What's up with you?"

"Nothing."

"Any deals?"

"No. You?"

"Nada. Couple leads, that's about it."

"So what you're telling me is, you're basically dead in the water."

"Yeah. I guess so."

And that's the way it had gone for the last few years. It used to be a hotbed of activity here. A busy time of wheels and deals, of excited home buyers talking move-in dates and kitchen remodels and closing costs. Now the only people who called me on this line were my dad and the Artist.

Maybe that's why I'd kept the machine. I still liked to dream.

I checked the message. It was from my seventy-nine-year-old father calling about my Christmas plans. I took a seat at my desk, picked up the phone and called, staring up at the brown water stains on the ceiling. There was a new one, I noticed. And I couldn't decide if it looked more like the map of Syria or a cow skull. After a minute of vigilant study, I concluded that it looked like Syria. Something not yet dead.

"Hello."

"Oh, hey, Dad," I said, not expecting a first-ring answer. "I got your message, was just checking in."

"Good," he said. "How'd the interview go?"

"Not great. It turns out there's no guarantee. Just commission and cold calls."

"You can do that yourself," he said.

"I know. So we soldier on."

"I have faith in you, son."

"I'm glad someone does. Anyway, you said something about Christmas."

"Oh, yes. You remember my friend Alan? From school?"

"Yeah. The Pan Am pilot. The guy you used to get drunk with all night. Play Bread's *Baby I'm-a Want You* album and smoke cigars. Or was it Glen Campbell?"

He laughed. "All of the above. And that was the early seventies. We've toned it down since then."

"Okay," I said. "Does that mean I don't have to rake the shag carpet?"

"You still remember that, huh?"

"How could I forget? It was like wading through the jungle every morning."

"Yeah…I guess it wasn't your favorite chore."

"So what about him?" I asked, placing a new mini-cassette tape into the message machine.

"Who?"

"Alan."

"Oh, yes, Alan. Well, we're thinking about a fishing trip around Christmas."

"Where?"

"Cabo San Lucas. You're more than welcome to join us."

"It sounds good, Dad," I said, "but I've already promised Mom I'd help her with the party."

My mother and father had long since divorced, but they were still great friends. We all tried to coordinate the holidays, but as we got older we sometimes went our separate ways. Or me splitting time between the two. And, yes, I am an only child.

"Well, if you change your mind, we'd be happy to have you. I'm sure Alan would love to see you again."

"I'll keep you posted," I said. I wadded up a piece of notebook paper and scored two in the wastebasket. "How's your health? You feeling good?"

"Pretty good. Knee hurts a tad, but I think I'll live."

"That's good. You need anything? Need me to come by?"

He thought a moment.

"No," he said. "Right now everything seems to be under control. Say, how's Jimmy doing?"

"He's hanging in there like the rest of us," I said. "Hand to mouth."

My father paused to blow his nose, then said, "Uh-huh. How's Rose? She lighting the world on fire?"

"She's great," I said. "But I need to make money to keep it that way. School's expensive."

"I understand."

I heard him cleaning his teeth with his tongue and cheek, a clicking and sucking sound. Then he said something that shook me. "Say…how's your friend Jimmy doing? The Artist?"

"Dad, you just asked me that."

"I did? Huh. I've got so much on my plate right now, I'm…kind of scattered. Planning this fishing trip and all. Comparing these travel sites is tedious. Expedia this. Orbitz that."

"I hear you. He's a…" And for a minute I lost my train of thought, still thinking about what had just happened. I'm usually not a worrier by nature, but for some reason alarm bells rang. "He's a…doing all right," I said. "But times are tough."

"I know they are, son. But that Jimmy sure is talented. I sure hope he makes it one day."

"Me too, Dad. Me too."

"Look, son, if you need a little help, feel free to ask. You know I'm here for you."

"I appreciate it, Dad, but I'm sure I'll make do."

My father didn't have a lot of money. Most of what he did have was locked up in an IRA with tax implications and mandatory distributions. And since he didn't believe in the stock market, he was earning zero return on the money in a bank account. His principal, like that of the rest of us savers, was eroding quickly. If the Federal Reserve didn't change its policy soon, he'd be tapped out in a couple of years.

"Well," he said. "I'm just a phone call away."

"I know, Dad. I'll check in on you soon."

I said goodbye and hung up the phone. Then I lay back on the bed, staring at the map of Syria on the ceiling. I wondered how to move forward. People kept telling me to "expand my brand," and I kept asking myself, what *is* my brand? How can I thrive in a new world that's foreign to me? Where does a middle-aged bald man go to find his brand? LinkedIn? Facebook? God forbid, Twitter?

I had to trust that these questions would be answered in time.

Meanwhile, what do you do when your whole world has been rocked? When your life is stuck between a skateboard and the end of times?

Do you start picking up dog shit for eight bucks an hour?

Fuck no.

You start drinking. And it doesn't matter how or where. Throw on a Lakers jersey and paint your face purple and gold and get smashed at the local sports bar. Splay out in the dim, mothering light of your own living room, slumped in your favorite easy chair. The result is the same.

Blasted.

I remember sitting on the couch that night, in between beers, and picking up a piece of notebook paper that Bales had doodled on—which he often did, to our amusement, when he was drunk. This cartoon that he'd sketched pretty much summed up what we all felt at the time:

Zero Dark Thirty

THE NEXT MORNING, I woke with a stinging hangover. I had drunk myself silly watching an episode of *Intervention*, some meth-head loser bossing his mom around between crying jags and fits of rage. I vaguely remembered a Quasimodo stagger down to CVS at midnight in a driving rain to buy another bottle of wine, the wide-eyed Filipina checker recoiling in horror at the sight of my inebriated mug. I must have resembled some wild beast, ready to attack if its needs weren't met. I sort of recalled a foggy image of myself in the mirror when I got home, my wine-stained teeth the color of Fresno plums.

Thank God for Pavarotti, who serenaded my morning pain with "Vesti la Giubba," a gift from my next-door neighbor, the sad clown. I pulled myself out of bed and read the *Los Angeles Times* online, then checked my Yahoo horoscope. Any guidance without judgment was always welcome:

Saturday, November 10, 2012.

When numerous alignments occur within one twenty-four-hour period, many changes are in the process of manifesting. Your job is to steer clear of confusion and chaos.

At 11 a.m. I reached for the wine jug. I didn't bother with a glass. I hoisted up the big bottle with two hands and took a long chug and let the spillage run down the sides of my mouth.

That ought to get me through the confusion and chaos, I thought.

Exiting my apartment late afternoon with my beach cruiser, I ran into Paula, my favorite Southie chick. She looked concerned, her gray hair pushed up into a bun.

"Are you okay?" she said, her thick New England accent in full blossom.

"Yeah, why?"

"Because I heard a loud thud from your apartment last night, and I rushed over to your window"—she pronounced it *winda*—"and the TV was on, but I didn't see you on the couch. But then I looked down and saw you rolling around on the floor eating French fries, *like David fuckin' Hasselhoff!*"

I forgot how insanely ravenous pot made me. Where I got the fries was anybody's guess.

"The munchies," I said, shrugging.

She laughed.

"How's your brother?" I said.

"He's still suffering from PESD. He voted for Romney."

"PESD?"

"Post-Election Stress Disorder." She pronounced disorder like *dis-awhr-da.*

I smiled and hopped on my bike. "Seems to be a lot of that going around."

As I pedaled north on the Venice Beach boardwalk, I saw the ocean was flat and greenish dark, stretching out to infinity against the burning autumn sky. At that moment I was alone on the bike path, a homeless head streaking toward the sunset.

After an invigorating, contemplative, wind-in-my-face ride, I arrived late evening at the Santa Monica Pier. I found the Artist set up with a five-by-five canvas anchored on a sturdy wooden easel in the amusement park. He stood west under the Ferris wheel, his brushstrokes animated yet smooth.

A boisterous group of Asian tourists with cameras and long lenses had stopped to watch him paint. Clucking and clicking. Clucking and clicking.

I skidded my bike to a stop, and he smiled when he saw me.

"What's up?" he said.

"Just checking in on the Artist. These people bothering you?"

"No," he said. "Who am I to deny greatness?"

We laughed.

Then I turned to the crowd, pointed at the painting, and yelled, "Eight grand! Do I hear eight grand? C'mon now! Which of you kind people are patrons of the arts?"

If they understood, they didn't let on. Most just smiled dumbly, a little uncomfortably. Nodding their heads as if freshly brainwashed.

"Hey," the Artist said, his Southern accent more regal in tone. "Did you hear Michaels is closing?"

"The crafts store?"

He zipped up his hoodie. "Yeah. Twenty-six years. The manager said it was because of the high rents."

"Wow. What are you gonna do about art supplies?"

"I don't know," he said. He looked down at his black Converse sneakers. "I don't know."

"You'll think of something."

"Yeah, I guess. Hey, sorry about your interview."

"Thanks," I said, "but there was nothing there anyway."

I dismounted my beach cruiser and laid it down on the pier. "Did I tell you I started wrestling again?"

"Oh yeah?" he said. "I figured it was only a matter of time before the Iceman came out of retirement. Everybody else is."

I smiled and walked over to the Artist, positioning myself behind him. "Check this out."

"Wait. What are you doing?"

"Drop the brush for a minute," I said. "I want to show you this new move I learned from my MMA buddy."

"Why do I always have to be the training dummy?"

The Artist never liked these grappling demonstrations. Over the years it was he who bore the brunt of my practice. In 2000 I had almost broken his arm while working on the Granby roll. No wonder he was skittish.

"I'm not going to hurt you," I said. "It's just a walk-through. Powder puff stuff. God forbid I ever have to use it."

"God forbid."

Still standing behind him, I placed my forearm under his chin. I felt his body stiffen. "Relax," I said. I gently locked my arms around his neck and arched his back with my knee. "The beauty of this move," I said, "is that the more the opponent struggles, the more they get choked out. In seconds, you'll be gasping for air like a dying fish on a dry lake bed. Then it's night-night."

"Can't wait," the Artist said.

I whispered playfully in his ear, "Are you ready to go to sleep?"

"No, I'm good," he said. "Really. But thank you for asking."

I released him, watched him grab his brush and resume painting. Then he looked at me and rolled his eyes.

"What?" I said. "I'm just trying to get back in shape. And you never know when I might meet a terrorist on the bus or something."

The Artist dabbed his brush into the cobalt blue on his oval wooden palette. "*Or something*," he said. "I just don't want to be around when it happens."

"Fair enough," I said. I took a seat on an Adirondack chair, crossed my legs, and got comfortable. "What about you? Any sales? Any action at all?"

"Well," the Artist said, "you know that Orange County photographer I was telling you about?"

"The guy with the large vocal sac? Looks like a tree frog?"

"Yeah. That's him. That dick let a rhino eat my backdrop."

Hoping to earn some extra bucks, the Artist had started painting backdrops for photographers. But as most seasoned pros know, photographers don't have any money. Which makes them notoriously cheap.

"Is that the same guy who shot that Czech model with all those exotic animals?"

"Yes. So, he returns my backdrop. And first off, it's ripped in two. Dirty hoof marks all over it. And then he has the nerve to tell me that I shouldn't sweat it, because it's good exposure for me. That people are going to see my work. Can you believe that? That backdrop is one of my bestsellers."

"What an asshole."

"I know. Then he says he can't pay me until Wednesday. Do you know how many times I've heard that? I mean, I don't even recognize how business is conducted anymore. I don't know, man. I'm irritated."

My phone dinged and I checked it. It was a text from Bales. It read:

Dogs and cats sharing bowls.
Sunnis and Shias sharing toothbrushes.
Generations of great expectations dashed.
Warning: Destruction ahead.
We're all melting icebergs.
Truly, the end of days, Clean.

"Who is it?" said the Artist.

"Bales."

"What'd he say?"

I pushed the phone up to the Artist's face. He bent down and read the text message, squinting in the swampy light.

"Do you think he's really crazy?" he said. "I mean, that shit with the sword. That was freaky."

"I told you. He's banging a nasty drum."

The Artist grabbed a clean paintbrush. "You know, sometimes he reminds me of a serial killer. He's got that look. That *Zero Dark Thirty* look."

"That's because he's high on drugs twenty-four seven," I said. "*Hard drugs*."

"Maybe so. Guess what he told me last night."

"What?"

"He said he killed a monkey at the zoo. When he was sixteen. Twisted its neck off right in front of the handler."

"I'm not sure you can believe anything he says. Monkeys are incredibly strong."

"Yeah, that's probably true." The Artist puffed out both cheeks. "Anyway, I got bigger problems."

"I'm not sure I wanna hear 'em."

"You got no choice. I gotta tell somebody. It's killing me."

I leaned forward in my chair. "What did you muck up this time?"

He looked at me, shivering in the cool ocean air. "Shit," he said. "I did something really bad yesterday. I don't know what I was thinking."

He hesitated, and I heard screams drop from the roller coaster.

"Now that you've got me all wet," I said, "tell me."

"You really want to know?"

"You didn't hurt anybody, did you?"

"No. Well, kinda. I staged a phony car accident on Wilshire. Or...Bales did."

"Why?"

"For the insurance money. Bales said these rich people around here deserve it. He took my Jeep and we parked on Wilshire close to Lincoln, and we waited for a luxury vehicle. Waited for someone looking for a parking spot. And when this woman in a Mercedes got close, Bales pulled out from the curb and she hit our front end. Bales told me to hold my neck. The police report documented everything."

I slapped my knee. "Oh, goddammit, Jimmy!" I said. "What were you thinking? That's a *felony*. A big-time clusterfuck."

"I know. I know. It's just that sometimes he can be...so...*intoxicating*."

"You know what?" I said. "I don't want to know any more." I shook my head. "You better wean yourself off his shit, bro. You're getting in deep."

"You heard what he said. There's no jobs. Nobody's buying anything. I need the money."

"You've got your art," I said. "It will sell. You've just got to give yourself a chance."

"What if it doesn't? Then what? I'm out on the streets."

"Frickin' A, Jimmy. What if Bales can't bail you out again? We're almost halfway through November. December rent's coming up. *Think*, do you have anybody that owes you money?"

He didn't think long.

"Yeah. That guy in Silver Lake."

"The guy whose restaurant you decorated?"

"Yeah, I've got three paintings in there. He said he's gonna have the money after Thanksgiving."

"How much is that?"

"Three thousand. That's if he pays me."

"Oh, he'll pay you," I said. "If he doesn't, I'm taking the paintings."

I was tired of the exploitation in this town. Squeezing service people and artists. Somebody had to take a stand. And I figured there was nobody better than a bald man.

But the Artist didn't see it that way. He tried to squelch my growing aggression. "We'll see," he said, laughing uneasily.

"Yeah, we will see," I said. "Because I'm going over there if you don't get the money."

Like all artists, he had a low threshold for sausage-making commerce.

"Let me help you," I said. "I know someone in the art world. Or used to. It's a long shot. But let me call her. See if she'll take a look at your work."

"I don't know," he said.

I sprang from my chair and got up in his face. "What do you mean you don't know? What else have you got? Bales and his schemes?"

"Look at you," he said. "You did that eBay thing with him because you needed the money."

"That's different," I said. "It was an arm's-length transaction."

"How do you know? The shoes could have been stolen...or fake. You don't know."

I paused in the dusk, a chilly wind blowing off the black ocean.

"No," I said, "I guess I don't."

"Jesus, Richard. What are we doing?"

I looked away toward a lone fisherman casting his line off the pier.

"We're drifting."

Back in the High
Life Again

I CONTINUED MY job search, but a week later nothing had materialized. I scoured the Internet, checking Indeed, Craigslist, and Monster. Nothing but Glengarry scams and hiring freezes across the board. On the news, President Obama was saying he wasn't sure how the fiscal cliff was going to affect small business. He should have called me. I could've told him.

As per the property management guy's suggestion, I again plowed through my old client list. I called everybody I knew and some I didn't, but most had either moved away or were staying the course. "Riding it out" was how one man put it.

Many afternoons I sat on my bed watching dust particles float in a slat of sunshine as I pondered how to make some money. My only experience was in sales. And the only sales jobs with a lucrative salary anymore were technology jobs, none of which I was qualified for. The sad truth was, I could easily learn the product (whatever it might be) and get up to speed quickly, but in the current economic climate, and with our youth-oriented culture, I knew I would never even receive that opportunity.

Bales put it to me this way: "Being over fifty in an industry that changes in a nanosecond is like trying to outrun the speed of sound. Ain't gonna happen." He said that once you're out of a job more than three months in the tech sector, you're done. I didn't argue with his assessment. It wasn't my bailiwick and never would be. Like the fat guy in the interview said, "Try not to beat yourself up."

I tried not to, but it was hard. Capitalism does that to you—if you're not earning money, you're worth nothing. Might as well collect cans and call it a day.

So. *What to do? What to do?* I was getting tired of drumming out my fate with my fingers on the desk, racking my brain over what to do next.

One day I read in the *Pasadena Star-News* that a doomsday cult was offering people with special skills substantial sums of money to join and help rebuild after the apocalypse. All I had to offer were my hunting and fishing skills, which quite frankly were a little rusty, along with my fishing pole.

Another day I heard the sounds of box cutting and tape tearing from next door. A young gay couple had recently bought and renovated the fourteen-hundred-square-foot house and were now in the process of moving in. Paula told me they paid $960,000 for the place. One of them was a hotshot entertainment lawyer and the other a senior programmer with a raucous stutter. I could only imagine their welcome-to-the-neighborhood housewarming party. "Oh, nice to meet you," the lawyer says. "And what do you do?"

"Well, right now, I mainly drum my fingers on the desk."

"For *eight hours*?"

"Sometimes I work overtime."

You see how it is? Floating into old age without a safety net. It sucks.

Soon I could hear the prosperous couple hosting dinner parties and arguing before their guests arrived, the lawyer pressing the programmer to remember that Steve didn't like mayonnaise, or that Raymond had a preference for gluten-free polenta. Too precious by half, but it took me back to a more comfortable time when *I* enjoyed fine dining with friends. A time when I could actually afford to host, and so could my friends. I knew damn well that if I had the money I'd do it all over again. It was money well spent. Friendships are priceless.

On more than one occasion, my new neighbors' well-fixed banter prompted me to play Steve Winwood's "Back in the High Life Again"—mainly for my own motivation, but also to drown out that discordant stammer. And then as the dark came on, I found myself hanging on to their dinner parties' hushed whispers, the subtle tinkle of silverware on china, the clinking of expensive wineglasses, the smooth jazz, the shards of laughter suddenly cutting through the night air. But my envy would soon fade with the primal masculine sounds that invariably shook the neighborhood around 11 p.m. I have nothing against a midnight cowboy, but it doesn't mean I have to go along for the ride.

As I said earlier, I had decided to start a journal, though so far I hadn't actually done anything about it. Partly I wanted something to help occupy my time, and partly I hoped it would help me figure out some of this shit—this shit being the rest of my life.

On Thursday I recorded my first entry:

Los Angeles, November 15, 2012

The Artist worries about the economy, that he heard Macy's had a bad financial quarter. He worries that JCPenney will shutter its doors, although he hasn't stepped inside the department store in years. Not since childhood, in fact. It seems, he says, that people aren't buying clothes anymore. A pastime he wistfully remembers as a hobby of his once upon a time. He says that all of the 70-percent-off sales have spoiled the people, driving down prices that won't ever recover. He speaks of himself in the third person and says, "The Artist used to wear suits to meetings. He'd buy ten at a time and have them tailored in Culver City by a guy named Manny. Hugo Boss was his favorite designer. But now, like most people, he shows up to meetings in a T-shirt, sometimes dirty. 'Why bother?' he says. Nobody gives a shit. The people don't care what you look like now. They only care about extracting a service for the cheapest price possible. And as long as you don't smell to the point of your customers fleeing the building with noses held, then you're good to go. Good to transact business freely, if unprofitably, and certainly not fruitfully to your benefit."

He tells me that maybe he is too old-fashioned but also realizes that real change is taking place in this country. He tells me that we have reverted back to third-world politics, cronyism, and that most young people today, without the proper education and connections, will have no shot of tasting the American dream. He says he is not sure where it all went wrong, but he is quite certain that if things continue on this path, we will see an uprising, not dissimilar to what we have witnessed in the Arab Spring. Then he quotes future trends forecaster Gerald Celente. "When people have nothing left to lose, THEY LOSE IT!"

He points to a rash of home invasion robberies in Beverly Hills and Westwood. And he says it is bad to think this, but he does, that he somehow sympathizes with the robbers. How long can you be squashed into squalor? How long can you watch the privileged fighting for parking places at Whole Foods when you're fighting for your life? And then I hear him hawk a loogie and spit it out, and I think to myself that he must be trying to expel the bad taste in his mouth that has been lingering for far too long.

He tells me a couple of big online retailers are entering the art market, and that maybe he should look into getting his work on one of their sites. But then he catches himself and curses, saying he would be succumbing to the evil empire of greed. And that technology doesn't give a shit about art, only money. And I say it might be good exposure. And he says, "What do you know? You're a dumb-ass realtor." But then he goes rogue and says that you can never underestimate the fragility of the human race and our capacity for deterioration. And that if you don't see it coming you're just as arrogant as that T. rex who strutted around like a cocksure carnivore, only to be vaporized by a meteor while pleasurably, but not without some difficulty, shitting out that triceratops it feasted on last night. I then remind him to take a deep breath and go watch the sunset over Palisades Park, let the beauty take him somewhere else, as it always does. And he agrees with me that people come from all over the world just to glimpse the sun setting over the ocean in beautiful Santa Monica.

But then I say something really stupid and suggest that maybe he move in a different direction with his art, maybe add some words or phrases into the piece. And he is silent for a long moment, and then he tells me the conversation is over and that the best thing I can do now is "pound sand."

Twenty minutes later he calls me back and says he's sorry, he's just a little worked up today. Then I tell him that a Mark Rothko painting just sold for $25 million at a Sotheby's auction. I tell him he has *something to shoot for. He laughs, and then he asks me if I've seen the movie* Lincoln. *I say no, and then he says, "I'll tell you what. Sally Field can still rock the nightgown. She looked kinda hot."*

Game of Thrones

WEEKENDS AT THE Artist's apartment were the best of times. Free from the pressures of weekday commerce, we were able to enjoy our time off guilt-free like the rest of America. At least on the weekends the engines of empire didn't remind us all that we were becoming functionally obsolete.

The weather had stayed warm and dry through most of November, and as a result several red flag warnings were issued. During those Indian summer days we would ride our bicycles down to the Manhattan Beach Pier and drink tall Heinekens out of paper bags and watch seagulls air-surf the waves. Bales loved it there. He used to refer to it as "the sun-splashed exclusivity." He said that if he ever got his shit together again, he was going to move to Manhattan Beach. We all agreed that it was a lovely place to put down roots.

On Sunday, the eighteenth of November, the Artist invited the gang over to watch the Chargers play the Broncos. Bales, wearing a Boone's Farm Original T-shirt, was camped out in his usual spot on the couch. Hashtag and the Artist sat front and center before the big screen. "Mr. Clean," said Bales, "how goes the job hunt, brother? Or should I say, the nihilistic ritual of beating one's head against the wall."

I noticed that Bales still wore a cloth dressing on his wounded right hand.

"Your concern for my well-being touches me," I said.

"I hear the oil sands is hiring," he said. "Welders making ten grand a week."

"Where's that?" asked Hashtag, a computer on his lap, a cell phone in his hand.

"Canada," I said.

"Oh," he said, his dull green eyes darting between the screens. "That sounds awfully cold. Why don't you think about teaching in Thailand? A friend of mine got his TEFL and loves it. Said the place is full of hookers."

"You fungoid fuck," said Bales. "What do you know about Thailand? Have you ever been?"

Hashtag cupped his junk. "No."

"Then stop picking at your crotch crust and shut up. I'm tired of small-minded nimrods positing their views and perceptions of a very cool, very dynamic country based on a fucking movie."

"*Hangover II* didn't help matters," I said.

"You're just as clueless." Bales jerked his head. "Hashtag, go get us some beer and food."

"Why do I always have to buy?"

"Because you're rich and fat. That's what you people do. Help us little people. It's called philanthropy."

"You were the high school bully, weren't you?"

"Please," Bales said. "Don't tease me about my glory days. Besides, you should be paying for our company. This gathering of great minds."

Bales's superior intellect was his currency. Those who dove into his mental slipstream drowned. The rest of us clung to the edge.

On the big screen, Peyton Manning was busy directing traffic, telling some clueless back the snap count.

Bales said, "Subway sound good? Everybody?"

We all nodded.

"Hashtag," Bales said. "What am I having?"

This was a ritual. A test. Hashtag made several food runs for the group during this period (my waistline was proof) and Bales had very particular tastes. He liked his order perfect, just so, and anything less would result in a run back to the fast-food establishment to get the order right. In-N-Out Burger. Subway. Domino's Pizza. Del Taco (when In-N-Out was closed). If as much as one less slice of this or one spread of that was missing, Hashtag caught hell.

"Hashtag," Bales said. "I'm tired of hearing myself talk. What am I having?"

Hashtag rose from the couch. "Uhh. Turkey on wheat. No cheese, no mayo. Extra olives with two—"

"Three!"

"—three slices of avocado."

I waved my hand. "I'll have the foot-long tuna. Everything on it."

Hashtag nodded, as if receiving orders from the ship's captain. "Everything on it."

Bales said, "And you know what the Artist likes."

Hashtag rummaged his brain, scratching his temple with a fat forefinger. "Um…chicken?"

"Are you sure?" Bales said. "Or are you just pulling it out of that extra-large ass of yours?"

"Um. Pretty sure."

"*Pretty sure?* Do you need to write it down? Do you need to scratch your ball cleavage?"

"No, I got it."

"Then repeat his order."

Hashtag stood straight, like a pledge reciting the fraternal oath. "Chicken on white bread with lettuce and tomato only."

"And?"

"Light mustard."

"What kind of mustard?"

"Spicy mustard…?"

"Are you positive, round man? Do you need your comfort pillow?"

Hashtag pumped a fist. "Spicy mustard!"

The Artist clapped, and Hashtag took a bow.

"You got it, Lumpy," Bales said. "Now waddle-walk outta here, and get the food. Do it now."

Hashtag grabbed his phone and lumbered out playing a game of Candy Crush, his shoulders slumped like a primordial sloth.

"Hapless," Bales muttered. "Totally hapless."

In a sadistic sort of way, I enjoyed the Hashtag bashing. He was an easy foil for Bales during this time. He was soft, oblivious. He had never held down a real job in his life, only the occasional movie extra gig when they needed a goofy-looking fat guy on set. And by his own admission, he had come from a long line of lazy people. For him, life was easy. A check arrived in the mail every month like clock-work. It didn't get any better than that, and Bales never let him forget it.

Hashtag never got glandular about things, though. He always remained calm under pressure. One Sunday morning Bales made oatmeal for an unsuspecting Hashtag and sprinkled dead fruit flies on top. When he asked what they were, Bales told him they were flax seeds. Hashtag chowed it down with gusto, licked his slightly swollen lips, and requested seconds. It was then that Bales christened him with his new Indian nickname: Two Chins.

Later that evening, Bales picked up a dry house spider off the floor and stuffed it into the Artist's glass bong. Hashtag was told it was a new strain of medicinal marijuana from The Farmacy, the over-priced Venice Beach dispensary. Bales lit the bowl and Hashtag enthusiastically bonged the nasty arach-nid, and when he exhaled he smacked his lips and said, "Yum. Woodsy with a hint of pepper. Indica?"

You don't get to be a man of his size without the love of food. Already equipped with an exceptional sense of smell, he also possessed the uncanny gift of being able to hear the handling and opening of any foodstuff on the planet. He was like a deer in the woods—head snapping at the slightest sound. The obvious would send him running—the crunch through an apple, a knife chopping—but it was the subtle culinary noises that pricked his jug ears. The distant rustle of a popcorn bag, the intimate crinkle of a cookie wrapper, the slightest tear of packaging from a TV dinner. He could be fast asleep, but the second you unwrapped a taco he'd lurch up and say, "Whoa. I must have dozed off." And then he'd missile-lock on your taco, looking at it like a caged animal. But even when you knew his game, meaning you didn't give in to a bite, you'd still have to endure that insatiable stare, that stare that would follow the taco to your mouth and into your gullet. And then he'd ask, "Is it any good?" And you'd always say, "No. It's terrible." But he knew you were lying and would wait patiently for a giblet to drop. Patience being one of his strong suits. And when you'd finished your food, he would pick up the wrapper, smell it, maybe lick it, and if he was particularly lucky on that day, find a discarded piece of chewed gristle and pop it into his mouth.

Hashtag was the kind of guy who would walk into your kitchen and squeeze your avocados. Open your fridge and pantry. Make jewelry out of a chicken bone and spend hours sucking the marrow. But even with all his faults and lack of street smarts, he was a pretty decent guy. His temperate personality was his biggest asset. I saw him get upset only one time. That was when Bales broke into his apartment, while he was away housesitting in Malibu, and fucked his Colombian maid on the couch. Hashtag was pissed, saying Bales went all *Game of Thrones* on him. At least that's what Hashtag told us. Bales denied it.

It was clear that Bales regarded Hashtag as nothing more than a casual house companion, someone who cooked and cleaned and paid the bills. And if that ever stopped, he was as easily discarded as the lowly, besotted servant who'd been caught nipping at the liquor cabinet.

That Sunday afternoon Bales said, "I got a painful thigh cramp beating off this morning. Screamed so fucking loud Foreskin pounded on the ceiling."

"Were you sitting at the computer?" I said.

"Yeah."

"Laptop leg," I said. "That's why I got an iPad. You get to lie back in bed, old-school style."

But when Hashtag tried to relate his own masturbation adventure, Bales stopped him cold. "Shut up, woman. Nobody wants to hear about your sickly trickle."

I remember we had a lot of laughs that day. It was one of the times when Bales seemed almost like a normal dude. No drama, no dire consequences, just one of the guys watching a ballgame and ribbing his pals.

It was during these unguarded, semilucid Bales moments that I started looking for clues to what made him tick. The Artist had been told that Bales had an IQ of 165, and I didn't doubt that, based on his dossier, his sharp wit. He was, as the Artist had said, intoxicating at times. But the character flaws I'd already observed were quite disturbing. The insurance scam, the alleged sexual assault, the stolen brooch, his increasing drug use, his blatant disregard for all authority. Certainly it was intriguing on some level, but I grossly underestimated the dangerous game he was playing.

This much I knew: he was a dazzling wordsmith and an outstanding liar. I got the feeling that he was acting his way through life, that it was all a joke. It got me to thinking: was he a product of the times? Or was something lurking deep inside his DNA? I used to be good at solving mysteries—beating Kojak to the punch or Columbo at his game. But it didn't matter what hat I put on with Bales: sleuth, cop, sociologist, psychologist, or psychiatrist, I still couldn't crack the code.

Unfortunately, I failed to detect the symptoms of his madness. Something I still live with every day.

Everything is Brilliant

THE NEXT MORNING I got up and turned on CNBC. Why? I don't know. I'd been raiding my 401(k) for over a year now, lying to myself that things would get better. I noticed the Dow was down eighty-five. That used to mean something to me. But now it was just numbers. Manipulated numbers. Numbers that saps like you and me got duped into believing would grow larger, but instead just disappeared.

I was particularly cranky that Monday morning, watching the financial bull-throwers drone on about spending cuts and long-term employment targets. Unfortunately for him, my financial advisor picked that time to call.

"Hello."

"Richard, good morning. It's Bob."

I didn't like his tone already.

"Yes, Bob," I said, pain in my voice. "How can I help you?"

"Frankly, it's more about helping yourself. And I don't want to come off as reading you the riot act, but this constant withdrawal of funds from your retirement account has got to stop. You've less than ten thousand left."

"No kidding, Bob. It seems you've done it again. Blown the lid off finance."

I couldn't remember the name of his firm, but Pump and Dump Financial sounded about right.

"Richard, *you're killing* your financial future."

"My financial future? Or yours? Because the last time I checked, you work for me."

I glimpsed the bald, white-bearded Federal Reserve chairman on the TV, and it infuriated me.

"And tell that idiot Bernanke to raise interest rates. *He's* killing me."

"You're killing yourself."

"You know what, Bob?" I said, now pacing the room. "The only time you call me is when there's no money coming in. Just once it would be nice if you called and said, 'Hey, Richard, how are you? Everything good?' And I would say, 'No. No, Bob, it's not, because I don't have a job, and I'm not earning any money. And that's why I'm robbing my 401(k).

Robbing Peter to pay Paul.' But does any of that concern you? Apparently not. Because all you're worried about is your fucking fees. Charging me over two percent a year with subpar performance. It's outrageous!"

"But, Richard—"

"No *but Richard*s. How many times have you bought a stock for me at fifty, only for it to open at forty-eight the next day? And stay there for months! Huh? Tell me. How many times can I watch you front-run my money? Flash-crash my cash? The answer is no more, Bob. Nada. Zip. Zilch. Wall Street's a shell game. I'm tired of it—I'm out."

"Richard, listen—"

"I will say this, you have the uncanny ability to buy me in at the top. I'll give you that. And what about all those shill publications you had me sub-scribe to? *Barron's*, the *Wall Street Journal, Money*. Talk about leading hogs to slaughter. Aside from the advertising bias, these frauds make stock rec-ommendations that lure in little guys like me. And when all us little guys have bought in, Wall Street shorts the market. It's a great game, Bob. Quick, let me grab my jai alai racket."

"But these publications are—"

"Toilet paper. I'd rather go apeshit with my money at the track than let you do it for me. At least I'd have a good time."

"I highly—"

"And speaking of highly, why do you think real estate is going through the roof? Because the rich aren't in this market. They know it's rigged. They're not stupid. So instead you've got to pick the pocket of the little guy, dazzle him with your fucking pie chart and cozy commercials with aged, sellout actors. It's despicable is what it is."

"If you'd just let me—"

"I don't have to let you do anything. *You're fired, Bob.* Don't ever call me again. Do you understand? Because I got better shit to do. Shit like bus surfing or booty grazing. Can that calculator brain of yours grasp this simple concept?"

"Yes."

"Then compute this, you slimy lizard. Fuck off!"

I heaved my cell phone against the couch cushion.

Needless to say, he raised my blood pressure. I pulled out my home monitor and anxiously clocked a 145/92. And I thought to myself, there's nothing remotely glamorous about an old white man with a preexisting condition. There never is. Never was. So before bed that night, I logged in some thoughts of the day. And to my surprise, I found that writing relaxed me.

Los Angeles, November 19, 2012
11:30 p.m.

For the first time I realize I am not young anymore. Don't get me wrong, I am still strong, but I see age creeping into the mirror. And if I can see it, you damn well know the younger generation can see it. I am a pair of old skis to their snowboard. A pay phone to a smartphone. They can spot me a mile away because I don't have the posture, that lean-in swagger. I don't look like a guy who knows his way around a smartphone. That old phrase, Let me make some calls, sounds as ancient as By Jove! or Groovy, man. Because everyone knows that in order to get information today you look on the Internet. You don't make calls until you actually have to talk with someone. And yesterday when I was walking down the Third Street Promenade, I asked this young guy— who was gawking at his phone—if he knew where the Apple store was. It was a simple question. And he looked at me, frozen. He didn't know what to say. You could see he didn't know what to say. He kept looking down at the ground, kicking pebbles with his skate shoes, hoping this old man would just dis-

appear. And I wanted to say, Dude, look at me. Talk to me. I'm right here. Right fucking here. And, yes, you will have to deal with me. You cannot text me away or email me into oblivion. Can't delete me or tweet me.

And do you know what? I can't recall if he ever said anything, because I was so hot under the collar I just walked away.

I feel alone. Will I be alone for the rest of my life? But if I do find someone to share it with, will I be able to care for them? Will I have enough money to pay for the basic needs of an aging companion? Not to mention myself. If not, I will have to stay alone. I search how long do hermits live? Maybe because I have become disillusioned with politics, by society as a whole. I hope this will pass. But right now I am contemplating a life of asceticism, free from materialism. Maybe I'll work for a rich man. Become an ornamental hermit, assigned to one of his many grottoes to be gawked at or fed at arm's length. Have handlers poke sticks at me at feeding time. Maybe I'll wear a camel-hair robe, buy a Montana cabin, not cut my hair, beard, or nails. Walk around with a fleece flap for the groin in summer. And then ask myself in winter, "Is companionship always a prerequisite for happiness?"

I don't even know myself anymore. For the first time in my life I am starting to doubt my abilities. I find myself envious of teachers, firefighters, and police officers. Anyone with a pension. And then I think, shame on me for thinking I was better than them all those years. And how certain I was of luxurious outcomes and fluffy towels, and for an apartment that was meant to be a way station but instead became your home where you aged out of the game and into middle age. The same home where you once tried Rogaine to help with that bald spot, but instead watched that bald spot spread across your cranium like pancake batter, destroying all follicles in its wake. The same apartment where you considered a hair transplant—were diagnosed with gout. The same apartment where you raised your daughter on weekends. Where you'd given her the bedroom and you'd slept on the couch. The same paper-thin apartment that every day and night brings you a symphony of quotidian sounds, sounds that grate, gnaw, and amuse.

Every ropy, gargling piss, every toilet flushed, every squeaky knob turned, every phlegm ball hawked, and every cold shower taken leaves you perpetually locked in some unwanted waltz with your debt-ridden neighbors. All embraced by this star-loved city.

This City of Angels.

It's as if I've been sleepwalking through life. How could I have let it get this far? My thoughts drift to Edmonton, Canada. Am I too old to learn welding? Maybe not. Just have to be careful on the scaffolding.

As I was about to turn off the light, my daughter Rose called from New York. She said school was good but stressful. And that she had met a boy that she thought "might be the one." I told her I was happy for her and asked about her mother. She said she was on some eat-pray-love journey and was currently in Kuta humping smooth, young Balinese men. I told Rose I wasn't surprised.

Lying in the dark before sleep, I was suddenly struck by the memory of something a German man with a big gray handlebar mustache said to me one night years before in Munich. We were at the Hofbrau House seated across a wooden communal table from each other. Next to him, a Japanese man was hacking away at a pork knuckle. When my eyes met the German's, I smiled. I asked him how he was doing. "Everything is brilliant," he said.

Everything is brilliant.

I closed my eyes, hoping it was still so.

The Blair Witch
Project

ON THANKSGIVING NIGHT, after we'd all done the family
thing, Bales told the gang to meet him at his apartment. He said he had a plan. A plan to get our sorry
asses back in the game. And while I was skeptical
at the time, I was in no position to turn down any
plausible opportunity, no matter how absurd.

I knocked on his front door around 9 p.m., a
six-pack of Heineken cradled under my arm, my
Dodgers cap high on my head. From inside I heard
Elvis Costello's "Accidents Will Happen" playing
softly on the radio. I waited on the porch a moment,
then pounded harder. I peered into his window but
saw nothing but black calm, so I turned the knob and

walked into blackness, the smell of cooked cocaine searing my nostrils.

"Bales?" I called, standing in the dark.

I heard a scratchy click. My head jerked toward the sound. A Bic lighter flared, its flame dipped and danced, and then Bales's lean face appeared in profile, his Anglo-Norman nose jutting toward the fire, the neck of a glass bong resting comfortably on his chin.

"Bales?"

He sat on the sofa and spoke softly in the orange light. "Did I ever tell you I put a guy's eye out with a Daisy BB gun when I was nine?"

I stood mute.

"My parents told everybody in the neighborhood it was an accident. They told me over and over it was an accident…but it was a lie."

He placed the bong to his lips, set the flame over the pipe bowl, and took a hit. I heard the water inside the glass apparatus bubbling and gurgling. Watched the cherry breathe fire.

He held the smoke in a moment, then blew out a thick, milky plume.

"I was aiming for the fucker," he said. "Blasted his cornea in two." He threw his head back and laughed, his body heaving with pleasure at the thought of it. "Fucking Bobby Dalloway. What an asshole."

I didn't know how to respond to that.

"Sounds like you're a real crack shot, Bales," I finally said.

"More than you know, Clean." He flicked the lighter again, holding the flame up to his face, looking at me through tendrils of smoke. "You know what happens when you die, Clean?"

"No."

"Nothing. Because death doesn't give a shit who you are. Whether you're an Oscar winner, a Grammy winner, or some captain of industry. All you are is one last tribute on an awards show—scattered applause at best. Your picture's right up there with Dave Brubeck and all the other dead people. But you know the difference between you and Dave Brubeck?"

"Tell me."

"Nothing. You're both fucking dead. And do you know what song they sing when your obit picture is scrolling on the screen with all the other stiffs?"

"No, I don't."

"They play you out with the Band's 'The Weight.'"

He flicked on the light and stood up, his pupils like two black pearls floating in red Jell-O. "And just like that it's over. The load's off."

I held his gaze a long moment, then said, "Where's the Artist?"

"At the restaurant."

"Which restaurant?"

"The infamous El Cholo."

"Why aren't you there?"

He held out his hands, palms to the floor, nails up.

"A manicure. One has to be civilized, Clean." He smiled, more like a man in charge than the junkie he'd become. "That's what separates us."

. . . .

BALES AND I walked a couple of blocks up Wilshire through a patchy sea fog and entered El Cholo Mexican restaurant. Hashtag and the Artist were seated at the bar eating salsa and chips when we arrived. Bales requested a private booth because he said the hefty bartender "Big Mike" had big ears, big tits, and liked to talk. We settled in a dark corner of the old-world dining room and Bales ordered Patrón shots with Corona beer backs.

"Have you spent all your money yet?" I asked.

"No," he said, "but my ex-wife has. Try servicing a thirty-K monthly nut. See how many opportunities you have to fund it."

"So what brings us together, then?" I said. "A brodak moment? Or you want to wish us all a happy Thanksgiving?"

Bales smiled in the soft lighting. "I've got an idea how to make some money…some real money."

The Artist said playfully, "I told you I'm not driving the getaway car."

Hashtag laughed, snorting beer through his nose.

"Quiet, idiot," Bales said. "Let me game plan this thing." He turned to the Artist. "A, you wanna make some real money? Or do you want to spend the rest of your life hunting quarters in the couch?"

"Is it legal?" I said.

Bales gave me a hard look.

"Simple question," I said.

Bales appeared amused. "You know, Clean, you strike me as the kinda guy who was always afraid to cut the cake."

"Yeah?" I said. "This coming from a tweeker who drinks thirty beers a day. Smokes coke on a dime."

His eyes grabbed mine. "I'm wise beyond my beers, Clean. Besides, you think I've done this my whole life? We've known each other for what? Maybe six weeks? Granted, I have not presented myself in the best of lights, but maybe I should remind you of the fact that I worked for corporate America for *thirty fucking years*. How many sick days?"

He held up three fingers.

"Three," said Hashtag, not looking up.

"Three," Bales said. "So stop making snap judgments until you hear me out."

I nodded, realizing that was exactly what I was doing. Making snap judgments. Something I never used to do.

"Fair enough," I said. "The floor's all yours. *Dazzle me*."

Bales cleared his throat, waiting for a waitress to pass by with a steaming plate of fajitas. Then he swung his eyes toward the Artist. "Are you ready to be rich and famous?"

The Artist said, "Rich would be nice, famous not so much."

Bales said, "That's a start. So listen, I want to make a documentary."

"About what?" asked Hashtag, stuffing chips into his mouth.

"Please shut up," Bales said softly. "I'll let you know when to reach for the wallet."

Hashtag dropped his head, resuming his relentless pursuit of wired distraction.

"What about?" said the Artist.

"About you," Bales said. "I want to call it, *The Artist of Santa Monica*. I want to shoot it on the iPhone, guerrilla style. Black and white. Hashtag's funding it."

Hashtag raised his head. "What?"

"It won't cost much," Bales said. "You'll be a fucking producer. Stop whining and focus on portion control. Just because it's all-you-can-eat doesn't mean you have to." Bales continued. "Now. You all remember that movie *Pollock*—with Ed Harris?"

We all nodded.

"About how it chronicled Pollock's life, his struggles to make a living as a starving artist? I want to do something similar here, where we document the Artist's plight during the Great Recession. We watch him paint, we listen to his hopes and dreams, we watch him go broke, descend into despair, and finally reach a breaking point…"

Bales leaned into the table, his voice low and persuasive. "And then we watch him kill himself."

The Artist looked shocked. "Excuse me?"

"It's staged," Bales said. "But the audience won't know that. Kind of like *The Blair Witch Project*, where you believe something to be true, but instead it's a hoax."

"And how will that benefit the Artist?" I asked, spinning my Dodgers cap on my finger.

"The point is," Bales said, "that a lot of famous painters didn't make any money during their lifetime. Van Gogh. El Greco. Johannes Vermeer. They only became rich and famous *after* their deaths."

The Artist nibbled on a chip. "Which doesn't interest me any."

"Exactly, who wants to die penniless?"

"Especially on the Westside," Hashtag said.

Bales elbowed him.

"So, how are we gonna make money?" asked the Artist. "Sell the movie?"

"Yes," Bales said, "that's one revenue stream. We'll go viral on YouTube first. I know a couple of really brilliant programmers that can help with that. Then once it becomes a hit, we license it."

"And then the demand for his paintings skyrockets," I said.

Bales launched a conspiratorial smile. "That's how it usually goes. We make this movie so heart-wrenching, so gut-busting, that people will scramble to purchase his work at any price. People love to discover dead artists. The whole package could be worth a few million, if done right."

"How's he gonna do it?" Hashtag asked. "You know, kill himself."

Bales crossed his arms. "I like hara-kiri," he said. "He'll disembowel himself on-screen with his samurai sword. Maybe a murder."

The Artist winced, scratching his blond flattop. "Ouch," he said. "I prefer sleeping pills and vodka. The Russian nap. You know, something more sedate."

"Or you could blow your brains out," I said. "Spray the screen red with splatter. Cut to black."

Bales grinned. "Full-on *Onion Field*. I like it."

In a lighter moment, we all shared our methods of death.

I leaned back in the red leather booth and finally said, "It all sounds very theatrical, but why not just shoot a straight documentary?"

"Because it won't work," Bales said. "Nobody gives a shit about a nobody. We've got to make him a somebody first."

"Sounds pretty cockamamie," I said.

"Yeah, and what happens when people find out I'm a fraud?" the Artist asked.

"You're not actually considering this?" I said.

The Artist looked off, swimming in his mind awhile.

Bales answered with, "Who gives a shit? We'll already have the money."

"I give a shit," said the Artist, his eyes widening. "It's my life."

Bales slid a toothpick into the side of his mouth and attacked the argument from a different angle. "Listen," he said, "when I got fired, I told my wife in jest that I was going to become a porn star to support the family. You know what she said?"

"Tell us," I said.

Bales sighed, as if the memory unnerved him. "She said, 'I don't give a fuck where the money comes from. Just bring it home.'"

"Harsh," said Hashtag.

"It *was* harsh. But she was right. The point is, that's where we are now, guys. This is America. It's get yours or get fucked. The money's all that matters." Bales motioned for a waitress. "Look, after we make it big, we release a statement to the press about art. About how art imitates life. We'll spin it then."

"If I'm dead," the Artist said, "I can't be walking around."

"My dad's got a house in Puerto Vallarta," Bales said. "You can stay there for a few months—lie low until things blow over."

"I don't know," the Artist said. He dipped a tortilla chip into the salsa. "I've got to think about it."

"Think about what?" Bales said. "You want to keep living this life? Sit out front of Home Depot hustling with the Mexicans for low wages? Flat-paint some dude's apartment for two hundred bucks? Face it, A, these are the times we live in."

A profound silence.

"Tell me," Bales said, shaking his toothpick at the Artist. "How long can you let society fuck you in the ass before you finally get your nut? You're the star of the show now. Take the spotlight. This is your time...*your time*."

"He said he wants to think about it," I said.

Bales flicked his nasty gaze my way. "I didn't ask you the question."

I felt a sudden burst of adrenaline. "Yeah, but I answered it."

An unstable smile crossed his face, his eyes black and glistening. "You're a violent man, aren't you, Clean? Deep down you want to hit me." He thrust his chin at me across the table, repeatedly poking it with his forefinger. "C'mon, *big man*. Wipe my ass. Save me from this fucking nightmare."

"C'mon, B," Hashtag pleaded.

Bales stopped him with a halting hand.

"You get any closer and I'll drop you like a bag of rocks," I said, my fists clenched, legs pumping under the table.

I watched his right hand grip the dinner knife, watched his eyes dart around the room. And after a moment of intense silence, Bales finally released the knife and exhaled, then leaned back in the booth and chugged his Corona. "I refuse to participate in a race to the bottom," he said softly. He placed his empty bottle on the table and stood up. His dramatic eyes were as dark and hard as black ice. "The rest of you losers can do what you want."

Driving Miss Uber

THE NEXT MORNING, I picked up the Artist and drove over the Sepulveda Pass on the 405 freeway, barreling into Sherman Oaks to have lunch with my father. The Artist sat in the passenger seat wearing a black lambskin leather jacket over a white T-shirt, cleaning his aviator sunglasses with a soft blue cloth. "You know," he said, "that documentary thing just might work. I mean, it wouldn't cost that much money. And Hashtag said he'd finance it. And if we did it right, Bales said we could release it on the festival circuit. Besides, it might be kinda fun."

I checked the rearview mirror of my Lexus and changed lanes. "Dude," I said, my eyes firmly on the road ahead. "Let me ask you a question. How many reality TV villains do you know that have gone on to do great things?"

I felt his eyes searching my face, his thoughts churning for answers. "Go ahead. Name one," I said. "Because you will be the villain in this film. The guy that misleads a trusting public for his own profit and greed. And I guarantee you that once those poor souls who bought your act and paintings find out they've been played, they will demand their money back. And you as an artist, and your work, will be finished. And that's a fact." I smiled. "You read an Elmore Leonard novel. You don't star in one."

He thought a moment as the Lexus descended into the urbanized valley, the Santa Susana Mountains ringing the dirt-brown basin.

"Yeah, maybe you're right," he said, hooking on his sunglasses.

"I hate to be right all the time," I said. "But if you're going to do a reality show, then you have to play the good guy. *Always*. Because when the show ends and the money runs dry, and you need a job, people will embrace you as the likeable character that you are. Villains are unhirable."

"So what do they do?"

"What can they do? They go on to seminary school. Thump Bibles in backwater towns."

He laughed.

"You know, you should be a teacher. You missed your calling."

"Funny you should say that," I said, "because my grandmother said I should be a judge. I guess I missed a few callings."

I exited on Ventura Boulevard and pulled into the Blue Dog Tavern, a craft beer and hamburger joint nestled on a quiet side street in high-toned Sherman Oaks. The tall oak trees were dappled in sunlight, and a filmy layer of commercial haze hugged the mountains like a dirty beige blanket.

"We're here," I said.

My father had become a foodie in his advancing years and had heard the Blue Dog had some of the best gourmet burgers in the Valley. Besides, he was springing for lunch. Who was I to argue?

The tavern was warm and rustic inside with exposed beams of oak and pine. Dog photos nailed to the walls. The boisterous lunch crowd was mostly young and handsome, a film and TV kind catching up on the gossip of the day.

"Do you see your dad?" said the Artist.

I craned my neck, my eyes roaming over the shacklike space. "Not yet. C'mon, let's get a table."

The waitress seated us in the back of the restaurant, and I ordered two Scrimshaw Pilsners.

"Does your dad still have the painting he bought from me?" the Artist asked, slipping off his black leather jacket.

"Are you kidding?" I said. "It's hanging in his bedroom. He loves it."

It was my father who had instilled the love of the fine arts in me. For many years as principal of Van Nuys High, he fought to save the art programs at school. He said it was the artist who possessed that truly special gift to inspire people, more so than any man of commerce ever could. While he stressed the importance of math and science, he firmly believed in a well-rounded education. Said communities needed creative people in order to survive and thrive.

During the lean years when funding dried up, he reached into his own pocket. And he didn't discriminate on whether you had talent or not. If you were a committed artist, an absolute, then he would provide the supplies for you to master your craft. But better yet, he would purchase the piece after you finished it. He told me that this instilled a level of confidence that all young artists needed at the beginning of a career.

And do you know what? His house is filled with rich and wonderful sculptures, paintings, and thrown clay pots—all pieces from grateful former students.

Some still stop by to say thank you, others just to say hi. A few, like a woman sculptor in San Francisco, have gone on to become quite famous.

I checked my watch. It was half past noon. My dad was fifteen minutes late.

And he's never late.

"I wonder where he is," I said, pushing up in my chair and scoping the eatery.

"He's retired," the Artist said. "Give him a break."

"Yeah, I guess. It is hard to park in this place."

The Artist said, "So how is he? Everything good? His health?"

"All good," I said. "His body is as strong as a horse. Still eats like one, too." I scanned the restaurant again. "I just hope he didn't get in an accident."

"Can he drive okay?"

I don't know why, but I felt offended by the question. "What do you mean? Of course he can drive okay."

"Just checkin'," the Artist said, "because my brother Charles had to take the keys away from our mother last year."

"Why? I mean, how did he know it was time?"

"It wasn't hard. She kept ramming the walls of the garage. Swiped a neighbor's parked car. Got out and left the engine running. Stuff like that."

"Did she put up a fight?"

"A little. But she knew in her heart it was time. She actually likes it now. Just orders a rideshare and off she goes. She calls it *Driving Miss Uber.*"

"How old is she again?"

"Seventy-eight. About the same age as your dad."

It's easy to take your parents for granted. Easy to believe they are somehow infallible or invincible. That they will live forever. But the moment you sense chinks in the armor, as you eventually will, you must act.

The Artist said, "You didn't make that call to your art dealer friend yet, did you?"

"Not yet. I've got to dig up her number."

"Good. Because I've been thinking now might not be a good time."

"When is a good time?"

I was getting agitated, not so much at the Artist, but at the absence of my father. The Artist just happened to be in the line of fire, someone to bear the brunt.

"I don't know," he said. "Maybe after the New Year. Let me kinda work up to it."

"Don't start with this shit," I said. "It's time for you to sell your art *now*. And to stop listening to your *fucking affected* next-door neighbor."

He dropped his head in a menu. My harsh tone had scaled him like a fish.

"Sorry, man," I said. "Just worried about my pops."

"I understand," he said. "I bet he'll be here any minute."

I nodded and picked up a menu. The bacon cheeseburger looked good.

The Artist said, "You know, Bales is starting to bug me."

"You and everyone else."

"I saw him this morning with his family. And do you know that he didn't even introduce me to his mother and father. I was just standing there in the courtyard waiting, like I was a butler or something. No acknowledgment. No wave. No this-is-my-friend-and-neighbor. Just a conceited rich guy smirk. What's up with that?"

I lost it. "Because he doesn't give a shit about you! Don't you see? He thinks we are below his station. What do you think I've been trying to tell you? God, you're thick."

The Artist looked at me as if I'd run over his dog.

"I'm sorry," I said, standing up. "If you'll excuse me, I've got to call my dad."

I flung my napkin on the chair and walked outside. Then I leaned against the building with one leg propped back and dialed my father.

He answered four rings later.

"Hello?"

"Hi, Dad," I said, my heart fluttering. "Where are you?"

"I'm in the garden with my tomatoes. It really is a lovely day."

"Dad, you were supposed to meet me and Jimmy for lunch today at the Blue Dog."

"Oh, the Blue Dog," he said, his voice migrating north. "I've been wanting to try that burger everyone's been raving about."

"Yeah, I know. That's why we're here."

He paused.

"Hmm. I thought there was something I forgot. I'm sorry, son. It must have slipped my mind."

I cracked my neck, my nerves jangled.

"That's all right, Dad. I was just worried that something might have happened to you. Didn't you write it down in your daily planner?"

"Uhh. I, uh…" His words drifted, as if his cord had been cut from the space station. "I guess…I stopped planning after I retired."

"That's not like you. You've used your planner religiously for sixty years."

"I know. I guess I've just gotten away from that. Look, if you give me half an hour, I can get cleaned up and meet you two."

I stared up into a crooked oak tree, watched goldfinches branch hopping.

"No, that's okay, Dad," I said. "Jimmy's got to get back to work. We'll do it another time. Enjoy your afternoon."

"Thank you, son, and tell Jimmy I said hello."

"Will do, bye."

And just like that, a new worry spun from the sky.

I tapped off the cell phone and walked back inside.

"Everything all right?" the Artist asked, his look of concern matching mine.

"He forgot about lunch."

"That happens with age."

"I know, but it's never happened to him before." My gaze landed on a pine knot in the wall. I tried to bore a hole through it with my eyes.

"Was he okay yesterday?"

"Yeah, everything was great. We had Thanksgiving Day brunch and watched some football. Sharp as ever."

"I'm sure he's fine," said the Artist.

"I'm sure he is."

My mouth pinched closed and my mind turned inward. For the rest of the afternoon I wrestled with sunless thoughts that had been lurking beneath the surface for some time. Murky thoughts—gasping for air—kicking toward the radiance like a deep-sea diver afraid of the bends.

Skeptical and Searching

AS THE LATE fall days grew shorter, the Artist became increasingly fragile. He told me he didn't even recognize his surroundings anymore. His house phone had been shut off, and it was later revealed that Bales had been paying for the cable bill. Each day, it seemed, I had to talk him off some proverbial cliff. I told him that there were no shortcuts to where we were going (wherever that was) and that whatever Bales proposed was not in his best interest. I had convinced him that making a film about his life and tricking the public would go against all that his art stood for—process and purity. That his legacy would be as thin as the dog painter's on the Venice boardwalk.

He told me Bales had called me a "noxious influence," a negative force to be squashed. The irony— Bales told him that immediately after hurling a pumpkin through Hashtag's window.

"I don't give a shit about Bales," I said. "He's as insignificant as the last loogie I hawked." I also told the Artist I was going to call my art dealer friend, Beth Rothstein. It was time for him to get his sorry ass back out into the world. And this time I didn't care about hurting his feelings, because his window was closing, just like mine.

Kicking and screaming, he reluctantly agreed. He finally gave me the green light to give him one last shot.

One morning I sat down at my kitchen table with my old Rolodex and rotated the spindle. I found the number and called Beth, a "friend" from college. It was 10 a.m. I was a little apprehensive, which was to be expected after thirty-five years. But surprisingly, she took my call.

"Is this the same guy who schtupped me in the fraternity house and then snuck out the fire escape?"

As I said earlier, I prefer direct women. At least you know where you stand.

"Guilty as charged," I said. "It was a lousy thing to do."

"I had a hunch you weren't coming back when I heard the engine of your squash-yellow 1978 Gremlin whining through the dark at three in the morning."

We both laughed. A laugh that we'd shared often during our junior year before I bolted.

"It was a long time ago," she said. "How are you?"

"Skeptical and searching."

"I see nothing's changed."

"Yeah…you?"

"Great," she said. "I almost feel guilty about saying that during these times, but it's true. The art world is crazy good."

"You deserve it. Nobody's more passionate about art than you."

"Thank you," she said. "How's your dad? He still collecting?"

Beth used to get along famously with my father. Both could talk for hours about a Lee Krasner collage, or Richter's photorealistic paintings, while I happily dozed off to Johnny Carson's monologue.

"He's good," I said. "Still loves art. Still has his collection. But he's mostly retired now. Except for the occasional garage-sale find. But he's not getting any younger. I'm starting to worry about him, you know?"

"Yeah, I know. Tell him I said hi, will you? I really enjoyed our conversations."

"I'll do that."

She paused, and I knew what she was thinking. She was running through our history, still picturing me in her mind's eye as that hunky athlete with a full head of windswept brown hair. The same athlete who made love to her in the bathroom of the freshman girls' dorm. The same athlete who she said looked like Steve McQueen in *Bullitt*.

"So," she said, after a nostalgic moment. "Did you call to talk about art, or what might have been?"

I flicked through the business cards in my Rolodex. "I actually have an artist friend of mine that I want you to take a look at. His name's Jimmy Miller."

Silence, as she processed the name.

"I remember him. Basquiat comparisons. Mid-nineties. Dennis Hopper bought some of his early work."

"So did my dad," I said.

"Really? Which one?"

"The orange-and-green one."

"I remember that one. Bold graffiti tags, rhythmic lines."

"Yeah. My dad still has it hanging above his bed."

"I love that piece. But I also remember that Jimmy Miller had a panic attack, or some kind of meltdown, at his last show. Stormed out, then dropped off the face of the earth. Last I heard he was painting houses."

"He was, but he's back to fine art now. He's matured a lot since then—producing some of the best work of his life. I want you to see it. Tell me what you think."

She cleared her throat. "Is he still cantankerous, overly sensitive, and difficult?"

"Aren't they all?"

"Yes! But I love it. Tell you what," she said. "I have a show coming up on December twenty-first at Bergamot Station. Let me take a look at his work, and if I like what I see, maybe we can figure something out. *Maybe.*"

"December twenty-first? Doomsday? Please don't tell me the show's called some facsimile of Armageddon. Because my doomsday fuse is running short."

"You're such a party pooper. I bet the song '1999' still sets you off."

"I've killed for less. And I like Prince!"

She laughed.

"Well, sorry to disappoint, buster, but the show is titled, 'A Light at the End of the World.' It's a multi-artist exhibition. We'll be showcasing new and emerging talent, as well as mid-career artists looking to break out."

"That'd be great," I said. "Just promise me you won't play that R.E.M. song. I swear to God if I hear it one more time, I'm going to drown myself in a bowl of cheese dip."

"Note to self," she said. "No R.E.M. songs. And definitely no cheese dip. All good?"

I rose from the kitchen table and walked into my bathroom. "Sounds like a plan. And by the way, he lives in Santa Monica, near Bergamot."

"Great. The logistics are perfect. I'll call you next week to set up a time to view the paintings. And I hope to see you there."

I checked my teeth in the bathroom mirror, not knowing why.

"I'll be there," I said. "With bells on. And I promise I won't sneak out this time."

. . . .

LATER THAT AFTERNOON a guy called me about my car. The unthinkable was about to go down. I'd had it listed on Craigslist for about a month and had received several emails, but I hadn't responded to any of them. I was secretly holding out for some-

thing—*anything*—to save me from this decision—
that is, until I was finally pushed over my own fiscal
cliff. My daughter phoned and reminded me that she
needed a $1,200 deposit for the Christmas vacation
to Aspen that I had promised her. My duties as the
Great Provider had been called upon once again.
So I had no choice. The car had to go. Reluctantly,
I recorded the transaction in my journal before I
retired that night.

Los Angeles, November 26, 2012

*Everyone thinks I'm insane. That my methods
are...unbalanced. Only eight hours ago my life was
different. I owned a car. Now my garage sits vacant,
its emptiness a testament to another life of mobil-
ity and pleasure in a city that worships the auto-
mobile. It is Monday, November 26, and America
is teetering on the brink of another Great Depression. But my friends in L.A. have been temporarily sidetracked in their struggle for survival. That's
because they are talking about me, the nutjob who
will now navigate this intricate city without a ride.
I am happy to provide them the entertainment that
they so crave.*

How will you get to the market? they ask.

It's down the street, I say. Four of them, actually.

What about your dentist appointment? It's all the way in Hermosa Beach.

I'll take the bus.

A long pause.

Dude, you have fucking lost it!

Perhaps I have, I think, as I sweep out the garage. My strokes are steady and precise, and after a moment I realize that I am free. The recession has clouded America's judgment. But not mine. I am on a long journey, realizing, as Buddha teaches, that everything is temporary. But Buddha doesn't buy my car. It's a guy named Steve. He shows up with ten grand sealed in plastic. It looks slightly larger than a green deck of cards. Before I know it, I am counting out one-hundred-dollar bills on the passenger seat. One…two…three…

It's all there, Steve says, his silver hair shining in the morning sun. My credit union's pretty good that way.

I smile. That's what Bank of America told me.

Steve is an amicable enough guy, with a disarming grin and an easy air. In short, the perfect person to sell my car to.

It's all there, I say. Ten thousand. All there.

We sign the bill of sale, and I hand over the title to Steve. I sigh. Take good care of her. She is a woman, you know. Doesn't like to kick over in the cold right away.

No problem, he says. So what kind of car are you going to get?

In L.A., everybody assumes that you'll have another car immediately.

Not sure yet, I lie. Maybe a BMW.

Cool. Hey, thanks, man, Steve says. And just so you know, I'm not the kind of guy who's gonna call you up if something breaks down. I don't roll like that.

I'm sure you don't.

We shake hands and I pat the car on the bumper. Nice meeting you, I say. Not really knowing if it is Steve or the car I am talking to.

Steve says, You too. He hops in the car and drives away. I watch the taillights of my baby fade down the alley. I am free now, I think…or insane.

These Are the Times
We Live In

LOSING A CAR in L.A. is like losing a loved one. Not only do you grieve, but everyone grieves with you. I tried to convince people that I was "going green." Saving the environment. But nobody bought it, not even me. I remember sweeping out my empty garage as my neighbor edged her Honda Pilot closer to the crime scene. She instinctively knew that something was wrong. Her lips trembled when she spoke, her eyes wide plates of horror.

"Wha…wha…what happened to your car?"

"I sold it."

Stunned.

"*Oh…my…God*. What happened?"

Once you lose your car in Los Angeles, you realize you've been reduced to a second-class citizen. A streetwalker, a night stalker, someone who moves through the shadows. Unlike other American cities, where commuters are praised for their sacrifice, here you're just another moving target in the crosswalk.

It was the last day of November, and I was waiting for the bus in the rain. There were eight of us huddled at the bus stop with umbrellas and rain gear. All except one middle-aged black woman who appeared drunk. She was soaking wet in a green Day-Glo T-shirt and yelling at a well-groomed black man wearing a dark suit and round glasses. The man stood without judgment beneath his umbrella, his prophetic face holding the long-suffering gaze of a preacher, as if at any moment he could break out the collection plate or a hellfire sermon.

The bawdy black woman poked his breastbone with a hard forefinger and said, "I don't need some goddamn naysayer on my team. Questioning me about my influence actions."

"I just said you was drunk," the black man said.

She got up and pressed her nose to his, spit and venom flying. "You crazy motherfucker! You think I need chew? You ain't nothing but a sorry mother-fuckin' house bitch. Get out my face fool!"

Nobody dared intervene. She was big and inebriated, and I'm quite sure packed a wallop. We were all saved from further escalation when the bus hissed to a stop at the corner of Lincoln and Maxella. I climbed aboard and thought, welcome to the streets of Los Angeles. Where there's no rhyme or reason, no heartbeat or pulse, just happenstance and blurred lines.

This is why nobody walks in L.A.

I took the Number 3 bus up Lincoln Boulevard heading for Brentwood. The only thing that took the sting out of the miserable, crowded ride was the eight grand in my pocket. It would get me through the rest of the year and into 2013. Give me a chance at a fresh start. I decided to take a part-time job for the holidays, just to keep the engines fired until I could find something more permanent. *If* I could find something more permanent.

It was a boiler room job on San Vicente near Whole Foods Market. Slinging hash, selling kitchen remodels over the phone. I sat next to a burly chick with scars on her face and a black T-shirt with white letters that boldly stated: I SURVIVED BLACK FRIDAY. And by the look of her meaty body, I deduced that others hadn't.

We read from a script that started something like this:

Hello, is this Mr. Jones?

Yes.

Hello, Mr. Jones, my name is Richard. Glad I got ya! The reason for the call is sometime back you responded to one of our programs for information...

After several phone calls of people telling me they had never responded to anything (or simply telling me to DROP DEAD!), I realized it was a scam. The big-boned chick confirmed as much, basically saying it was a cold call. "You get used to the lies," she said. "The money's all that matters."

My disillusionment had reached new lows. And just when I was about to bail, the young floor manager stood up on a chair and addressed the room.

"Listen up, people," he said, waving his right hand to quiet the mumbling salespeople. "Listen up."

And I remember thinking at the time, here we go again. Another kid on a skateboard. The youthful boss sported arm-sleeve tattoos under a white T-shirt, and his dark hair was clipped to the skull. He showcased a single diamond stud earring in his left ear, a shiny stone that winked at you when it hit the light. And while I am not a certified gemologist, I appraised the diamond more Zales than Tiffany.

Which should have told me all I needed to know about this fly-by-night operation.

"It has come to my attention," the manager said, "that several of you are still talking to the women of the household. And as I told you before, *do not pitch the bitch*. I repeat. *Do not... pitch...the bitch*. They never buy."

I raised my hand.

"Yes, Richard."

"I read somewhere that women make up more than sixty percent of all purchasing decisions in the home now. Probably more. You would think they might be interested in what we're selling."

"Maybe in the real world," he said. "But they don't buy over the phone. Need a lot of touchy-feely, and too much finger-banging. We're a one-call-close shop. Got it?"

We all nodded our heads.

"Great, now get back to work."

I decided to finish out the day. Take home the extra pay. But instead of actually trying to sell something, I ignored the manager's advice and chatted freely with several nice women. One in Oregon said I sounded sweet, and that if I ever got out to Bend, to give her a call. She said the golfing was amazing. I pocketed the number for future reference, trying to remember the last time I'd been to a driving range.

For the next hour I fake-dialed or hung up when someone answered. And then around 11 a.m. I took my break and got stoned out of my gourd. Rolled a fattie in the parking garage and shared it with the chief attendant, a jovial Mexican man with a Super Mario Bros. mustache.

When I got back to the office, I was magic carpet flying.

The tattooed sales manager said in passing, "Is that marijuana I smell?"

I froze at the reception desk, spaced and confused. The manager's lips were moving, but I couldn't hear what he was saying. My throat was dry and constricted, my tongue glued to my palate.

"Huh?" was all I could manage.

"Richard, is that the stench of THC?"

"It's medicinal," I finally said. "I believe the strain is called...*Train Wreck*." I swatted at some imaginary fly. "By the way, do you guys provide free lunches?"

He eyeballed me and crossed his arms, his Bengal tiger tattoo threatening to pounce. "I thought you told me you were a game-changer, Richard."

"Um...yeah," I said, loose-jawed, staring up into the square fluorescent ceiling lights. "I guess I, uh... changed a few games."

"You're stoned. Highly unacceptable, Richard. And if you ever—"

"The name's Clean," I interrupted. "*Mr. Clean.*"

He didn't mince words.

"Thank you for sharing the holidays with us…*Mr. Clean.* Now get the hell out! *You're fired.*"

I shrugged. "Another professional relationship goes up in smoke."

He seemed astonished at my response.

"Why so cavalier?"

I stared at him glass-eyed.

"Because these are the times we live in."

I shouldered my backpack and walked out, left him standing there shaking his clipped skull.

It would be my last job of the year.

AFTER THAT I went home and got shitfaced watching spiders on the wall. Spacing out to the Steve Miller Band singing "Fly Like an Eagle."

Outside, a relentless drizzle tap-danced against my window. I watched the rain sluice down the glass and at that moment made a staunch decision to drop out. No longer to add to the landscape. I would simply blend in.

Just when I was about to test the boundaries of my new high and sink into the depths of nocturnal despair, I got a knock on the front door. It was around 10 p.m. I opened it slowly, peeking out for trouble. It was my neighbor, Norma, the knob checker and chicken choker. Or Ms. OCD as we sometimes called her.

"Oh, hey, Norma," I said, pulling down my Dodgers cap to hide the slits that once were my eyes. "What's up?"

"I'm so sorry to bother you, but I just needed to tell someone."

"Tell them what?"

She crossed her arms, her eyes blinking frantically.

"That I just lost my only dog-walking job."

"What?"

"You know the attorney in Westchester, the guy I've been working for for five years?"

I leaned one arm up against the doorjamb, signaling that she would not be invited in.

"Yeah."

"He fired me today."

"Why?"

She hopped under the landing, out of the rain. "He said he couldn't afford me anymore. He said his work was slow, and he had to cut back. I billed him eight hundred dollars last month. I don't know what I'm going to do. He said his dogs really love me. He has the cutest pugs. Lily and Booby. I'm really going to miss them."

I said, "You'll get another client."

You'll get another client. You'll make rent. Just stay positive. Everything will work out.

I smiled a lot when I told people these things. The fact of the matter was, I didn't know shit.

She leaned in and we hugged.

"I know, I know," she said. "I just have to make it to the shift."

I reared back.

"The shift? You been talking to Paula?"

"She's been talking to me. We're going to form a drum circle on Venice Beach the evening of the twentieth. A group meditation. You're welcome to join us. If the world does end, we'll all be there in love, holding hands."

"I see."

For a moment I searched my pot-fueled brain for excuses, anything to keep me away from aging mystics and drum circle hacks, and then I remembered I already had one. My mother's Christmas party. *Bingo.*

"I appreciate your thinking of me, Norma," I said, "but I'm gonna be in Las Vegas at my mom's house." I bared teeth. "It's a family affair."

She nodded five times, not two, not four, but five exactly. Same as she always did.

She said, "Well, if your plans change."

"They won't. But I'll keep you posted."

"Please do."

She said good night and walked up the concrete stairs in a light drizzle and entered her apartment. I heard the door shut, then heard the deadbolt slide.

Then I waited for it. Waited for her to do her thing, make sure the door was locked.

Bum bum bum bum bum

One.

Bum bum bum bum bum

Two.

Bum bum bum bum bum

Three.

Two more checks and she was home free. Five was the magic number. Shake, rattle, and roll. Classic OCD. She made it look so easy. And if you were a casual observer of the mundane and saw her walking dogs on the street, then you might think that she was a fairly attractive woman of forty-five. Norma on her best day looked like Olive Oyl on crystal

meth. Frantic, fried eyes and a long, lean body—
without curves—that stretched for the sky like an
Edwardian streetlamp. Her short, lank black hair was
always wet, and if you were horny and saw her in a
pair of tight gray yoga pants, then you might say to
yourself, *Gee, I'd like to hit that.* But then it would
be your turn to take her down to LAX and watch
her count the planes coming in every morning at
5:30 a.m. Sixty-two, to be exact. And then it would
be on to downtown to count the UPS trucks exiting
the bay, where no fewer than eighty-six would be
logged. Not once a week, but *every day.*

I live here. I know who she is. Which shelters
me from falling into that trap. That sexual trap of
pursuing a woman with a mind like a stoned clock.
The parts are all there and moving, but they're hor-
ribly out of sync. I've seen the meltdowns. But then
you see the poor saps trudging up our apartment
steps fresh from scoring a date on Plenty of Fish,
where she advertises for "fit men only" and they
never are, and then you just want to say to the guy,
"Dude, don't do it. She's fucking cuckoo." And then
you never see the guy trudging up the stairs again,
because he went downtown on a date to count the
UPS trucks. And that's what I tell people when they
ask me, "Why don't you give her the time? She likes

you. She lives in your building." And then I tell them there is no such thing as free pussy. And any middle-aged man that believes there is is fooling himself. Just ask the Donald.

The entire complex fell asleep to Norma that night rattling and shaking and checking her doorknob to make sure it was locked. We all would've been happy to assure her that it was. But somehow the certainty of the daily ritual provided us all with a sense of calm and normalcy.

Giant Steps

THE RAIN STAYED with us into the first week of December. And just like the headlines of our day, the Artist was growing more edgy by the hour. He said as long as this "water torture drizzle" continued, he was "out of business." No longer able to paint outside in the alley, he spent his time drinking, chewing nails, and worrying about outcomes beyond his control. It was Tuesday, the fourth of December, when I paid a visit. I got right down to it, tired of the dance.

"You make rent?"

"Not yet," he said, nervously wiping down a metal easel with a paper towel. "I'm three hundred short."

"Did that guy in Silver Lake come through?"

"Not yet."

I clenched my teeth. "That tool. I swear to God, I'm gonna waterboard his ass."

Wound tight, the Artist paced the room, saying over and over, "I don't know what I'm going to do. I don't know what I'm going to do. I don't know what I'm going to do. The landlord *will for sure* kick me out this time if I'm late."

I watched him pace another minute, then tried to coax a smile.

"Hey," I said. "Did you see that picture of Romney pumping gas in La Jolla? It was classic."

He wasn't listening, just raking the sides of his hair like he was crawling out of his skin. "Jesus Christ! I'm so tired of this rain! It's been like…*five days*." He turned and looked at me like a wounded animal. Sounded like one, too. "Did Beth call?"

"Not yet. But she'll call."

He stared off into the kitchen, perturbed. "I told you," he said, "you *never* bang somebody and run. Who does that?"

I knew what was going on. He was nervous about missing rent, but he was doubly nervous about showing his work. You have to be a brave spirit to be a fine artist in Los Angeles, where the cult of fame and celebrity trumps all. It's easy to get lost in this town of hype, pitches, and loglines. Easy to let the sarcasm chip away at your soul.

"You know," I said, "sometimes you have to take a risk. And you have to risk failure. You have to know that going in. If people don't look at your work and say, 'Oh, this is a piece of crap,' or '*I* could do that,' then you're not learning, man. You're not growing as an artist."

He kicked a newspaper on the floor. "Screw that! I'm not chasing profits."

"Then forget the profits," I said. "And focus on paying rent, will ya."

It was startling how much I sounded like my father.

"Arrrgggh," he said, running a stiff hand through his flattop. "I'm just so overwhelmed."

By now you should know that the Artist is a proud Southern man, raised never to accept a handout. He is famous for saying, "If I ever take government cheese, put me down like Old Yeller." So if you wanted to help him, you had to cloak your philanthropy in such a way as not to offend him. Or you had to buy one of his paintings. And since the only paintings I wanted were valued at more than a thousand dollars, I had to take a different route. The holidays gave me that opportunity. Plus, I was in the gift-giving mood. And, at the time, it was the right thing to do.

"Let me ease the pain," I said.

I pulled out my wallet and dropped three one-hundred-dollar bills onto the kitchen table.

"I can't take that," he drawled. "You know I don't take charity."

"It's not charity," I said. "It's an early Christmas present. Take it." I smiled. "But don't kid yourself. I'm expecting a gift this holiday, too. I'm thinking about a big spread across the street at the fish place."

"Yeah?"

"Yeah. I'm talking fine wine. Hundred-dollar-bottle shit. Blue crabs and lobster. You sell some paintings, you take care of your buddy."

The Artist was ogling the money when my phone rang. I looked at the number and saw it was Beth. I pointed at my cell. "It's her."

The Artist took a deep breath, fanning his flushed face with both hands.

"Well, hello there," I answered.

"Hey," Beth said.

We had a short but pleasant talk, during which she revealed that she'd been happily married to a CAA agent for the last nineteen years. They had two kids and lived off Bellagio Road in Bel Air. Unlike us, she was living the good life. We agreed to meet on Monday, December 10. It didn't help matters that the Artist was bobbing and weaving and farting and pacing and grimacing and biting his bare knuckles during the entire conversation.

When I hung up I said, "It's all good. She's coming by next week to view the painterly magic."

"When?" the Artist asked.

I tried to sound as calm and cool as possible. "Your birthday."

The Artist hyperventilated. "I don't know if I'm ready for this."

"Sure you are," I said, handing him a small brown paper bag. "You got nowhere else to go. You're fifty."

· · · · · · · · · · · · · · ·

I DIDN'T HAVE anywhere else to go either. So later that night while preparing some chamomile tea before bed, I got to thinking. Is there any way I can still be a productive member of society without stoop labor, still earn a decent living wage, and retain some semblance of dignity? I'm not asking for a lot here. Remember, I'm a boomer, raised on caviar dreams and millionaire wishes. But I'll settle now. Cry uncle for the simple life, no longer intent on ruling the world.

I know others would consider that extravagant still, but when you've grown up singing the theme song to *The Mary Tyler Moore Show* and drinking Coke slurpees from 7-Eleven, there are just some things in life you won't forgo. Or can't. So while sipping tea and watching Anthony Bourdain on the Travel Channel somewhere in Philly, a greasy cheesesteak smeared across his face, I was struck with an idea for a book that I might like to write. A nonfiction book about America. I recorded the thoughts in my journal.

> *Los Angeles, December 4, 2012*
>
> *Since everyone thinks I like to hear myself talk (Okay, I'm a blowhard. You happy now?) I've come up with an idea about writing a book on how to achieve success in America today. I am happy to give you a teaser, but only a teaser, because I intend to compile these gems into a self-help book, although I hesitate to call it a self-help book because self-help books generally don't help you. They give you a jumping-off platform into the "Rah rah go team" tactics on how to think positive and how to visualize wealth, but they are almost always generic in terms of location and time. And let's face it, nobody can magically visualize wealth (except the Federal Reserve).*

If you don't have the skills or resources today, no amount of mental technique will make you rich. I'll give you an example of what I mean by that. I saw a news piece on the unrest in Tunisia the other day and how all the young people were desperate for jobs. One young man said, "All the revolution brought us was freedom of expression. That's it." And then he pitched a hardback copy of Anthony Robbins's book Giant Steps *into an oil-drum fire, effectively stoking the flame and warming his hands. Apparently giant steps were not what was needed at the time, but rather baby steps, third-world steps, not four-hour work weeks and tango dancing in Argentina. And I'm sure during the time the book was written, which was on borrowed time, it actually helped rescue a few bewildered people from their American funk. But it held absolutely no value in today's world.*

These books do, however, make for excellent firewood substitutes. Great kindling to roast a city pigeon or country squirrel.

But back to making a go of it in America today. First off, I want to say that I feel sorry for the kids growing up during these times. They are like digital samples under a microscope. Here to be studied and observed. And despite where I have ended up today,

I would not trade my era for theirs—no way. I'm a private person by nature, and the thought of me taking a naked selfie of myself in the bathroom and sticking my tongue out at the world for all to see is something simply too disturbing for me to fathom. So with that, I'll give you my advice. And for the time being, it's free.

LIVE LIKE AN IMMIGRANT*. Let me be frank. Most of you will never be able to afford a house in some of the glamour cities of America. It doesn't mean that it can't be done, but you are going to have to be really lucky or, like the rest of us, work insanely hard and sacrifice. The old days of leverage are out. What is in is paying cash. Just like the Great Depression. Your goal now is to own property free and clear, meaning no loans against it. So how do you get the cash when you're working for eight bucks an hour? That's the million-dollar question.*

The answer is, you live like an immigrant. Meaning instead of living alone in an eight-hundred-square-foot flat, you live with five or ten other people. Just like those families have done for decades crossing our borders. You can either save collectively as a group, or you can save on your own. It's up to you. And before you dismiss me as some pothead loser boomer (as I appear to be), remember I have

234

been in real estate for over thirty years. Take that as you want.

LEARN TO MAKE OR FIX SOMETHING WITH YOUR HANDS. *That way you can never be outsourced or replaced by a machine. Learn to tie a fishing knot. Rope a calf. Farm the land. Become a midnight plumber. Fix air conditioners in the desert. Because your hands can't lie about what you produce. Can't manipulate the labor with derivatives or algorithms. Now do you see why I'm fighting for the Artist? Craftsmanship. Working with your hands is no longer respected in America, but it is making a comeback. So make something that people want or have to pay for. Give them something they can't get online. Stretch the boundaries of your frugalness. Because the machines are marching on, and they will escort you to the outhouse of time if you don't acquire a skill that has survived since the beginning of mankind. Remember this: you cannot compete with software. If you do, you will lose. So become the best handyman on the block. (A once respectable trade in America.) And if your clients can't pay cash, then barter for food, clothing, or shelter. Beer occasionally.*

PROTECT YOUR DIGITAL REPUTATION. *I can't stress this enough. In the old days it took* *months, even years to ruin a reputation. Now it takes a click, tap, or tweet for the powers that be to declare war on your economic future. One innocent online boudoir photo of your wife in stockings can be doctored by cutting and pasting penises all around her face, and the next thing you know she is the lead-off hitter for a porn site buried deep inside a Soviet Republic server. And then once she has been exposed for the dirty slut they always believed her to be, she will never again find another job. And once they (the technology corporations, because that's who controls most of the country now) strip you of that economic road to success, then you will have no choice but to produce something of value with your hands (or body) that people will pay you for regardless of your past transgressions. Don't let the digital imperialists own your future. Fight for it now.*

The End of White Men

ON DECEMBER 5, 2012, it became official. I became one of them: a street person, an untouchable. It'd been over a week since I parted with my Lexus LS 400, but already the street people had sized me up and claimed me as one of their own. I was just another guy on a bicycle now. Somebody who knew every crack in the sidewalk, every dangerous intersection, and every dried piece of gum caked on the pavement.

I was out there all right. And I belonged to them. Homeless people, slack actors, spindly-legged geezers, dead-eyed psychics, blown-out screenwriters, dopers, maids, drunks, pimps, punks, and star-spangled runaways who'd never had, and never would have, a shot, shell-shocked vets, campus gropers, cart pushers, limping whores, and the guy living in a Vanagon down by the ocean. They can all spot you. And they approach.

Case in point.

I rode my bike to Trader Joe's this morning, and I was standing in the checkout line when this whacked-out sixty-year-old derelict tapped me on the shoulder.

I turned around.

"Yeah," I said.

He invaded my space and pointed at his blood-shot eyes.

"Do I have bags? Dark circles?"

"You look fine," I said.

He didn't. He looked like an Ice Age mummy.

"Are you sure?" he said. "Because this is a company town. It's about image, man. You know that."

I thought a moment, appraising his dirty, frayed jeans, his greasy maroon sweater and unruly dark hair.

"Let me ask you something," I said, already knowing what he was going to say. "Does hard work and loyalty ever trump beauty?"

He recoiled and gulped as if he'd just swallowed a fly.

"Hell, no," he said, clear voiced, wide-eyed. "Hell the fuck no."

Then I patted his grimy back and told him what he wanted to hear.

"*You look great.*"

He lowered his head. "Thanks, bro. I do the stairs three times a week."

This twisted town.

I wanted to scream at these people.

Leave me alone!

I am not one of you!

I am saving the environment!

I am a green elite, leaving behind a smaller carbon footprint!

You don't understand, dammit!

"*I GO MEATLESS ON MONDAYS!*"

· · · · · · · · · · · · · · · · · ·

LATER THAT NIGHT I got a text from the Artist to meet up at JP's Grill on Wilshire. It was a neighborhood hangout with a rough past. A hole-in-the-wall, darts and pool. A dim place for gilded Westside youth to slum it with professional drunkards and angry old men. There were no airs here, no L.A. pretensions. Just moral decay and cold beer. It was the last outpost on the beach where you had a hint of real danger, the last shot at a fistfight.

I spotted Bales at the bar, holding court with his merry band of idiots—Hashtag, Big Salad, and Homegrown. Hashtag was slumped over the phone, wearing his usual food-stained polo. Homegrown just stood there in a Radiohead T-shirt, tall, skinny, and pasty, like steam belched from a manhole. I could barely make out Big Salad, but Bales looked sharp in a purple gingham oxford, his gray hair jelled up in spikes.

"Gentlemen," I said, approaching.

"Ah, Clean," Bales said, clutching a pint. "Hear you lost your ride. What's next, brother? A scooter?"

They all laughed.

"Where's the Artist?" I asked.

"He had to chuck a leak," Bales said.

A scrawny hipster with a ducktail beard and a sock hat tried to slip through the crowd. Bales grabbed him by the elbow and jerked him back. "You look like a fucking Portland type."

The skinny kid was stunned. He tried to speak but couldn't. "Wha…wha…"

Shit happens when you slum it.

"Goddammit, Bales," I said. "Let him go. Just once can you dispense with the drama?"

Bales released the kid and told him, "Haul ass, beardo."

"Sorry, man," I said to the sock hat. "He's drunk."

"*He's drunk*," Bales said, mocking me. "Shit, you remind me of my ex-wife." He snapped his head toward the bar. "Hashtag, get me another beer!"

"Number twenty?" I said.

"It's no fun to count." He burped. "So the Artist tells me you've got some big shot looking at his work."

"Yeah, he's on the verge."

"So what are you saying? He's the next Jasper Johns? Larry Bell?"

"Could be."

Bales nodded. "Looks like one of us might make it out alive, huh, Clean?"

"I guess so. It couldn't happen to a better guy."

I looked out into the sottish crowd, Van Halen's "Running with the Devil" cranking over the sound system.

"Fuckin' A," Bales said. "I got to take a piss."

We watched him forcefully push his way through the packed house, winding around the pool tables.

I turned to Homegrown. "What's he on?"

"Meth and Xanax…some edibles. What I know about anyway."

"Great," I said. "Another heart attack."

Homegrown looked mystified, his junky little fingers nervously tugging at his T-shirt.

"He…he didn't tell you?"

"Tell me what?"

"That he…that he faked that heart attack."

I looked surprised. "Faked it? Why would he do that?"

"So he could buy some time on the rent, bro. The landlord gave him like, an extra three weeks. On account of his health and all."

I shook my head.

My God, I thought. Who else was he playing? Did he indeed have some kind of master plan? Or was all this simply a means to entertain his own warped sense of humor? I'd met his wealthy, nihilistic kind before. But never anybody this destructive. And then I recalled what my father had taught me—that the root word of confidence is con.

Somebody bear-hugged me from behind.

"Let me guess," I said.

"Clean, whuz happening!"

It was the Artist, drunk. A happy drunk. And who could blame him? He finally had prospects.

He released me and I turned around. We high-fived. Then somebody accidentally bumped him from behind and he spilled beer on his dingo boots.

"Ah, shit," he said, laughing.

"You happy now?" I asked. "You want to call me Mr. Sunshine?"

"Yeah," he said, a stupid farm grin on his face.

"The sun's back," I said. "You can work outside again. You're on the brink, baby. What more could you want?"

I clapped him on the shoulder and he burped like he was holding down puke. "Pujols," he said.

The Artist was still smarting from the Albert Pujols trade to the Los Angeles Angels.

"It's going to be a good holiday season, buddy," I said. "Cheers."

We clinked beer mugs, and I spotted Big Salad and his man bun heading for the door.

"Where's he going?" I said.

"Home," said Hashtag. "He's got a problem with his bowels."

"Constipation," added Homegrown. "Said he pushed so hard last night he cracked his back. Saw stars."

I wondered how a guy with a diet of organic greens and salad dressing could be constipated. I wouldn't be able to stay off the can.

Bales shouldered his way over. He stopped and got up in the face of this young, fashionable Asian man.

"You, my friend, haven't made anything worthwhile since the Walkman." The young stranger looked puzzled, batting his eyes, as if stumped in a spelling bee. "Process it all you want," Bales said, "but it's the truth."

I grabbed Bales by the arm and yanked him over. Then I side-mouthed the word "crazy" to the Asian dude.

Bales mumbled, "One fucking night. Just one night. Why can't you have a good time?"

I held my iPhone tight enough to crush it, and looked away. "I don't have anything to celebrate."

Hashtag started laughing.

"What?" I said.

Homegrown pointed at Bales's nose. He had what looked to be a cotton ball stuck in his left nostril.

"May all your Christmases be white," Bales said, cackling.

"What the fuck—"

"A two-gram rock of cocaine," Homegrown said flatly. "Well…it used to be two grams."

Bales tossed his head back and howled like a wolf. Then he started shouting "motherfucker." Sounding off like some wild tropical bird. Cawing at the top of his lungs, head and neck bobbing. "Moth-

erfuck—ahh!…CAW! CAW! Motherfuck—ahh!…
CAW! CAW! Motherfuck—ahh!…CAW! CAW!"

In an ordinary bar this might have caused some concern. Not here. Not among these payday drunks. He was just another guy having fun, letting off some steam.

Bales turned to me all hopped up and said, "Take a look around, Clean. What do you see?"

I didn't have to look around. I stared him straight in the eye. "A drunkie."

"That may be true," he said. "No, in fact it is true. But look closely and what you'll find here are Asian faces, Latin faces, the *Shahs of Sunset* faces, and the latest arrivals to the beach…*Arab* faces. And what do they all have in common?"

"What?"

"They don't give a shit about us. None of them. Because *we* are the minority now."

"So?"

"So Gidget's dead, Clean. Our time's over. It's bye-bye *Beach Blanket Bingo*. Along with hobby shops, golf, America's Cup…"

"Classic rock," added Hashtag.

"All history," Bales said. "Because the only good white—*is a lobotomized white*." His eyes were wild and raw, his jaw grinding on a wire. "It's the end of white men, boys. Tag us and bag us. Archive us all. Because we're museum-bound. All of us. Right next to the fucking blond guy with a surfboard."

We all gnawed on that unpleasant thought a moment.

Then Hashtag leaned against the bar and said, "I read the other day that several new mosques are being built in the San Gabriel Valley and all the way down to Corona. The Muslims are coming. Only a matter of time before they take the beach."

"Tell me about it, bro," Homegrown said. "I was in Starbucks yesterday and it was *packed* with Middle Easterners. And I swear to God, they were playing that hijack music inside. I mean, I got kinda scared."

"Not to worry, Homegrown," Bales said. "They don't have to kill us anymore. They can buy us now."

"The Jews aren't gonna let that happen," I said.

Bales scoffed, his beer-free hand sweeping the air. "Jumpin' jihad, Clean, who kicked sand in your Shawarma? Open your eyes. They're pushing the Jews back to Manhattan Beach. The white man's last stand. Once they break that, it's clear sailing down the coast."

I noticed the Artist was fading. He was rocking back on his heels, trying to keep his eyes open. They fluttered, struggling for half-mast.

"The Artist is finished," I said. "I'm gonna get him home. How much does he owe?"

"I got this, bitches," Bales said. "You two ladies have a fine walk. And try not to get your heads lopped off."

"Are you sure?" I said, reaching for my wallet. "Because I got cash."

Bales slugged his beer and waved me off. "I told you I got it. Now get Cinderfella home before he turns into a pumpkin. Beat it."

"All right," I said. "I'm not going to argue with you. Later."

I pointed the Artist toward the door, and we headed for the exit.

I didn't know it then, but I was picking up dimes in front of a bulldozer. Playing Gallant to Bales's Goofus.

The Great Displacement

I GOT A call from the Artist the next morning. He
said he lost his wallet and wondered by chance if
I had it. I said no, it was probably at JP's. So we
agreed to meet for lunch at noon. See if they had
his wallet. I told him it didn't matter if it was lost
or stolen because it held nothing of value. Just a
few old grocery coupons and a phone number from
some Malibu MILF who liked to suck his toes. But
he didn't find my observation funny and told me to
get my ass over to JP's—pronto.

We arrived at the same time and took a seat at
the bar. The bartender's name was Chris Beeks, a
bald, middle-aged steroid jockey with a Polynesian
scalp tattoo and biceps the size of howitzers. He wore

tight jeans and showcased his Muscle Beach guns in a Judas Priest T-shirt. The Artist said he used to be a bouncer at the Forum in Inglewood, but got fired after he fucked up some dude at a KISS concert.

I had been instructed not to mess with the guy.

"What's up, Beeks?" said the Artist, folding his hands on the bar.

"Hey, Jimmy," he said stoically. Flat-eyed.

The Artist gestured toward me. "This is my friend—"

"Clean," Beeks said, interrupting. "Yeah, I know. I met him last night."

"Why so glum?" said the Artist. "No tips?"

Beeks reached into his back pocket and tossed a wallet onto the counter. "Yours?"

The Artist looked at Beeks, then down at the thin brown leather billfold.

"Looks like it."

"If it's empty," I said, "it's his."

The Artist checked his wallet. "Yeah, that's it. Looks like it's all there."

"What?" I said. "They didn't steal your Triple A card? I'm shocked."

Beeks had other things on his mind. He smoothed a hand over his tattooed dome and said, "You've got bigger problems, Jimmy."

The Artist looked up, eyebrows arched. "Oh, yeah? What's that?"

"Your friend fucked up," Beeks said. "And that means you fucked up."

"What are you talking about?"

"Follow me."

We looked at each other.

Beeks stepped out from behind the bar and led us into the kitchen and pointed at a TV monitor. The Artist looked at me with trepidation as Beeks grabbed a remote and rewound the tape. He stopped on Bales at the bar, froze the screen, and pointed at the image.

"Is that your friend?"

"It's his neighbor," I answered.

"Neighbor, friend, it's all the same. Watch."

Beeks pushed the remote button and started the video. I hadn't realized how loud it was in there last night. Amazing how alcohol dulled the senses. No wonder my ears were still buzzing.

On the screen, Beeks was seen setting down a black leather guest check holder on the bar in front of a big, brown-haired man. The credit card peeked halfway out from inside the fold. The brown-haired man was drinking and laughing with another patron and ignoring the bill. Then we watched as Bales slowly slid his left hand over the wooden bar top and pinched the guy's credit card with his thumb and forefinger. Then we watched him drop it into the front pocket of his dress shirt. He rose quickly, but not hurriedly, and casually walked out the door.

"Ah, man," I said.

The Artist just stood there slack-jawed, struck dumb.

"He's a bad news bear," Beeks said, clicking off the TV monitor. "He clipped one of my regulars for eight hundred bucks before he canceled the card. Then the fucker has the balls to skip out on his bill."

"The credit card company will reimburse the guy," I said.

"I'm sure they will. But the damage has been done." Beeks crossed his pumped arms. "The guy's not going to file charges," he said. "And neither are we. But you tell that fucktard if I see him around here again, I'm going to break his face. Then he's going to jail. You tell him that."

"I'm real sorry, Beeks," the Artist said, his Southern accent as thick as creamed corn. "But he's been through a real rough patch."

"Who hasn't? But they don't go around stealing credit cards. I'm sorry, Jimmy. But we're going to have to take a break. This is not from me, mind you, but straight from the owner."

"What?"

"Are you saying," I said, "that we're *banned* from here?"

"Like I said, it's the owner's call. Not mine."

I pleaded our case. "But Jimmy doesn't have anything to do with him. It's his *neighbor*."

Beeks shrugged. "I'm not saying it's forever. It's just what's best for now."

"Christ," I said in a low voice. "How much does he owe you?"

Beeks laid the bill down on the bar. "Two hundred fifty-six bucks. Without tip."

I reached for my wallet, which I had done more times than I'd cared to back then, and counted out three hundred dollars in crisp twenties. Three hundred I didn't have.

I dropped the cash on the counter and told Beeks we were real sorry, that one day I hoped we could repair the damage. But that wasn't in the cards.

I never stepped foot inside JP's again.

Neither did the Artist.

AFTER WE LEFT the bar that afternoon, we went to Palisades Park. We stood high on the steep coastal bluffs of Santa Monica, leaning against the concrete railing, staring out over the Pacific Ocean. The sea was dark and flat, a smooth line under a bright blue sky.

The Artist rested his arms over the rail, head hung low.

"I'm humiliated," he said. "I mean, that's my *Stammtisch*."

"How many times can a guy shit in your backyard?" I said.

The Artist looked south toward Catalina Island, his paradisal dream shattered.

"I don't know if Bales is still giving you money," I said, "but I'd caution against taking anything more from him. You've got too much to lose now. I know he's your neighbor. You got this bromance thing going. He's helped you. You've helped him. But it's over. It's time to cut him loose. You hear what I'm saying?"

The Artist wrestled with his thoughts.

"You know," he said finally. "For some strange reason I'm not mad at him. He's just got major problems he's working through. And it's a much bigger issue than him."

"Yeah, tell that to yourself when you're sitting in county wearing an orange jumpsuit."

He looked at me, his aviator sunglasses reflecting majestic palms.

"You think Bales is right about us?"

"About what?"

"The end of white men?"

"You don't have to worry about that," I said. "You're an artist. You transcend color." I looked up the coast, staring off into the Santa Monica Mountains, the craggy brown peaks rising from the beach like a sculpted sandcastle. "But he's right about one thing. Times are changing."

"I don't even recognize Santa Monica anymore," the Artist said. "It's no longer a sleepy beach town. We used to have all this space. That's why I moved west. For the space."

"Yeah, the beach used to be a lifestyle," I said. "Now it's a commodity. A tourist trap. The multinationals are building this place out. High-rises and security doors. In ten years you won't recognize it. It could Dubai or Vegas…or anywhere. It's big business now. Sunshine and profits, the eternal dance."

"Who's buying all these places?"

"People with more money than us."

The Artist nodded. "It's outta control, man. Razing these iconic bungalows. Building McMansions. It's tragic."

"L.A. doesn't give a shit. It recycles people like us."

The Artist looked off, watching an old woman feeding the pigeons. "I used to spot all the actors reading their lines here," he said. "Now I can't even remember the last time I saw a guy with a script walking around. All you see now is foreign tourists, drug dealers…and dot-com dorks talking codes and technobabble. It makes you long for the good ol' days of the Hells Angels."

"That was many moons ago," I said.

The Artist took a deep breath and theatrically extended his arms toward the Santa Monica Bay. "No matter what happens, they can't take this."

"Arguably one of the best sunsets in the world."

"I'd move," the Artist said. "But I could never leave this. It's my therapy, man. My inspiration."

"Your paintings reflect that," I said.

The Artist pointed up to the sky.

"You see that?"

"What?"

"Those cirrus clouds."

I stared up at the thin wispy strands, curling like old gray fingers.

"What about it?"

"If you look real close, and use a little imagination, you can make out the Archer. My sun sign, Sagittarius. See?" He traced the clouds with his forefinger. "You see the arrow there?"

"Where?"

He pointed with emphasis. "*Right there.*"

"Kinda," I said. But I'm not sure that I did.

We took in the breathtaking view a moment, watching whitecaps on the steely water.

The Artist said, "I guess I thought it would be different, you know? I'm going to be fifty in a few days, but I don't feel any different. I don't feel old."

Los Angeles is a city where people come to work out who they are. We were still working out who we were.

"Fifty's a tricky birthday," I said. "It fools you into thinking you're still young. Truth is, you're not that far off from enjoying PBS doo-wop specials."

He laughed, then turned serious again.

"I asked Bales the other day what it was like to be rich. You know what he told me?"

"Another lie?"

"Maybe. But he said the better question would be...what's it like *not* to be rich."

"Don't feel sorry for a guy like Bales. He was weaned on cynicism. He made his bed. And he knows it more than anybody."

I watched an old Mexican man with a straw cowboy hat strumming his guitar on a nearby park bench.

The Artist said, "What do you think I should wear to the show?"

"I'd go all black."

"The Ed Ruscha look?"

"Yeah. Black T-shirt. Dark jeans."

"That's my comfort zone."

"It is indeed."

I closed my eyes and turned my face toward the sun, catching some vitamin D.

"Hey," the Artist said. "I'm thinking about growing a beard. What do you think about that?"

"What kind? The hipster Civil War beard, or the craft brew beard?"

He smiled.

"I was thinking more like the *Miami Vice* stubble. What about you?"

"Grow a beard?"

"Yeah."

"No, my beard's white. There would be nothing hip about it. I'd look like the fucking Fed chairman.

258

But maybe I'll let the sides of my hair grow long. Rock the Viking donut."

"That'd be a strong look."

"One you definitely have to own."

The Artist checked his watch, then looked at me.

"Can you believe it? We got kicked out of JP's. I mean, nobody gets kicked out of JP's."

"Yeah," I said. "We're a couple of real outlaws."

· · · · · · · · · · · · · · · · ·

SPEAKING OF OUTLAWS, I planned on confronting Bales later that evening. I wanted my three hundred dollars back. I didn't appreciate other people taking food off my table. So I had the Artist set up a time to meet somewhere later in Venice. But when I got home I had another surprise waiting for me. It announced itself as a short potbellied man wearing a pair of comfortable Dockers and a blue blazer shaped like a moving box. As I got closer to the entrance of my apartment building, I could see the portly stranger bent over with a measuring tape. I knew exactly who he was. He was a real estate appraiser. Which meant one of two things. The owner was either going to sell the building or refinance it.

At this point, all I could do was speculate.

Walking up the concrete steps of the building, I saw Paula jogging toward me in her brightly colored workout suit and electric-yellow Nike running shoes, her silver hair tucked proudly under a navy-blue Boston Red Sox cap. She intercepted me by the battered aluminum mailboxes in the front entryway, slightly out of breath.

"Did you hear?" she said.

"Hear what?"

Her eyes grew big and she gently shoved me in the chest with both hands. "They sold the building."

I looked over at the fat man, his measuring tape stretched out against the side of the beige structure. "I knew something was up when I saw him," I said.

"Yeah. Do you know what Andrew told me?"

"The doomsday prepper?"

"Yes."

"What? That he's the demon beast?"

I tried to fit the laughs in when I could, but the world kept beating them back.

"Yes," she said, catching herself. "I mean, no. He said he's moving out. And he asked the manager if he repaired some of the damage that he'd done to his unit, would he get his entire deposit back? And do you know what the manager told him?"

I shook my head.

"He told him don't bother with repairs. Because they're never going to rent out that unit again. *Ever.*" She blew a droplet of sweat off her nose. "What do you think he meant by that?"

"It means they're going to tear down the building," I said. "They want us out. We're just flies in the soup now."

I knew what was happening. I'd seen it before in my line of work. The new owners were going to bleed us out. One by one. We'd either move by choice, at their request, with some form of payment (bribe), or we'd stay and fight. But whatever route we chose, the outcome would be the same. We would be gone from our apartments. It was just a matter of time. And like I said earlier, when you lose your apartment, you lose your community. That's because you can never afford to buy back in.

It was happening all up and down the California coast. I'd never seen anything like it. The gentrification—this great consolidation of wealth. Wall Street speculators and international money were gobbling up older buildings at record prices and knocking them down and erecting smaller, luxury housing units, literally transforming cities overnight. The poor were thrown out like street dogs, left to fend for themselves. From San Francisco to San Diego, the great displacement was underway.

"What's gonna happen to us?" Paula asked, a note of anger in her voice.

"We'll get evicted."

"When?"

I opened my mailbox and reached for a handful of bills. "A year. Maybe longer. Depends on how fast their project gets approval, and how fast they can get everybody out."

"What about us? Don't we have rights?"

"Not if they invoke the Ellis Act."

"What's that?"

"A little gift from the California legislature to landlords. I guess it seemed like a good idea at the time, but now it's uprooting seniors and disabled people."

She clutched my wrist and looked at me like the Red Sox were down to their last out.

"We must have some chance."

"Maybe a procedural defense. But that's about as slim as winning the lottery. These landlords are slippery. Like moss on rock. They'll cover their ass. We'll just have to be happy with the relocation fee. Hope for something better."

"And how much is that?"

I flipped through my mail. "Twelve grand. Maybe a little more."

"But then what? That's only five months' rent. One-bedrooms are going for three thousand now. I can't afford that. Where am I gonna go?"

I shrugged, looking up at a small plane flying overhead.

"I don't know."

Where am I going to go?

That's a question we all have to answer on our own. And for some, the ride will be long and emotional. Most will never live on the coast again. At least not alone. The lucky ones will have a place to go. But most will not. The early transition will find them landing with relatives, or on a friend's couch, before finally settling inland with an unwanted roommate to age out as gracefully as one can. The diehard tenants, those most likely to have called the place home for more than thirty years, will lawyer up and fight. But they'll spend their last dime fighting for a lost cause. In the meantime, if you are a diehard, you'll watch the lights in the units go out one by one, until you are alone in an abandoned, graffiti-tagged building. And if you were one of the tenants who liked to garden, then you'll watch your tomato plants that you tended lovingly for the last five years trampled underfoot. And each day that you hang on, the new owner tortures you with the presence of realtors, learned men, engineers, architects, appraisers, contractors of all stripes, and they'll all walk by laughing and squashing your garden and making notes and sketching things out that you do not understand. And not one of them will look at you, let alone speak to you, because all you are is the last termite to be exterminated. Something to be pushed toward hotter and colder climes. And eventually *you will* get the final court order to vacate the unit, and you'll think about how all those years you meticulously cared for the building and the property, and then you'll soon realize it meant nothing. Not a damn thing, just one day closer to death.

Don't Fear the Reaper

LATER THAT NIGHT I met the Artist at the Brig in Venice. For over fifty years it had been a funky, seedy fixture on Abbot Kinney Boulevard, a neighborhood beer bar for the rough-and-tumble crowd. It was founded by a hard-hitting featherweight prizefighter named Babe Brandelli, whose crouching pugilistic silhouette still remained on the sign outside. But that was all that remained of the "Old Venice" haunt. About ten years ago it had received a chic facelift, remodeled into a slick hipster haven. Now it was just another hotspot on the college barhopping tour.

The Artist was seated at the space-age metallic bar when I arrived, plunged in violet light and drinking a bottle of Budweiser. His threadbare black hoodie looked oddly out of place among the twenty-something crowd, a throwback between yesterday and today.

"What's up, man?" he said, extending his right arm out with a balled fist.

I met him, and we bumped knuckles softly.

"Look at this place," I said. "I haven't been here in ten years. It's unrecognizable." I looked out into the young, trendy crowd. Beautiful and privileged women, shrieking and sharing drinks. Not a sea hag in sight. Prissy men with skinny-fit jeans and short-cropped beards playing pool, peacocking in tight flannel shirts and black military boots.

"Yeah, like the whole street," he said. "From swearing sailor to Urban Outfitters. Talk about a loss of flavor. But the drinks are still reasonable."

"Cool," I said. "Where's Bales?"

"He said he was coming."

"Did you confront him about last night?"

"No," the Artist said. "To be honest, he's starting to freak me out. He's getting darker. And his eyes are always shifty. It's like he's about to pull a job or something. I thought you might help me talk to him."

"I've got no problem with that," I said. "Maybe he can get us kicked out of here."

I took a seat and flagged down the bartender.

"Guess what?" I said.

"What?"

"They sold my building."

The Artist smacked the bar top with the flat of his hand. "No fucking way! It's happening all over, man. What are you going to do?"

I paid for my beer and took a sip. "Nothing I can do. Just wait until they offer me some relo money."

The Artist flexed his jaw. "I'm tired of this town, dude. Anything older than ten years and they want to knock it down. We're talking about people's lives here."

"Don't sweat it, bro," I said. "It's my time."

"Do you know who's buying the place? Maybe they'll keep the tenants."

"Fat chance. My neighbor says it's a Chinese firm. Based out of Beijing." I raised my glass. "Bring on the earth-moving equipment."

"That sucks."

I watched a guy break the rack on the pool table. "There are over four billion people in Asia," I said. "Two hundred million more in Brazil, and they all want what I have. Or had. A better life. That's who's buying up a lot of these properties. The scions of the wealthy. As well as a few lucky tech punks. It's a billionaire's playground now. It's time for me to go."

And I meant it. I'd been trying to leave that rat-infested dump since the minute I'd moved into it—ten years ago. Which was right after my divorce, right after we sold the house. Each year I said this year will be better, this year will be the year that I move out and buy a house. But each year the economy got worse and prices rose. Leaving me frozen in a 1970s time warp. I hadn't thought too much about it until I saw Bales that day lying on the floor in tears, the pain on his face of losing everything a reminder of all that went wrong. I knew the feeling, the gut-wrenching heartache, and it brought back memories of my downsizing, my impending sense of failure.

I didn't know where I was going to go, or how I was going to live, but my time was coming to an end there. Fate had intervened and was kicking me out. All of us out. Maybe I'd pioneer some strange new land. Some distant mountainous region or exotic jungle. Resort to cannibalism for survival. And I hear you asking me the question, "Would you really eat people?" And my answer would be, "Depends on who it is."

The Artist said, "Yeah, but what about your neighbors? I know they don't have anywhere to go."

"Nothing they can do. The deck's stacked against us."

"Landlords. Soulless moneychangers is what they are."

I watched a young beauty lope across the dance floor like a gazelle.

"You can stay on my couch anytime, bro," the Artist said.

"Thanks," I said, "but I'm sure I'll figure something out."

I looked around the bar, hoping for somebody to rescue me, but life preservers were in short supply.

"Hey, did you hear?" said the Artist. "They're knocking down Norms. Gonna build more high-density rat cages."

"The diner?"

"Yeah. It's practically a landmark. Old-school California." He grabbed his bottle of Budweiser and picked at the label, then looked at me. "I guess I just miss the way it used to be."

I hoisted up a pint of the local brew and took a healthy chug. "Don't we all?"

"Yeah, I guess. You know, when I was striving toward the dream, all I could think about was wanting more. Now all I dream about is having what I used to have. Funny, huh?"

I raised an eyebrow like Spock. "Hilarious."

The Artist's phone chirped. He picked it up and read the text message. "It's Bales," he said. "He's on his way."

"Great. He better have my money."

The Artist nodded, still lost in the past. "You remember how authentic this bar used to be? A real dive. Dark, with cool characters and surfer-painters. I mean, not like that idiot." He pointed at a young guy in a porkpie hat wearing a skinny tie and rolled-up jeans, dancing alone to the hip-hop music. His eyes were closed and his head bobbed like he was tripping on E. "Twenty years ago that guy would have got his ass beat. Fucking pastry chef."

"The bohemian rhapsody's over," I said. "Or maybe we're just getting old."

The Artist looked up into the purple lights. "Yeah, I guess. I got a problem with change."

"Cue the Streisand music."

"Maybe so."

I watched the Artist remove his Cardinals baseball cap and place it down on the counter. It was dirty and wrinkled, as was his hoodie. And for the first time in the dingy light of the bar, I could see the ravages of Father Time, economics, and the many days of working outdoors, finally taking their toll. His face was rough and windblown, like cracked red leather. The contortions of eternity carved in his brow.

He looked like something that had been left out in the sun too long.

"Dude," I said, "you look like an old salty dog."

He smiled. "I was just going to say the same thing about you."

We laughed.

"Funny," I said. "Just when we've grown into the look, they remodel the place."

"Do you think we look that old?"

"You serious? Kids are looking at us like we're dinosaurs."

"No."

"*Yeah*. They're writing up a Yelp report as we speak. *Warning*, gross old men at the bar."

"No, they're not."

The Artist, like most in L.A., suffered from a touch of the Peter Pan syndrome.

"Hey," he said. "Would you ever consider plastic surgery?"

"No. Wouldn't help. Bald men can't hide the scars. But we do wear them well. Adds to the mystique."

The Artist's phone sounded and he checked it. "It's Bales," he said. "He's here. He wants us to meet him outside at the food truck."

. . . .

WE EXITED THE Brig at 9:30 and spilled onto Abbot Kinney Boulevard. The fall night was mild, a cool ocean breeze shaking the palms. As we stood on the bustling sidewalk looking for Bales, I felt as though I were from another time, another place. I felt like a stranger in my hometown, someone who didn't even speak the language. It was definitely not the gritty Venice of my youth. More like shiny Rodeo Drive.

"You see him?" the Artist said.

"No. Every lumbersexual looks the same. Did Bales say which truck he was at?"

The Artist shook his head. "He just said he was outside."

"Maybe he's in the back parking lot," I said. "Follow me."

We pushed our way through the drunk, hungry crowd, dodged a skateboarder on the sidewalk, and wandered into the Brig's back parking lot. It was packed. Long lines of boisterous club kids, digital nerds, and Airbnb tourists stretched around the block, most waiting patiently at the Korean BBQ truck. I smelled a fusion of flavors surfing the sea air, everything from short-rib tacos to organic turkey dogs. We stopped in the middle of the crowd, and then I was certain that the haughty voice I heard cutting through the night emitted from him.

"Over there," I said, pointing. We walked back to a French gourmet truck parked under a clump of palm trees. And there he was, appearing out of the haze of food smoke, lively and slack-limbed, wearing white sneakers, fitted dark jeans, and a light gray Gucci sweater. I could tell he was drunk, wearing Wayfarer sunglasses at night.

"I don't give a shit about your farm-to-table food," Bales was saying. "I'm telling you it sucks." He stood at the order window, shouting at the chef, his silver head flashing like a beacon. If I'd been a rooftop sniper, I'd have had a clear shot. And I would've taken it.

Bales was screaming, causing a scene, which, to any person who got to know him, was something he excelled at. "I want my fucking money back," he said, tossing his paper plate on the ground. "This is dog crap." He kicked over the chalkboard of specials. "You pretentious fucks, with your salmon and bacon crepes."

As we approached, I heard organ meat hissing on the grill, smelled shallots and leeks in the air.

"Fresh-baked my ass," Bales rambled. "This baguette tastes like it came from Smart and Final. Or the dollar store. What else are you skimping on, Pierre?" He turned and addressed the young crowd waiting in line. "Hey, people," he said, "guess who's duping your nascent palate?"

"Bales!" I called, walking toward him. I saw his sunglasses swing my way, but it didn't mean he saw me.

"Fuck you," Bales said to the chef, then stumbled toward us. "Heyyy," he said in his baby voice. "I've been a bad, bad boy, Daddy. I am so sorry. I promise I won't do it again. Don't send me to military school. Don't do it, Daddy." He laughed, then threw his arms around the Artist and bear-hugged him. "A, who's your daddy? Am I your daddy?"

The Artist smiled. The affection, however calculated, satiated his need for human touch.

Party pooper that I was, I dug into my pants pocket and pulled out the check from JP's. I shoved it toward his face. "This look familiar?"

He released the Artist and took two steps toward me and stopped. He leaned into the paper, flipped up the Wayfarers high on his head, and squinted at the bill.

"Never seen it," he said.

"You got that right," I said. "Because you walked out before you ever received it."

An alcoholic grin laced his face. "Okay, Clean. Question. How many times can the bald man be cast as the small-town sheriff?"

"It was a role I was born to play," I said.

"I admit, you do play it well. But so what?" He staggered back. "So fucking what? What do you fucking care about my bill? It's none of your damn business."

"You made it my business. We went in for lunch today. And do you know what we saw?"

Bales smiled. "Dead people?"

I lunged forward and grabbed him by the neck of his sweater. "You stole a guy's credit card. They have it all on film. And they're going to press charges if you—*or we*—go back in there again." I shoved him backward. "I paid your fucking bill. You owe me three hundred bucks."

Bales straightened his sweater. "I'll get you your three hundred bucks. You cheap fuck. I don't give a shit."

"Yeah, but I do," I said. "And the Artist does. That's his bar. He's been going in there for years. And in one night you ruin a lifetime of goodwill."

Bales swung his Wayfarers at the Artist, who up until now had been a docile pile of goo. "I'm sorry, A. I was drunk. I'll make it up to you. I'll pay everybody." He palmed his chest. "It's my bad. My bad."

The Artist looked away into the night scene, then looked back and said, "You know, John, I just wish you wouldn't drink so much. I think it makes you do stupid things. Now, I'm willing to forgive you, but I want you to promise me that you'll think about other people before you act."

Bales bowed repeatedly with both hands together, like a servant in rising Asia. "I totally agree. I promise. I *swear* to God, I'll never hurt you again. *Swear to God.*"

"What about me?" I said, waiting for an apology.

But it never came.

Bales wagged an inebriated finger at me and said, "*You…you…*I got something for *you.*"

"My money?"

"Better than that. Watch this."

He fleered at us. Then blindly walked backward, arms at his sides, hypnotic eyes locked on ours, and slowly waded out into the oncoming Abbot Kinney traffic. His silver hair floated across the busy arterial street like a white-hot flame, horns blaring and tires skidding.

A woman screamed.

"My God," the Artist said.

Bales miraculously made it to the other side of the boulevard unscathed. He megaphoned his mouth with both hands and shouted over the din of traffic. "Hey, Clean! Can't you see? We're dodos! It's passed us by!" He spread his arms and smiled. "It's our time to fly!" Then he turned on his heels and scampered up the sidewalk, disappearing into the folds of the night. And I remember standing there, someone's car radio blaring Blue Oyster Cult's "Don't Fear the Reaper," wondering what the heck just happened. I could have understood if he'd tried to dodge the rush of cars, confident in his athletic ability, but he made no attempt at a move of any kind. His body ramrod straight, walking stiffly as if positioning himself before a firing squad. The only thing I could attribute that insane act to was the alcohol I smelled on his breath—otherwise it made no sense. But later on I came to know that it was one of many bread-crumbs Bales dropped along the trail as clues.

Clues that I kept missing.

Midnight Train
to Georgia

I DIDN'T TELL anybody I had a guy living on my couch. His name was Carter Daggett and he rode in from Kerrville, Texas, on a Triumph Bonneville motorcycle. All he had was a North Face sleeping bag and a dirty canvas Dopp kit. I found him on Craigslist, and he paid me $450 for the month of December. Which was a steal. Couches were going for six hundred on the Westside. He said a bad divorce rocked him pretty good, and he just wanted to come out to California and clear his head. Smoke some good weed. I understood that and agreed to take him on for the month.

He was a quiet young man, an all-American kid, with a jean jacket and a John Deere cap. The kind of *Friday Night Lights* guy you'd run into at the foot-ball game. He said he was twenty-three, and I didn't doubt that, with his lanky frame and thin face. He usually left before I got up in the morning (which was nothing out of the ordinary because I rose half-drunk at ten). Normally he would sit at the dinner table with his computer and headphones watching YouTube videos or movies on Netflix. I knew he didn't have much money. Occasionally he'd look back at me getting snockered in my brown leather armchair, with my long legs outstretched in front of me and my head knocked back from too much grog.

One rainy night I told him to "get the fuck over here and join me for a goddamned drink." I was tired of talking to myself. Which was true. I got a half bottle of jug wine in him and got him to open up. Pried where I could. Then he flopped down on the couch and asked me about my ex-wife.

"What was she like?"

"Hard and angular," I said. "Like her veneer. And so many quirks."

"Like what?"

"Like she could only shit in elongated toilets."

"Wait…what?"

"I kid you not. One trip up to San Francisco I stopped six times before we found one that she was comfortable with. I think it was in Solvang."

"No. Really?"

"Yeah, and not only did she need the right toilet, but she couldn't shit with someone else in a public bathroom, either. One time she and this other woman were locked in a bathroom stalemate for a half hour. It was like a game of chess in there. Both needed to go, but neither one dared. I finally stuck my head in and directed traffic. Told my wife to get out to let the other crazy do her business, then watched the door for my wife."

He shook his head.

"Wow. That's crazy."

"Yeah, it was. What about you? You said you were married?"

"Once. When I was twenty-one. Lasted about a year."

"What happened?"

He beamed. "You mean after the hot jungle sex or before?"

"After," I said.

"We didn't have much to talk about. She liked to shop and I didn't. So we got drunk and fought. And when she got really wasted she liked to beat on me."

I poured him a glass of wine.

"You hit her back?"

"Not me," he said. "I was raised never to hit a lady. Although I thought about it a few times. I guess I couldn't give her what she wanted."

"Sounds like she didn't know what she wanted."

He nodded.

"Yessir. Maybe so."

I walked into the kitchen and fetched a small glass pipe from the utensil drawer and packed a bowl. We got stoned and watched the news. The top story of the night was about the latest string of liquor store robberies in West L.A.

"You hear about this guy?" I said. "Wearing a Romney mask? He hit a liquor store on Washington last week. Three blocks from here."

"Yeah. I heard they said he might be tied to a murder in Hollywood."

I looked at him, slightly paranoid. "You'd tell me if you were the Westside robber?"

He laughed. "Dude, I'm not crazy. I just try to give you your space."

I appreciated the fact that he was a true Texan. Not some diluted accent from Austin.

"You running from anything?" I said.

"Just myself."

I held his gaze a long moment, then took a mammoth toke. "Join the club."

I passed him the pipe.

"You know, you're not half-bad for an old dude," he said.

"Thanks," I said. "These days I take compliments any way I can get them."

I was great at telling everyone else their destiny, but I didn't have a clue as to mine.

"You didn't murder anybody, did you?" I was half-serious. That's the space I was in.

"No."

"Good. Did you have a job back in Kerrville?"

"I did. Worked at Costco a while, drove forty miles to get there, but the manager was an asshole…so I quit. I'm thinking about going back to school. Study to be a land man." He paused. "I like open spaces."

"Uh-huh. You thought about looking for work here?"

"Maybe."

Outside, the rain softened, then pounded harder.

"You know what L.A. weather does to tourists?"

"What?"

"It lures them to stay one month longer than they should have. Two months you're taking a sabbatical from work. Six months you're relocating. And the next thing you know, your life has passed you by."

He laughed, then stopped when he saw I was serious.

"You rich?" I said.

"I wouldn't be here if I was."

"Do you know your way around a computer?"

"Facebook. A few games…that's about it."

"Hmm. What about Spanish? You speak Spanish?"

"A little Taco Bell."

His attempt at humor.

"Strike two," I said, leaning back in my chair and crossing my legs. "And would I be going out on a limb if I guessed you don't speak Mandarin?"

A dopey laugh. "No."

"Another whiff," I said. "What about showbiz? You thinking about that?"

"I'd be lying if I said I wasn't. Maybe acting."

"I'm not an agent," I said. "But I think we can both agree you're no leading man."

He nodded and looked down.

"Which leaves you with character actor roles that don't pay shit. So I'd forget that."

"I don't know," he said, taking off his John Deere cap and clawing at his hair. "I might be able to make something happen."

"Maybe. But the way I see it is, you fall somewhere between too good-looking and not good-looking enough. It's a tough spot to find yourself in. Hard for casting agents to place."

"I at least owe it to myself to give it a try."

"Yeah, but for how long?"

"I don't know. Long enough, I guess."

"You see, that's what happens here. You don't think. Your sunstroked mind falls somewhere between the cracks, singed and seared, until eventually, and unceremoniously, you burn out. And then you play Gladys Knight and the Pips' 'Midnight Train to Georgia' and you think about buying a one-way ticket home. But you never do. You just stay here and hope for the best. And, you know, hope is never a strategy. But instead you just hang around and take what the city gives you, which is mostly scraps, and you learn to live with that." I stared him straight in the eye. "Does that sound like something you want?"

I held his gaze until he looked floorward at his motorcycle boots. "No."

"Then listen to me, kid. Do yourself a favor and hightail it back to Texas. Don't look back."

I don't think he expected a lecture that night, but that's what he got.

"That's your future," I said. "Vacation here all you want. But your opportunities are there. In the Lone Star State."

He peered down in his glass and swirled the wine, as if mimicking someone he'd seen in the movies. Then he looked up at me, his eyes red and bursting like Roman candles. "You really believe that?"

I nodded in the soft evening light.

"I do," I said. "I really do."

More Cuervo

ON THE NIGHT before the most important meeting of his life, the Artist lost it.

Carter Daggett was sitting at the kitchen table watching Bill Maher online, and I was sorting through bills when the call came in a little after ten. I had a hunch it was the Artist, because he always called after ten. Free minutes with Verizon.

When I answered the phone, I could barely hear him.

"It's closing in around me," he said.

His words were thin and feathery, paranoid.

"What? What's closing in around you?"

"Everything…my life."

"Did something happen today?"

I could hear the line crackling, feel the static between us.

"I'm paralyzed," the Artist said. "I've been paralyzed for years."

I heard the phone drop.

"Hello," I said. "Hello? You there?"

After a moment he whispered, "I used to have
people ask for me. Actually pay me for my work."
He sighed deeply. "I'm so fucking stressed. I need
some tequila. Hold on a sec."

"I'm here. I'm not going anywhere."

I heard him fumbling around in the kitchen.
Opening and closing cabinets.

Then when he got back on the line he said, "People
don't care anymore. They used to care, but they don't
anymore."

"About what?"

"About people. You know, I'm making fifty percent
of what I was making ten years ago."

"We all are."

"That's not true," he said. "I see it every day. The
rich stand in line for designer cupcakes, and the
poor stand in line at the food bank. It's a tale of two
Americas. I don't know how people aren't shocked
by that."

"It's amazing," I said.

"It is amazing. It is *amazing*. We are going back-
wards as a nation."

The Artist needed to talk, drink through it. And I was happy to be there for him.

"This disparity," he said. "This horrible disparity. Used to be the boss made fifty thousand, and his workers made twenty-five thousand. Now the boss makes twenty-five million, and the workers still make twenty-five thousand. It's mind-blowing, man."

"It is."

"Of course it is! And we're part of the problem. Letting athletes like Pujols make two hundred and fifty million dollars to play baseball. You know how much Mickey Mantle earned back in the day?"

"How much?"

"One hundred grand a year. You see what I'm talking about?"

"Yeah," I said. "It's messed up."

"Hey, wait a minute, hold your horses," he said. "I need more Cuervo."

I didn't know how long the Artist needed to vent, so I settled in for the evening. I rolled a tight doobie and poured a bubble glass of California red.

"Can you hear that?" the Artist said, back on the line.

"What?"

"The sound of social unrest. Revolution. My dad was union, man. And these teabagger Republican scabs are destroying this country. This fiscal cliff shit. This budget shit. They're keeping good people from good jobs. It's criminal. And for what? *For what?* Their own goddamn agenda."

I remained silent.

"I mean, I firmly believe these assholes will continue to debase the property and labor of others. How long before they police our thoughts? Continue to read our emails? Bug our phones? Hello! Hello! You fucks! Can you hear me? I'm still here! Shit. It's tyranny, man. Total tyranny." He took a deep breath. "You know what a guy in the alley said to me the other day?"

"No."

"He said, does anybody have change for a twenty? And I thought, hell, it's been years since I've been asked that question. Nobody has change for shit. Not even a dollar. I'm tapped out, bro. Sorry. Tapped out. Fuckin' tapped out. *Tap. Tap. Tap. Tap. Tap.*"

The tequila was starting to work its magic.

"You want to know what this other bum said to me?"

"Yeah."

"He said, first you lose your job, then you lose your teeth…then you lose your dignity."

"That's heavy."

"Of course it's heavy. It's *fucking* heavy."

He paused.

"I don't know what I'm going to do. Art is dead, Richard. What am I doing? I've wasted my life."

"You're not wasting your life," I said. "In fact, you have a really important meeting tomorrow that can change your life. My advice would be to lay off the tequila and get some rest."

He took a long, exhausted breath, then cleared his throat.

"I was walking down Abbot Kinney the other day and looking at all the junk they got. Dog paintings. Boardwalk pictures. Paintings of dead celebrities. It's all kitschy crap. These people don't get it. It's about the process, man. The *creative* process."

Most of the serious artists had long ago left the Westside. Only hacks, dilettantes, trust-fund babies, and money launderers remained. Maybe a few sleeper cells.

"Do you remember how electric L.A. felt thirty years ago?" he said. "The great clubs like Po Na Na Souk and Madame Wong's? Remember that?"

"I do," I said. "But the more nostalgia trips we take, the more we lose sight of the future."

"Yeah. Maybe so."

I changed the subject, steering him away from that dark place.

"Bales surface?"

"Yeah," he said. "Hashtag took us out for sushi last night. Know what he did?"

"I can only imagine."

"He took his dick out and started chumming the bar. He yelled, 'Who will have my swiveling cock!'"

"That's rude. Did they call the cops?"

"They didn't get a chance to. He ran out the back door like a drunk frat boy." The Artist chuckled, giving me an encouraging sign.

"What about you?" I asked.

"Hashtag told the Korean owner we didn't know him. That it was just some guy we met. He bought it. Then we paid the bill and left."

"Collateral damage," I murmured.

"And when we got home," the Artist said, "I heard him crying through the walls, dude. Not just crying. But *wailing*."

"He was crashing hard," I said.

"Whatever it was, it was creepy."

"Listen to me," I said. "Do not. Do *not*, under *any* circumstances, let him in tomorrow while we're showing your work. I don't want him meeting Beth."

"I'll try," he said. "But he lives next door. By the way, I've got your three hundred dollars. He gave it to me to give to you. He said he was drunk and to tell you that he was sorry about how all that went down at JP's."

"I'll let him do the apologizing," I said. "And I'd back off the tequila, hombre. Get some sleep. You okay?"

"Yeah, I'm fine."

"You sure? Excited about tomorrow?"

"I guess."

"Say yes! Say *yes, I'm super excited!* I'm ready to change my life!"

He laughed. "Okay, Mr. Sunshine," he said. "I'm excited."

I started singing "I'm So Excited" by the Pointer Sisters, and it seemed to make him feel better. Well, I hoped it made him feel better, because when I finished singing, the phone was dead.

Crouching Asshole,
Hidden Dick

I'D READ A study in a prestigious publication—which one, I can't recall—about happiness and money. The correlation had been opined by many before, but this study definitively concluded that as long as basic needs were met, $50,000 to $75,000 was all the money one needed to make to keep them happy. Anything over and above that simply provided angst. And Santa Monica was living proof of that, because on Monday when I stepped out into the crosswalk on Wilshire, I almost got T-boned by some glazed-out rich girl driving a black Audi SUV. If I hadn't jumped out of the way, I would have surely been squirrel meat.

Seventy-five thousand dollars, I thought. Shit. That wouldn't pay her gas bill.

It was December 10, the day the Artist turned fifty, when I showed up on his doorstep around 5:30 in the evening. Freshly shaved and carrying a bottle of tequila, I sported a blue Ferragamo blazer over a white T-shirt with straight-legged chinos. Prada loafers—no socks.

The door swung open and the Artist greeted me in all black, his blond flattop neatly trimmed.

"Happy birthday, bud," I said, handing him the bottle of booze.

"Thanks," he said, smiling. "And look at you. Casket sharp. All dolled up and nowhere to go."

I was pleasantly surprised to find him at ease. Maybe it was the relentless rain that had finally stopped for the first time in a week. I walked into his apartment and was blown away by what he'd done. He'd cleaned out all of his work except for the four pieces that hung neatly on his museum-white walls. Everything else was spotless.

"It looks like an art gallery in here," I said.

"If I'm going to do this," he said, "I'm going to do it right."

"I'll tell you what. I've got a hard-on. And it's been a while."

He smiled. "What, the iPad porn not working?"

I walked up and studied a painting, an abstracted Ferris wheel with primary colors bleeding off the edge.

"No. The Jackintosh works fine," I said. "It's me. Nothing gets me hard anymore. MILFs and cougars. College teens. Granny's pie. Nothing."

Just like everything else in my life, my dick was numb. Masturbation, once a pleasure, was now a chore. Something only to cleanse the prostate, oil the mechanism.

"Maybe a tequila shot will help. Or Beth."

"No, she's married," I said. "But it will be good to see her. But, yes, tequila should be explored."

The Artist poured a couple of shots.

"What time is it?" he asked.

I looked at my phone. "Five forty-five. She'll be here in fifteen minutes."

The Artist had Dr. Wayne Dyer on the TV. Said he calmed his nerves. We took a seat on the brown leather couch and clinked shot glasses. Then we tossed back the tequila, the burn stinging my throat.

"You ready to do this?" I asked.

"Yeah," he said, a serene voice in a quiet room. "I'm a divine being."

There was a shuffling noise outside. The wind began to howl. And then a horrible thought crossed my mind. I had a premonition that Bales was lurking, that he was listening in on our conversation—ear to the wall. I'll never forget that night. Because what happened next sounded like a sonic boom. Instantly, the front door exploded off its hinges and slammed hard against the foyer wall. I saw the Artist rock back on the couch like he'd just been shot; then I glimpsed the gun.

"Freeze, motherfuckers!"

The gun-waving intruder quickly moved across the room in a bright red ski mask, his dark shadow tracking on the wall.

I instinctively rose from the couch, hands up. Then the intruder trained the gun on my glistening forehead.

"Sit the fuck down, bald fuck."

I recognized the voice.

"It's cool, Bales," I said, slowly sitting down, hands still up.

"John, please," said the Artist. "Put the gun down."

He swung the piece.

"Shut up, bitch."

Beth was a stickler for order. And for some reason that was all I could think about. *Are the paintings straight?*

I glanced across the couch in the dim light. The Artist was bleeding from his left temple, hit in the face by a wood dagger from the burst front door.

Bales said, "You losers want to know who I am? Huh? What if I told you I was a mule for the Tijuana drug cartel? And that I'd just stolen six hundred thousand dollars. You think they'll come looking for me?"

"The Artist is hurt," I said.

"It's a fucking flesh wound. A scratch. What about me? Don't you think I hurt? You and your fucking high horse." Bales wagged the gun at me. "I ought to drop you right here. Isn't that what you told me the other night?"

He was high on something. And I remembered what my father had taught me. Never rattle a drunk or a junkie. Never lash out. They were sensitive, unpredictable, and extremely volatile.

"John, I'm hurt."

"Shut up, A. I'm tired of this starving artist bull-shit. Oh, woe is me, I don't have any money. My life is so *fucking* bad. Boo-the-fuck-hoo."

He turned his gaze on me.

"You know the score, Clean. We all do. He says he doesn't have any money to date. To go out, to lead a normal life. But you know what? I can see out my window. I got two fucking eyes. I know what's going on. Last week two hot Swedish chicks show up to watch him paint in the alley, and the deprived Artist here ends up fucking one on the couch. Poor me. And then he says he's been living on rice and beans for the last two years. Living like a dog. But what do I see? I see the granny neighbor June, a decent-looking GILF, bringing him a whole plate of lasagna. Not one time. Not two times. But *four* fucking times last week. Sound familiar, A?"

"John, please."

"When was the last time Clean got laid? Look at him. He's old, bald, looks like a fuckin' insurance salesman."

He turned back to me, the muzzle in my face. "Is that about the score, Clean?"

I nodded.

The sad thing was, he was right.

"And look at me," Bales said. "Look at fucking me."

He ripped off the ski mask, pointing at his ripened face. "Fifty-one years old. Broke with no prospects. My only asset a full head of gray hair. You think chicks are coming on to me? Wandering around the alley looking for some old dude to fuck? Shit. The only thing they want from me is to move my fucking car." He drew a difficult breath through his nose, his Gallic nostrils flaring. "Put me out on a street corner," he said, "*any* fucking street corner, and ask any stranger how old I look. And I guarantee you...*I guarantee you*, every one of them will say I'm at least sixty-five. So don't tell me about your so-called horrible life. I don't want to hear it."

He walked up to the Artist and leveled the gun right between his eyes. "And goddammit, A. Not once, not fuckin' once, has anyone ever brought me a *FUCKING PLATE OF LASAGNA!*"

At that moment, a woman's voice called through the open front door.

"Hell-oooo."

Bales jerked his head, giving me an opening. I Superman-rushed him. Flew across the room and grabbed both his wrists and body, slamming him up against the kitchen wall. I torqued his gun hand but received little resistance. The piece dropped helplessly from his grasp and skittered across the wide hardwood planks. And I remember thinking, *That was too easy*—as if he'd released it on its own. It was then I realized he wasn't fighting back, his poisoned body Play-Doh for my sandbox.

"Get the gun!" I shouted at the Artist. "Pick up the fucking gun and call the cops!"

The Artist leapt off the couch and scrambled for the piece.

I quickly took Bales from behind and thrust my arms under his armpits and extended my hands upward and held the back of his neck with a palm-to-palm grip, my fingers interlaced. The hold is called a full nelson. It's illegal in amateur wrestling. But the judges never said anything about a living room brawl.

Once I had Bales locked up, I called out the door, "Be there in a second, Beth!"

Bales grunted, coughed, then said, "Is this how the world ends, Clean? The arrival of a bald man in a sport coat?"

I cranked down on his neck, pushing him toward the floor. "Shut the fuck up, or I'll break it."

Bales coughed again.

"You're the Fourth Horseman, Clean. The Pale Rider, the horse of death. Do it…*break my neck*."

I was thinking about it. Beth outside waiting for a meeting, me inside contemplating killing a man. Now that was art. Performance art.

But then the Artist's voice stopped me cold.

"It's plastic," he said.

I snapped my head and saw the Artist holding the piece up like a feather, his thumb and forefinger pinching the tip of the barrel.

"What?"

"The gun," the Artist said, trembling. "It's plastic. Not the 3-D kind. It's a toy. A *fucking* toy."

My eyes went wide and I released Bales. He slumped down against the wall, laughing like a lunatic, stomping his legs and feet on the hardwood floor. "Oh, you should've seen your faces," he said. "I got all you bitches. It was priceless. Fucking priceless!"

"Goddammit, Bales," I said.

Now I wanted to kill him. And I had the skills to do it.

I thought hard about it for a second, glancing at the TV, Dr. Wayne Dyer droning on about "the divine mind at work. Can't you just feel the love?"

Sure, Dr. Wayne. Right after I snap this guy's neck.

But I didn't. I yanked Bales up and dragged his drunk body into the bedroom and threw him on the bed.

"I will not let you screw this up for the Artist," I said. "Someone's here to see his work. Just shut the fuck up, and please, please be quiet. And if you've ever cared about him, just give him these thirty minutes."

Bales sat up on the edge of the bed.

"Do you like the Eurythmics? I do. My favorite song is 'Sweet Dreams.'" He smiled and closed his eyes and started softly humming the hypnotic tune.

"Shut up," I said.

"Okay, Clean. But just so you know, some of us enjoy being abused. It's in our nature." He laughed and dropped his head on the pillow. "It don't mean shit anyway. History will erase us. Erase us all."

"I said *shut up*." I jerked my head toward the door and called out to Beth again. "Be there in a sec!"

I pointed at Bales. "You stay here. And I swear to God, if you move a muscle or make a sound, you will get your death wish."

Bales made a zip-your-lips gesture with his hand across his mouth. I turned out the lights and closed the bedroom door and raced out into the living room.

I took a look at the Artist, checked his left temple wound. Luckily, it was just a scratch. He'd live to paint another day.

"Get in the bathroom," I said. "Wash your face. I'll greet Beth. Take as much time as you need."

He didn't say anything, his pale blue eyes wide and frozen, quietly terrified. I grabbed his shoulders and squared them up to mine, locking our eyes.

"You good?"

He nodded his head yes. But like an obedient child, he meant no. He was in shock.

"Focus, Jimmy," I said. "You got this."

I shook him again.

"I'm okay," he said, his head lolling on his shoulders. "I'm okay...I'm good."

"You sure?"

He nodded. "Yeah."

"Good."

I patted him on the back and steered him toward the bathroom.

All right. Clear your head.

I blew a deep breath, then another, then wiped the sweat off my forehead with the sleeve of my blazer. That was one good thing about being bald. No bad hair days. Just towel yourself off and move on. So I did.

I had art to sell.

I removed the unhinged door from the entranceway and set it down on the big oak kitchen table. Then I met Beth standing on the stoop outside, her arms folded in the cool evening air.

"Hey," she said, smiling.

"Hey," I said, hugging her. "You look great."

"You, too." She pointed at my bald head. "I see you've gone postapocalyptic. I like it."

"You know me," I said. "I've always been a fan of *Blade Runner*. The end-of-the-world fade. C'mon in."

I kicked away the loose wood chips and crossed the threshold. "Watch your step," I said. "We had a little break-in an hour ago."

She gasped. "Oh my God."

"We're all right," I said. "Nobody got hurt."

"Oh my God. Are you sure?"

"Yeah. It was just some drunk punk. Too much eggnog. They got him."

I ushered her over to the leather couch. "Would you like something to drink?"

"No, thank you," she said, sitting and crossing her legs formally. "I'm meeting my husband for dinner."

In another time, I could've been that husband. But this wasn't that time. It was a shame, too, because she'd kept her body in rocking shape. Tall and slender with shoulder-length black hair, she looked cute and casual in riding boots and jeans. (She'd toned the wardrobe down just as I'd instructed, so as not to spook the Artist. He froze at anything too corporate.) Her trademark beauty was her chocolate-brown eyes and thick animated eyebrows that jumped and wiggled when she got excited. Like caterpillars on smack. Stalked you when you flirted, beckoned when you didn't.

I was thinking about other times when the Artist suddenly emerged from the bathroom looking peaked. Like he'd just bled out.

"This is the artist, Jimmy Miller," I said.

Beth rose and shook his limp hand. "It's so good to meet you. I've heard a lot about your work."

He lackadaisically threw up his arms, his face a dull canvas. "Well…here it is."

The Artist was Gumby. He was in no condition to speak, so I took the lead. "Abrupt, but well said."

I walked over and pushed up the dimmers on the wall switch, softly illuminating the paintings.

Beth turned and said, "Are these the pieces?"

"Yes," I said. "They're part of the Colors of the Pier series. The Santa Monica Pier."

Beth strolled over, standing in the muted light, her trained eye inspecting the pieces. "Aggressive brushwork. Reminds me of de Kooning. These are the latest?"

"Yes. All of the Ferris wheel at night. The Pacific Wheel."

"Brilliant streaks of color," she said. "The red and yellow spokes. I mean, wow. You can almost see it spinning. Like the movement of a second hand." She looked at me. "Oil or acrylic?"

"Both," I said. "With some alley patina. He paints outside with the canvas on the ground. Lets some of the natural elements cure the piece. The sun, the wind, a little rain, and whatever may blow by. Then he adds a mix of resin to pop the colors. It gives it that rich, textured look."

She slid on a pair of tortoiseshell glasses and leaned in. "Stunning," she said. "And there's something, and I don't want to say violent about it, but an 'apocalyptic end of the world carnival ride' vibe I'm feeling."

"It is Santa Monica," I said.

She laughed, and I remembered I had a disturbed man in the bedroom. I glanced over my shoulder and thought I saw a pair of black eyes peeking through the crack in the door. Mouse eyes, beady eyes, concentrated eyes.

Crouching asshole, hidden dick.

Beth said, "I had another artist last week with a similar style. That space somewhere between abstract figurative and Neo-Expressionism. Works of this size went out at forty thousand dollars at Bonhams and

Butterfields." She turned abruptly. "I want this for the show. All that you have. That is, if you're interested."

"He's interested," I said.

"Yeah," was all the Artist could manage.

"Fantastic," she said. "As I told Richard, the show is from seven to ten on December twenty-first. It's at Bergamot Station. We'll work out the details next week."

"Okay," the Artist said, his voice cracking.

"Great, I'm excited," she said. "Your work is incredible. And so honest. I'm sure you'll sell well."

I walked her out and she said, "He's fantastic, and he's lucky to have you as a friend."

"Thanks," I said.

We hugged goodbye on the porch, and our eyes met longer than they should have. "Well," Beth said, pushing back with a wistful smile. "It really was good to see you. I'm glad you called."

"I'm glad, too."

I watched her walk away into the dark, her musky scent lingering on my sport coat.

IT HAD BEEN a roller-coaster birthday for the Artist, but later that night we ditched Bales and I took

Jimmy to a little Thai place I knew off Washington in Culver City. In honor of his fiftieth I ordered Thai BBQ—all he could eat. We feasted on pork spare-ribs, fiery chicken falling off the bone, and crispy duck topped with honey and green chili sauce. And when our mouths got full and hot, we washed it all down with cold, sweaty bottles of Singha beer and Thai iced tea.

And I remember sitting at the table that night, my belly full of spicy goodness, and thinking I had somehow managed to pull it all together. But the question was, how long could I keep it together?

The Last of the

Mohicans

WHEN CIRCUMSTANCES TURN beyond your control, all any decent citizen can do is remain calm in assessing the situation. This is Los Angeles, and there are plenty of unstable people here. I was reserving judgment on what had transpired the evening of the Artist's birthday, but that didn't make it any less unsettling. I'd almost killed a man. I thought about the time my father's car broke down in South Central. Dad said that while waiting for the tow truck, he hadn't felt that uneasy since Vietnam. He could feel danger in the air. Zombies on the ground. Some people are like that. Their mere presence chills your bones. That's how I felt about Bales. I didn't want to see him again, but L.A. had other ideas.

My couchmate, Carter Daggett, rode up the coast to Santa Barbara, leaving me alone in the apartment for a few days. It would give me a chance to decompress and focus on my mind and body. When I woke that morning I ate cold pad kee mao and fortune cookies for breakfast, leftovers from last night's celebration. I broke open the cookie and pulled out the thin white paper, then grabbed my reading glasses. I placed them at the tip of my nose, picked up the tiny note, and read its message:

**YOU FIND BEAUTY IN ORDINARY THINGS.
DO NOT LOSE THIS ABILITY.**
Lucky numbers 09 18 27 54 72 63

I decided to put my good fortune to the test. With a screaming eagle hangover and a Louisville Slugger baseball bat, I walked across the street to pick up a copy of the *Los Angeles Times* from my favorite street corner dispenser. I say "favorite" with tongue in cheek, because this metal bastard had eaten plenty of my quarters in the past. It was a touchy machine. You had to drop the coins in just right. I slid the first quarter in and let it drop softly, playing it real smooth like a carnival game. Then I heard a click. Aha! The sound of success. I repeated this process three more times; then came the moment of truth. I reached for the door handle and gently tugged. No dice. It didn't open. I gave it a little shake just to be sure. And again, I was denied.

I was in no mood to play its game, hence the baseball bat. But because I'm a guy who believes in second chances, I decided to give it another try. I shook out my quarters from the machine and slid them into the slot. Each coin dropped with precision and tender loving care. But again the same result.

You motherfucker.

For a moment I just stood there in my sweatpants and T-shirt, the bat resting on my shoulder, a biblical fog swirling all around me.

I decided there would not be a third attempt.

And then I went ballistic.

"You treasonous heap of scrap metal!" I yelled. "You junkyard fuck! You're a dinosaur."

I swung the bat. Hitting that steel beast of burden right in its smug plastic face.

Bang!

"Ever hear of *The Last of the Mohicans*, you fuck!"

I swung again.

Bang!

"If I'm going down, then you're going down with me. Two old fucks in a museum."

Bang Bang!

"How does it feel?"

Bang!

"And when I call the *Times*—"

Bang!

"—and that nice lady answers and says we'll look into it—"

Bang Bang!

"—then you just smirk and eat more quarters. You lecherous piece of tin! You malleable fuck! You dung heap of hardware!"

Bang Bang Bang!

I beat that thing to a sorry pulp. Dented it beyond all recognition until it teetered on the brink of extinction. Its base loosened from its bolts, its smug plastic face in pieces scattered on the sidewalk. Quarters in the street, shimmering like grunion in the early morning light.

I stood there sweating and breathing heavy, the bat at my side. Ted Williams would have been proud.

After I collected myself, I scanned the neighborhood. And sure enough, there he was. An old man in a white golf cap and a mustard-yellow argyle sweater, frozen on the sidewalk, staring at me with mouth agape.

Some crazy motherfucker had interrupted his morning walk.

I didn't know what to say. So I reached inside the smashed window and plucked out the *Los Angeles Times*. I extended my right arm and held out the Tuesday edition in the upturned palm of my hand, as if on a silver platter.

"Free paper?" I said.

Old man bait.

Did he take it?

Of course he took it. He couldn't resist it. He snatched it, staring at the front page, squinting and grunting. He soon forgot all about me. All about the mangled news rack. He had the sports page now. Fuck everybody. A morning shit in sight.

He gave me a quick wink and smile and a vintage wave and continued on his walk, his white orthopedic trainers infused with an extra bounce in their step.

And as I walked back to my apartment, I thought, there's never been an old man in the history of humankind that refused a free paper.

Ever.

Not that I know of.

LATER THAT NIGHT I decided to squelch my growing anger. See if I could kill it. So I decided to get really blasted on jug wine and German beer. After dinner and washing the dishes, I got down to business. Started chugging, not sipping. I wanted to go high school big. Freshman year of college big. Get so blind drunk that I couldn't see straight big. Break the neighbor's window with a golf club big. Spin in bed. Burn the chicken. Throw something. Punch something. Kick something. Yell something…WHAT ARE YOU LOOKING AT, FUCKFACE!

At 11:15 I was well on my way. I staggered blindly, stiffly, over to the kitchen counter in my sweatpants and drunkenly tackled the wine jug.

Mumbling incoherently, I aimed for my glass.

Not too much. Not too much.

Shut the fuck up.

Half glass. Half glass.

What are you, a fucking pussy?

Half glass. Half glass.

It's a fuckin' thimble. I'll pour you a half glass.

No. No. Too much. Too much.

Just give me a full American pour!

The house phone rang and I fumbled for the cordless. "Fuck," I said, knocking it off its base. "Hold on."

I dropped to my knees and fished around the floor, and when I finally found the phone said, "Yello."

"Hey," the Artist said, "are you watching the news?"

I had wakeboarding on the TV.

"Yeah."

"I mean, this Westside robber is brazen, man. He knocked over Davy Jones Liquor Locker last night."

"On Navy Street?"

"Yeah, man. The guy in the Romney mask strikes again."

"You can't blame him. That Mormon fire still burns angry."

He laughed.

"Did Bales fix your door?" I said.

"Yeah, Home Depot came out this afternoon. It's sturdy, man. Top of the line. I mean this door could stop a Sherman."

I stood up, wobbled, collapsed on the couch.

He said, "You there?"

"Yeah," I said, rubbing my eyes. "Guess what?"

"What?"

"I beat up a dispenser this morning."

"A news rack?"

"Yeah. Those alien bastards."

"What happened?"

"The fucking thing ate my quarters."

"How many did you put in?"

"Four, like I always do."

"That's the problem," said the Artist. "The *Times* raised the daily to six quarters a few days ago."

"Motherfucker."

"It's expensive, man."

"I guess so. Silver Lake call you?"

"No. He's blowing me off."

"*Motherfuck.*"

The Artist paused. "You've been cussing a lot lately. That's not like you."

"I know. Maybe I've changed. Or the world changed me. But I do know this, we're getting the paintings or the money. One or the other. You call that idiot tomorrow. Tell him it's his choice. Paintings or the money."

"You know I'm—"

"He's got three of your paintings," I interrupted. "Has for nine months. Hasn't paid you a fucking dime."

"Yeah, but he said he's going to make good."

"Really? He used you. Duped you. Decorated his restaurant for free."

"He said he's trying to help sell them."

"Oh, bullshit, dude. Nine months? He's not trying to sell shit. Only bad food to hipsters."

"Well, but—"

"No fucking buts. Paintings or the money. *Say it.*"

"Excuse me?"

"*Say it!*"

"Paintings or the money?"

I blew a deep breath and waited a beat, this close to blowing a gasket.

"One more time," I said, trying to remain calm. "And give me gangster. Think Nucky Thompson."

He chuckled like a nervous crow.

"Okay," he said. "Here goes…paintings or the money."

"That's fucking weak!"

He paused. "Man, you're angry tonight."

"No, I'm drunk."

"You sure hold it well."

"Unfortunately, high tolerance runs in the family." I kicked off my loafers. "You sound better, though."

"I'm getting some major heat right now. I got this Peruvian girl's phone number at the Coffee Bean this morning."

"And like you always say—"

"Strange clears your mind."

"I can't argue. You're on a roll."

"I hope so," said the Artist. "But you know, I'm tired of living this up-and-down life. I want to be more like you. Even keel. Keep the highs and lows in check."

I tossed back my entire glass of red wine, then hiccupped.

"I'm flattered," I said, "but I'm kinda out of whack myself right now."

"No, really, I mean it. And I just wanted to say thank you, man. I really appreciate all you're doing for me. And I just wanted to let you know that. It's been a long time since somebody stepped up to the plate for me. Not just for my art. But for last night. I mean, Bales scared me, dude. I thought we were going to die. I froze when I saw the gun."

"Forget it," I said. "Artists aren't cut out for that shit. You never hear, *My God, can you believe it? Degas choked somebody out.*"

He laughed.

"You mean Warhol wasn't the town bully? Roaming the streets with a baseball bat and clubbing news racks?"

My first smile of the day. If I could register one, I was happy.

"Hey," he said. "Do you think my work's really gonna sell?"

"We'll find out in ten days. Unless the universe reams you, and we all get hit by an asteroid."

"That would suck."

"Dude, not gonna happen. I have no doubt you'll sell. It's just how much."

I stretched my arms and yawned.

"Look," he said. "I want to thank you again. And uh, well, I'm going to let you go. I know you're tired."

That was kind of him, but I'd already left. Passed out with him still on the line, my face buried deep in the sofa, wakeboarding on the TV.

Something Brewing

THE FOLLOWING DAY I recorded only one journal entry.

Los Angeles, December 12, 2012
  Still angry.

The End of the World
As We Know It

I SPENT MOST of Thursday stoned, watching eBay auctions on my iPad. Nothing exciting, like cars or houses or exotic antiques. Just small stuff, like plastic shipping bags and hand-crocheted doilies. And the real barn burner: one-hundred-percent cotton hand towels. *Okay, next up. A set of two luxurious cotton, kiwi-green hand towels. Used only once. Hey, I got one dollar—one dollar—one dollar—one dollar—oh heyyy—do I hear one twenty-five—one twenty-five—one twenty-five—SOLD! to the tall bald man in the back—one twenty-five!*

And when one auction ended, I would find another. And another, until I grabbed for the bag of weed and found it empty.

Motherfucker.

I called Homegrown immediately. No answer.

You feckless fuck! Pick up the phone! I need some dank!

Then I started crawling around on the floor on my hands and knees looking for stems, loose buds, or nuggets, anything that resembled marijuana. I thought I'd found something, struck gold, but upon closer inspection it revealed itself to be a chunk of a Clif Bar.

Motherfucker.

So I moved to wine. Sat in my easy chair listening to the rain fall, the room lighted only by the silvery ripple on the TV. Then the Artist called and asked if I was still mourning the death of Ravi Shankar. I said I was, and that I played "While My Guitar Gently Weeps" over and over until I passed out.

That was my Thursday.

If I'd known the Artist had only nine days left to live, I would have surely spent it with him.

ON FRIDAY THE skies cleared and I took a much-needed bike ride. Waiting for the light to change at the corner of Lincoln and Washington, I noticed a homeless man holding a hand-scrawled cardboard sign. It read:

PLEASE HELP
NEED FUEL FOR MY SPACESHIP

I gave him a buck and thanked him for his creativity, then asked if he had any extra seats.

I continued riding north on Lincoln Boulevard. Every crack in the dirty sidewalk, every bump or pothole in the road, every auto shop, body shop, nail salon, and bum dressed like Jesus greeted me like old friends.

Stopping at the red light at Lincoln and Venice, I glimpsed my favorite car wash. It had changed hands over the years, but it was still the same old car wash that used to clean my wheels. My cars in chronological order with nicknames: Toyota Celica (*Silver*. Not because of the color, the car was dark gray. But in reference to Hi-Yo, Silver!). Porsche Carrera (*Bob*). BMW 325 (*Mr. Black*. Obvious). Lexus LS 400 (*Eman*—name spelled backward for lack of creativity).

For more than two decades of Fridays, I would sit out under the thatched roof at the car wash (just like the people were doing now) waiting for my ride to be spit-shined and polished. And when it was finished, I would provide a generous tip and hop into my gleaming vehicle and drive west on Venice Boulevard, waving at all the bikinied hotties headed to the beach. Most of the time they waved back. But now I was on a blush-pink lady's bicycle with road grit in my teeth, the smell of hot metal and exhaust from the passing automobiles burning my nose. And I wasn't even on a good bike, like one of those fancy European road models they sell in boutiques on Abbot Kinney. I had a Huffy. A beat-up Huffy cruiser with a wobbly front tire and no hand grips.

Motherfucker.

I let a few lights change as I watched those shiny vehicles streaming out one by one, a team of attentive Latino men with sparkling white hand towels waiting for the detail.

And then I heard it.

I whipped my head from side to side, almost frothing at the mouth, searching for the origin of one of the most annoying tunes on earth. One more note and I was going to blast off, burn up in reentry.

Where is it? I thought. *Where is that fucking music coming from?*

And then I spotted the guy, stopped at the red light in his new metallic blue Camaro, radio blaring

R.E.M.'s "It's the End of the World as We Know It (And I Feel Fine)." God, I was tired of hearing that song. And I'm an R.E.M. fan. And I'd like to take this moment to sincerely apologize to the members of the band for my actions taken on that day. It wasn't your fault that the song became a marketing anthem. But somebody had to put a stop to it, and that somebody, of course, was me.

I jumped off my bicycle and threaded my way through the stationary traffic, found the guy, and stuck my head inside his open window like a crazy beach bum.

"Turn down that music!" I yelled. "Nobody feels fine, dickwad! You clichéd *fuck*."

And he did what most people would do in that situation—he freaked. He frantically rolled up his window, almost cutting my head off in the process, and violently gunned it. Tires squealed and rubber smoked. And I can assure you he didn't feel fine now. He would think twice before cranking that song again.

For a long minute I just stood there in the middle of the street, cars honking and people shaking their fists at me as they drove by. And all I could think about was what a beautiful car that Camaro was.

TWENTY-FIVE MINUTES LATER I pedaled up to the Artist's apartment. I found the gang huddled on the couch in sweaters and jackets watching TV. It was the first cold autumn evening of the year, and I remember it felt like a meat locker inside. And just as somber.

Bales was the first person I saw. He looked exhausted, or loaded, wearing a cream-colored shawl sweater and a Stanford beanie.

"What's up, Bales?" I asked.

"Ennui and upward," he said quietly.

I looked around the room and glanced at all the solemn faces. Hashtag (for the first time without his phone) clutched a throw pillow to his chest, his cloudy eyes glued to the TV.

"Did I miss something?" I said.

The Artist looked at me as if I was from another planet. He stuffed both hands inside his down vest and said, "Didn't you hear?"

"Hear what?"

"Some crazy guy just shot twenty kids in a school. In Connecticut."

"What?"

"It's a bad scene," Hashtag said. "One of the worst in history."

"Oh my God."

Bales held out a bottle of beer. I shook my head no. I was too numb to feel anything. It turned out I'd had my last drink of the year. My last hit of dope.

"It's those stupid video games," the Artist said. "They're killing people. I mean, people didn't go around killing kids in the Great Depression. What times are we living in?"

"The problem," Bales said, "is it's so easy with a gun."

"There's nothing easy about it," I said. "It's fuckin' crazy."

Bales stared at me like he'd been in the bush too long. "I just meant it was easy for some is all."

On the TV, a visibly shaken President Obama said, "How much more can our nation take?" Crushing unemployment. Tsunamis. Hurricanes. Earthquakes. Mass shootings. It was all too common now.

We all called our families to tell them that we loved them. Even that monster Bales.

Later, Hashtag bought Indian food for dinner, and we all sat in silence, the rain beating down on the roof, eating chicken tikka masala and garlic naan and licking our fingers and smacking our wet lips and pretending to be friends for one lonely, wretched night.

The only welcome sound, one tragically beautiful sound, was the neighbor's kid practicing "Amazing Grace" on a flute, off-key.

A Season in Hell

Los Angeles, December 16, 2012

11 a.m.

I am sitting in church singing "Onward Christian Soldiers" with the rest of the congregation. My neighbor Paula sits to my left. She looks over to check on me and smiles while she's singing. She knows I'm wound tight. A frail bird on a high wire. She has concluded, and rightly so, that after Friday's tragedy we need to start the healing process. Move forward—spiritually, mentally, physically.

I reluctantly agree to accompany her to a non-denominational church in Venice. I look down at my shaky hand, my alcohol-deprived hand. I have not had a drink in over forty hours. Paula sees this, checking on me as she would a small child, and takes my hand in hers. I am coming off a sixty-day binge, *a Rimbaudian odyssey. My own season in hell. I tell myself this is not about me. But it is! Oh, it is. Because who am I to think, arrogantly, that I can change the world for the better? Oh, I can try. But what if we pray for the victims and their families, try to make sense of it all, and find out that there is no hope? That like a broken record it just happens again and again. What if Rimbaud was right? That "everything we are taught is false."*

My mind races headlong into thoughts running over themselves to go somewhere they've never been before. To some rigged, crooked finish line that may or may not be there. So what's the point? Why care? Why fucking care? Because I want to! I have to! And I will get involved. Get back in the game. Whatever game that is. Because somewhere between the lies and reality is my destination. I know it. I'm a long-distance runner. Whether I find the answers in the scriptures, between the lines, on the top of a mountain, or in my own DNA, it does not matter.

But who is this modern man that I should become? How should he, I, shape the future? Our future? How can I break that final plane? That is something I'm going to have to work on.

Am I a fresh voice?

Maybe not.

Am I a true voice?

One hundred percent.

Never Get Out
of the Boat

I WOKE UP at ten the next day, my neighbor's one-year-old son shrieking like a wounded peacock. My body fried and wrung out. I was so sensitive that the sounds of silence would have unnerved me. I had woken at 2 a.m. shivering in a pool of my own putrid sweat, the tinny metallic taste of blood in my mouth. The inside of my cheek had been chewed like hamburger. I changed the sheets twice and had trouble going back to sleep, tossing and turning to dreams I mostly forgot. But I do remember one. I was a nuclear cockroach with a gas mask, crawling through the wreckage of some unknown catastrophic event. I was perched high on a rock, peering out over the ashen wasteland. And another cockroach asked me, "Where do we go, boss?"

And I said, "Anywhere but here."

Then it became clear to me, just as it had to Bales with his cartoon, that whatever new path I was going to take would require structure. I am a Capricorn, the logical son of pragmatic Saturn. Structure is in my bones, and I knew, instinctively, that the farther I got from the center, the harder it would be to find my way back. So I decided that from now on I would keep a regular schedule—nine to five. It didn't matter what I was doing, but I had to be doing *something*. Health would also play a major role in my comeback, and I was in the process of steeping some strawberry green tea when I got a call from the Artist.

"Hey, what's up?" I said.

"Not much, just wanted to check in."

"Did you call that guy?"

"Well," he drawled, "I'm not sure you wanna hear this."

"What? Bales screw up again?"

"No. I called him. That guy in Silver Lake."

"Yeah. What'd he say?"

"His name's Hector Gonzalez. I'm not sure, but I think he may be an ex-gang member. He's got a neck tattoo, and he's a pretty edgy dude."

"*What did he say?*"

He paused.

"He kinda told me to get lost."

Basic. Any sort of pressure and the Artist folded like origami.

"For Christ's sake, A," I said. "I'm tired of this peaceful warrior bullshit. Be ready at four. Get Bales and anybody else he's got. It's time to pay this clown a visit."

Certain acts call for reprisal. How could any man look himself in the mirror each morning knowing that he had a chance to make something right but instead hit the bottle, or chattered under the table— and once again let the unaltered world punch him in the face? We live in a society where people *flee* the scene when we should be striving to *steal* the scene.

Change something, motherfucker.

The Artist stuttered, "But but but but—"

"No more buts!" I said. "You've used them all up."

∙ ∙ ∙ ∙ ∙ ∙ ∙ ∙ ∙ ∙ ∙ ∙ ∙ ∙ ∙ ∙ ∙ ∙

AT 4:30 THAT afternoon we were rolling east on Sunset, five alpha dogs in the Artist's oxidized Jeep Cherokee. Well, four and a half if you count Hashtag. The fifth wheel was a ponytailed Russian named Ivan that Bales had brought along for backup (and who the Artist would later confirm was carrying a gun. A real gun. A Ruger .22 automatic). Bales said Homegrown asked to tag along, but Bales told him the job required muscle, and unfortunately that wasn't Homegrown's strong suit. Bales said he should stick to things he did best, like living a life of chemical servitude. Homegrown agreed.

We didn't talk much until we reached Sunset Junction. Then Bales looked out the window and said, "Silver Lake. Shoot me if I ever have to live here. It smells like skunk." He chugged a Coors tall boy and asked if anyone needed a beer.

We all passed.

The Russian stared straight ahead, the countenance of a smooth oval stone.

Hashtag played Scrabble on his mobile, oblivious to all but his next move.

The Artist chewed his nails, pensive and shaky at the wheel.

Me, quiet and intense, a blind rage barely harnessed. Locked and loaded, a bottle rocket in search of a light.

"Suit yourselves, ladies," Bales said.

He reached for the radio dial and cranked the Doors' "Break on Through."

I stared out the window, my jaw clenched tight as Jim Morrison's voice hacked my central nervous system into tiny pieces with a dull butter knife. The gritty urban jungle rolled by, frame by frame, raw and uncut, like some documentary film student's vision of dystopia: snarling pit bulls, tracksuit pushers, pud pullers, list tickers, box checkers, veiny-faced hipsters in tiny hats, navel gazers, crossdressers, hirsute dudes in girl jeans, student hookers, organic hopheads, vampires in hoodies, Two Buck Chuck disciples, motorcycle mamas, walking tattoos, cougars and crackers, bangers and beggars, skeletons walking to forget they're dead, bean bloggers, yogurt eaters, coyote cuddlers, Nashville sneaks, chicken whisperers, hot walkers, key janglers, and strung-out musicians with nowhere else to go because they were already *fucking* there.

Welcome to the hipster capital of America. Can I get you a cold PBR?

Fucking Silver Lake, I thought. Or is it Silverlake? One or two words? *Make up your fucking mind!*

And that hideous killer of a pit bull, grunting and panting its squatty body low to the ground to take a piss. An ugly, rotten beast that looks just like its bald, tattooed, broad-backed, fucking braindead owner who offers nothing more than the depletion of resources. And that flat, flat, blue perennial monotonous light that promises to be brighter every day, except that it isn't. And it makes you so downright angry that you want to clean the sky with a dish rag, wipe away that dull blue haze, begging, pleading for a lustrous, polished blue that never comes. And you hope that it comes, and you pray that it comes, but it never does. And that's when you say *fuck it*.

I am Martin Sheen in *Apocalypse Now*.

Clean on the machine gun.

Kurtz on the river.

Never get out of the boat. Never get out of the boat. *Never get out of the fucking boat!*

"Clean," Bales said. "Get out of your head. We're going in."

I snapped back into focus to see the Artist pulling into the alley behind a Mexican restaurant named Machos. When I asked where we were, Bales said somewhere off Glendale Boulevard, near the reservoir.

I took a deep breath and rolled up the car window. The air was cold outside and the sun was setting. Perfect weather for my burning, clear-eyed anger.

Bales wriggled into a brown cashmere sweater and scanned the full parking lot. "Dude, the place is packed," he said to the Artist. "I thought you told me dinner started at eight?"

The Artist said, "Maybe he changed hours. It doesn't feel right."

Bales glanced at the Russian. "What do you think, Ivan?"

"It is of no concern to me," Ivan said, sounding as thick as a Crimean warlord. "I get paid either way."

The Artist ran a nervous hand through his flattop. "I don't like the vibe, man. This is bad. We should bail."

"We're here," I said. "We're going in."

Bales smiled.

"Clean, going all Walter White. I like it." He continued. "Okay, gentlemen. Just like we talked about. The Artist goes in first. Then me, then Ivan, followed by Clean and Hashtag. We go in sweet—all smiles. Give him one last shot to make good. If he bucks, we go beastmode." He looked at the Russian. "And, Ivan, check for cameras."

Ivan nodded.

"All right, ladies. Let's clock in."

We hopped out of the Jeep and entered through the back of the kitchen like we were sneaking into a nightclub. *Swingers* style. Confident, not cocky.

The Artist led us past several dishwashers and one tried to speak, but Bales cut him off with a raised hand and said, "Easy, *señor*, we're not here to gentrify the neighborhood."

It didn't take long for Hector to spot us once we reached the door to the main dining hall. He stood in the frame vaping an e-cig, wearing a blue blazer and designer jeans, his head shaved, his face a pockmarked blob of brownish dough. I could see now why he got the neck tattoo. Cover up some of that shit. I guessed him around forty-five, his stocky body out of shape with a carbohydrate gut. He might have grown up tough on the streets of Boyle Heights once, but age, capitalism, and Tex-Mex dining had softened his edge.

Now all that remained was a pretentious Latin bohemian.

"Hey, Hector," the Artist said, slow and smooth. "We just wanted to stop by and see how you were doing."

Hector crossed his arms and said, "What is this, an ICE raid? I thought we got a chance to catch up this morning on the phone. I told you things are tight right now."

"Looks like a full house," I said. "Parking lot's jammed."

I stared at that fucking neck tattoo. A crude ink drawing of a sombrero with the colors of the Mexican flag.

Bales said, "I know it's the holidays, and Feliz Navidad is just around the corner, but what our artist friend is trying to say is that he's flat broke, and well, frankly, so are we. So we've come to offer you a little proposition."

Hector thought a moment, eyeing Bales. "Did anyone ever tell you, you look like that dude Roger from *Mad Men*?" He turned to one of the Mexican cooks. "Hey, José, don't he look like that *Mad Men* dude? That silver-haired vato?"

José nodded.

"*Mad Men*," said Bales. "Impressive, Hector. I didn't expect a man of such high culture. We should do lunch sometime—the Jonathan Club. You can bring your pit bull."

That was it for me. Enough of the small talk. I pushed Bales aside and got up in Hector's ruddy face, my hand raising a contract.

"Did you sign this?"

Bales leaned into me. "That's it, Clean. You're an alpha, not a beta."

Hector kept his composure, staring at me with the cold hard look of an assassin squinting down the barrel of an assault rifle.

"*Puto pelón?*" he asked coolly.

"Hashtag?" Bales said.

Hashtag translated. "Basically he asked who's the bald fuck?"

Everybody else had gone off. Now it was my turn.

"You got that right," I said. "Just some crazy old bald fuck that doesn't give a shit. Some stupid cracker that voted for Gary Johnson. So I'll ask you again, short time. Did you…or did you not…sign this?"

Hector hit the vaporizer, blowing smoke through his nose. "You ain't nothing but yesterday's man, bro."

"Yesterday's got nothing to do with it." My forefinger stabbed at his signature, practically poking a hole through the paper.

Hector glanced at the contract. "Yeah. It looks like I did. What do you know?"

I looked down at his hipster combat boots toe to toe with my black Vans slip-ons. Then I jerked my head up, pointing at the document.

"You see this clause, homie?"

He shrugged. "My eyes ain't so good right now."

"Let me read it to you, Hector. If a client is no longer able to pay the balance outstanding in full within six months, then the Artist has the right to remove the paintings from the premises at any time—anywhere."

"So," Hector said. "What's your proposition?"

I was at least six inches taller than he was, so I moved in closer, looking down on his roadkill face. "Two choices, amigo. Paintings or the money."

Hector chuckled with the confidence of a man secure in his own demographic skin, winked at his kitchen crew, then looked back at me.

"You think you're gonna come in here and dog me in my own house, ese?"

My cold eyes never left his. "*Paintings...or the money.*"

He raised his chin, his hard face to mine like two boxers at a weigh-in.

"Buff my shit, strawberry."

I grinned.

"Another time, slut chops. I'm here for the art."

I looked off a moment, my heart pounding wildly, then brazenly pushed my way out through the kitchen door and into the main dining room. I would have popped his ass right there, but I didn't intend on going to jail that night. Hector had to take the bait.

I heard Bales shout as I strode through the dining hall, "A, get the car!"

And then, "Let him go!"

Bales didn't care which dog ate which dog. All he cared about was that *a* dog would get eaten.

The three small paintings hung near the salsa bar. A series of brightly colored Mexican Day of the Dead sugar skulls. The restaurant was packed, and I had to turn sideways to slip through the long row of boisterous tables before finally arriving at the back wall.

My presence, up to this point, went largely unnoticed. That's because my light blue uniform and "Mike" name tag made me look like the local HVAC guy. Someone there to fix the heater. Last year's Halloween costume.

I reached for the first painting, a gorgeous Renaissance-blue Mexican skull floating in a black background, with yellow marigold flowers for eyes and lips sewn shut. I remembered the Artist varnishing this particular piece, informing me that the ancient Aztecs worshiped the skull not only as a symbol of death, but a promise of resurrection.

I unhooked the artwork, setting it down quickly but gently against the side of the bar.

That's when I heard Hashtag shout, "Clean!"

I turned abruptly and saw Hector stalking me. I backed up, hands up, as if to say, "Hey, bro, what the heck's going on here?"

I'd spotted the camera in the corner of the ceiling, my self-defense case locked.

I shuffled one step toward the second painting, hands still up, my eyes stuck on Hector, giving him one last chance to back off. But that neck tattoo and his unpolished Eastside bravado would be his undoing. He rushed me and took a wild ghetto swing at my head, and I blocked it with my forearm and spun him around. When he looked back over his shoulder, I chopped down on his bloated face with a fist the size of a cantaloupe. He staggered back, crashed into a table, then charged again. I waited, waited until he got close, waited until he was right up on me. Then I unloaded a straight right bomb to the nose—like Fat Man on Nagasaki. This time I felt the center of his face give way as if I'd just punched a hole through a cheap Styrofoam cooler.

There was a sharp *cr-aack!*

Hector hit the floor with a thud. A woman's scream pierced the air.

My hand was hot, wet, and sticky, sweat leaping from my pores. I could see nothing but blind anger, my entire field of vision a snowy white. And at this moment, I remember hearing the sounds inside the restaurant for the very first time. The hysterical shrieks and squeals and howls, all riding up my spine like a white-hot poker. The horrified clatter of dishes. Chairs yanked out, and the choppy, frightened footsteps of the fleeing masses.

And with all that, the Mexican slowly rose to his feet. His creamy brown core shaken but not stirred. And, yes, I could see the fire burning in his eyes—his baggy brown eyes peeking out from behind a Kabuki mask of blood. Refusing to be extinguished by some bald cracker on his home turf.

His eyes were talking to me, still talking shit.

You motherfucker. Dogging me in my own house!

Groggy and badly disoriented, he charged like a black rhino with his head down low and tried to tackle me, lunging for my knees. He wanted to grapple. Ha! He wanted to fucking grapple!

Guys like him are how I eat.

And at this point I almost laughed. Some demonic, sadistic laugh that seemed wildly inappropriate, yet so perfect for our time. But out of respect for the craft, I swallowed it.

You see, I hadn't totally gone to seed. Every couple of Sundays I practiced Brazilian jujitsu with some of my wrestling friends up at Mt. San Antonio College.

The submission technique called the Standing Rear Naked Choke is my specialty. A nasty chokehold that the Artist narrowly escaped, and one that would soon introduce Hector to his black swan moment.

Hector attempted a takedown and tried to sweep me off my feet. He drove me hard against the back wall, his shaven head burrowed deep in my chest. He threw a wild open right hand that boxed my ear. Then a left that stung my elbow.

I had him right where I wanted him. The same place I had Bart Order when I won state my junior year.

In one quick motion, I grabbed his shoulders and jerked him around so that his back was to me. Then I took my right arm and locked it around his neck, my forearm underneath his chin. I sunk the choke in deep by applying pressure by flexing my right arm. Then I walked him backward with my knee on his lower back, and sunk the chokehold even deeper. Squeezing like an anaconda. To his credit, he kept trying to stomp my feet with his combat boots and trying to elbow me in the groin, but it was too late. In ten seconds the blood supply would be cut off from his brain.

I squeezed with all my might. Squeezed until I was blue and he was purple.

Seconds later, I felt his body begin to convulse. His legs spasm. And then I listened for it. I wrenched his neck one last time, and then I heard it.

Heard him snoring.

And I knew he was gone.

I released him and let his limp, rag-doll body collapse to the ground, eyes rolled back, arms and legs grotesquely tangled beneath a twitching torso. Then I threw my head back in barbaric triumph and yelled, "STOP FUCKING THE ARTISTS!"

And for a second I stood over the quivering mess, chugging air in and out of my mouth, right fist cocked, the HVAC man daring him to get up. But there was no chance of that. Hector was out cold. Gone to sleep.

I collected myself, wiped my brow off with a forearm, and tucked in my shirt.

"Bales! Hashtag!" I called. "Get in here and get these paintings!"

I believe the last words I uttered that night while stepping over Hector's moaning body were, "Sorry we crashed your fiesta, *señor*. I'll try and make a reservation next time."

Paradigm Change

IT'D BEEN TWENTY-FOUR hours since I choked out Hector. I had no choice. He gave up his back. I'm not a violent man. If you can see past that, you can see past me. I'd only had three fights in my life, including Hector. Twice defending myself, the other defending the Artist. There were so many things that I wanted to say that night, but in retrospect it was nothing important.

Oh, there was one thing. I wanted to shout out at the top of my lungs to all those clueless hipsters that PBR beer is Pabst Blue Ribbon. PABST BLUE RIBBON! Hello! Are you friggin' kidding me? If the corporations have sold you on believing that that goat piss is actually drinkable, then I'd love to sell you a little doomsday bunker in Iowa in which to ride out the end of the world.

Take it from me. Try PBS, not PBR.

And speaking of beer, it'd been several days since I'd had a drop of alcohol. My body had finally adjusted, and I was no longer moody or hot to the temper. I was still twitchy, but, you'll be glad to know, not choke-out twitchy.

I kept the promise to myself to take better care of my body. Panda Express orange chicken (double order), as delicious as it is, was unfortunately off the menu. I instead found myself with the other health food nuts and geriatric hippies, going to Rainbow Acres market on Washington every morning and getting my favorite detox drink.

My body was getting stronger every day. If I could have, I'd have grown some dreadlocks.

On Tuesday, December 18, 2012, I'd just finished a sand run on the beach and was strolling down the Venice boardwalk when the Artist phoned around five.

"Hey," he said. "What's up, vegan boy?"

I smiled, weaving my way through pot merchants, skate punks, and professional weirdos.

"Sun's out, guns out," I said. "I'm on the Venice boardwalk counting all the marijuana dispensaries. Talk about a contact high."

He provided a short, curt laugh, but I could sense something was up.

"Hey," he said, "I just wanted to see what you thought about this. Get the wise bald man's opinion."

"I'm all scalp."

"Well, this morning," the Artist said, "I get a call, and then a hang-up. And then a minute later, the same number calls back. And when I said hello... nothing."

"Sounds like a wrong number to me."

"That's what I thought. But then that same person calls back again, and when I answered this time, a Mexican man with a thick accent says, 'Hector's going to kill you.' And then he hung up. Well, I freaked out. I called the number back. It must have rung twenty times, but he never answered. What do you think about that?"

A lady mime dressed in a white tutu and a painted red face stared at me with a frozen smile. I did not reciprocate.

"Was it Hector?"

"Could've been," he said, "but I don't think so. It didn't sound like him. What do you think I should do? I mean, should I call the police?"

I sighed.

"Did you call the restaurant?"

"No."

"Shit," I said. "My first thought is, he's just messing with you. I mean, I'm quite positive that wasn't Hector's first ass-kicking. Normally a guy like that moves on. I don't think he would risk losing everything just for revenge."

The Artist laughed uneasily.

"Yeah, but you didn't grow up on the streets."

"True," I said. "Maybe I should call him. Give him some heat. Threaten him with the illegals he's got working in the kitchen."

I felt bad. Now I was getting people death threats. Not just any people, but my people.

"Look," I said, striding past several T-shirt stalls and tattoo parlors, "I'm sorry about the other night, dude. I was wrapped tight."

"Oh, I'm not mad at you. He deserved to meet Jack Reacher. And I'm glad we got my paintings back. You were right, he was just using me. Just like all the other assholes who tell me it'll be 'great exposure.'"

"Look, I'll go down to the restaurant and apologize—"

"No," he said. "I'll figure something out. It's probably time I start fighting my own battles. I've got some old stuff I can give him."

"Why give him anything? He's the one that jacked you."

"Well," he said, "I'll...think about it. Hey, I've got an impromptu party at my place tonight. I want you to come by. You remember Claudia?"

"The Guatemalan chick?"

"Yeah, the one who rented the apartment near that overgrown lot because she said the view reminded her of home."

"You gotta love her for that."

"Well, she knows a shaman. Don't ask me how. But he's blessing her new place. Then he's coming over to my pad to bless the paintings for the show. For good luck. She's bringing food. And I might even convince her to get you some kale chips."

I laughed, stopping at the intersection of Eighteenth Place and Speedway. I stared up at the famous Jim Morrison mural. The legendary lead singer of the Doors—young and shirtless, full of swagger.

"I like Cool Ranch," I said. "I'll see you around seven. And look, don't worry about Hector. He's just blowing smoke."

"I hope so. See ya."

I got a text from Bales just as I hung up. It read:

times change
paradigms change
minds change
what are u going to do about it?
GET FUCKED UP!

Like always, I ignored his babble. Staring up at the Jim Morrison mural, I was reminded of something that I'd read on a prediction site. It said: *There will be desperate people who will look for shortcuts in order to survive. They will steal from others. Some people will take themselves out of the reality of hardship, pain, and stress, and will choose to lead a simpler life.*

If I could locate the author now, I would apologize to his face for secretly calling him a crackpot. Because that is exactly what happened.

And is still happening.

I Thought She Was
Into It

THE MAYAN SHAMAN arrived at eight, dressed in white linen and Mexican sandals. We stood in a semicircle in the frigid living room (the Artist had no central heat) facing the paintings in the glow of flickering candles. The white-haired shaman asked for all the names present, and one by one we sounded off: Me. The Artist. Bales. Hashtag. Homegrown. And finally Claudia, the short, stout, raven-haired Guatemalan neighbor who served as translator. She was dressed in a traditional square-cut Mayan blouse, with bold colors and embroidered flowers.

The shaman grunted.

"He wants us to close our eyes," Claudia said. "First he wants to cleanse the room, then he wants to cleanse us."

Claudia shook a pair of maracas, and the shaman began chanting.

"Ummm bye-ya. Ummm bye-ya Ummm bye-ya Ummm bye-ya..."

Deep, guttural sounds. Throaty and hypnotic.

After a few minutes Claudia said, "You may now open your eyes. The room and its people have been cleansed. We are now ready for the blessing of this beautiful work."

I opened my eyes, and just as I did, a cold wind billowed the stark white curtains.

We watched as Claudia sat down on the couch and placed a pair of bongos between her brown knees. She shook her arms out like a maestro, then started pounding the skins rhythmically, maniacally, infusing the room with a primal, sexual heat. The Mayan elder raised his arms and asked the sky gods for safe passage and good luck. Then he picked up a branch of olive leaves and shook it at the first painting. The hypnotic beat of the bongos grew louder, more intense, as the shaman whirled theatrically around the room. He danced and chanted, individually blessing each piece of art with an emphatic wave of the hand and a shake of the olive branch.

Moments later, Claudia halted the bongos.

And for what seemed like an eternity we stood in silence by candlelight, listening to the howling wind outside—a tree dipping its boughs against the windowpane. Claudia handed the shaman a spiral conch shell. He placed the sawed-off spire to his lips and held it out like a trumpet. And like so many had done before him, he blew a deep oceanic roar from its belly. One last call to the divine, one more battle won, one more evil spirit cast away.

And that was it.

Claudia said to the Artist, "You will have good luck with your work. You are truly blessed."

"Thank you," said the Artist, stepping out from the candlelit shadows. "I feel blessed. For the first time in a long time."

She smiled. "You're lucky. Most people never feel that way."

The shaman uttered something to Claudia, and she pointed in the direction of the bathroom.

"What's up?" I said to the group.

"I guess the shaman's got to take a shit," Bales said.

THE CEREMONY LASTED less than twenty minutes. Claudia packed up her bongos and maracas and headed home, promising to be at the show on Friday. The rest of us hung out in the afterglow of the shamanic blessing.

"Claudia is sweet on you," Bales said to the Artist. "You gonna slip her the hooded soldier?"

The Artist walked over to the fireplace and turned the gas key. Then he struck a long match and placed it under the logs, and red flames whooshed into being.

"You're a vile man, John," the Artist said. "But she is kinda cute. You know her mom's a maid in Toluca Lake. Saved enough money to buy a house. They're good people."

Bales sparked a joint. He stretched his arm across the couch and offered it to me.

"No, thanks," I said.

"So you've quit herb, too?"

"Maybe not forever," I said. "But it's called medicinal marijuana. It's legalized for pain. And since I don't have any pain, other than mentally, I figured it's best for now."

"Fuckin' Mr. Figs-and-Pine-Nuts here," Bales said. "Maybe I should quit."

Homegrown said, "Quit what? The crack and the hookers? Or the benzos and the booze?"

"Shut the fuck up, pole sniffer. I can't even look at your weak face anymore."

Homegrown stroked his lips with a delicate finger and looked down at his red Doc Martens boots. "That's kinda harsh, bro."

Bales drained a beer and slammed the empty down on the coffee table. "What is it, fucking ladies' night in here? Hashtag, draw two!"

"I'm not your maid," Hashtag said.

"Christ, Moobs. Who moved your stinky cheese? I'll get it myself. Oh, and don't bother to get up."

Hashtag made no attempt to get up. He just bit into an apple and stared pensively into the fire.

Bales rose from the sofa and started filming the paintings with his iPhone. Walking around, shooting all angles, getting close-ups, panning in and out.

"These are great, A," he said. "I bet these sell big-time."

Bales went into the kitchen and retrieved a sixer of Heineken and dropped it on the table. He opened a beer, then tossed the bottle opener on the floor.

"Help yourselves, you miserable serfs."

Bales aimed the phone at the Artist. "A, what are you gonna do if you don't sell any paintings?"

The Artist joked. "Probably shoot myself."

"Say it like you mean it."

"Like, as if I agreed to do your documentary?"

Bales flashed a stagey smile. "Clever boy."

The Artist laughed, then pushed his face toward the camera and said, "I will *fucking* shoot myself!" Then he put a finger to his head and pulled the trigger. "BANG!" He smiled sweetly and looked at Bales. "How's that?"

"That's good," Bales said, walking over to the fireplace. "But what if...*you didn't shoot yourself*?"

"What are you talking about?"

Bales slowly unsheathed the sword above the mantel. "What if someone chopped your head off? Say, maybe that Qatari dude across the street. Wouldn't that make the public more attuned to your death? More interested? I mean, murder could be *so much* more delicious." He dropped to his haunches and twisted the blade in the fire glow. "But the question is, will it work?"

A wave of panic broke over me. For the first time, I felt that he was serious. That he was capable of murder. But what did I really know? I had no proof, just a gut feeling. But I know one thing now—I should have spanked him right then. It was my last chance. But instead, I just yelled at him like a weak father reprimanding his ten-year-old son.

"Goddammit, Bales," I said, "we're not playing this game. I'm tired of you acting like a child. Put it back."

He aimed his hooded eyes at me, then gently sheathed the blade. "You're no fun," he said. "You never were."

Homegrown broke the tension. "If you don't sell anything," he said to the Artist, "you can always try the Venice boardwalk."

I threw my hands up. "Here we go."

The Artist gave Homegrown a paternal look. "Did you know, Bobby," he said, talking holy Southern, "that Ravi Shankar was asked to join the Beatles?"

"No."

"Well, he was. But he declined the invitation. Do you know why?"

Homegrown shrugged. "Because he didn't like to travel?"

"No. Because it would have *devalued* his body of work. He knew the Beatles took drugs, something he was adamantly against. And the *taint* of that would have cheapened everything he had accomplished, both as a man and as an artist. That's me and the boardwalk. Nothing but hacks and dog painters. Get it?"

"We get it," Bales said. "What's your schedule on Friday?"

"I'm leaving for the show at five."

"What time are you taking the paintings over?"

"Five."

"The night before?"

"Some, some the night of the show."

"The Artist is freakishly protective of his work," I said.

Bales walked over to the stereo and cranked Echo and the Bunnymen's "The Killing Moon." Then he excused himself "to his chambers."

He ducked into his apartment several times that night. It was no secret to any of us what he was doing—smoking his brain. The only questions were "what?" and "how much?"

Later on, after Bales had returned with eyes like a long-haul trucker's, the Artist turned on the eleven o'clock news. We all shared a passion for current events.

"Did you hear Zimmerman is suing NBC?" I said, staring at the TV.

"Yeah," Hashtag said. "He claims they edited his nine-one-one call. Made him sound like a racist."

"Oh, bullshit, dude!" said the Artist. "Of course he's a racist. He was *stalking* Martin. The kid was walking home, eating Skittles. They ought to fry that shooter. It's mind-blowing, man."

"Straight up," said Homegrown.

We watched the tube in silence for a few moments. The dark room splashed with the catastrophic images of the day. Then Bales slowly sat up on the couch, lit a joint, and said in a casual tone that frightened us, "There's a killer inside us all. It just comes out sometimes."

A chill shot through the room—our bodies froze.

"Just like that bitch I almost snuffed in the bathroom," Bales said. He flicked the ash off his joint onto the coffee table and spoke without emotion. "I had my dick halfway in her ass before she started screaming. She wouldn't shut up. So I tried to push her brain in. Palmed her head like a fucking basketball." He paused and sipped his beer carefully. "I thought she was into it. Turns out she wasn't. Fucking whore. Cost me my job."

Bales looked around the stunned room, staring each of us straight in the eye, as though he were trying to gauge the level of our fear. Then he broke out into rich, wild laughter. "Gotcha, you motherfuckers! So fucking gullible! I could buy and sell you all."

My heart pumped. "You're a real hoot, Bales," I said. "Why don't you go to bed?"

"I liked you better drunk," he said. "And that's not saying much."

"If you didn't live here, we wouldn't be friends."

"Who said we were? But if it makes you feel any better, you can follow me on Twitter."

I stood up. "Fuck you, Bales. My fist will apply pressure to your face."

Bales laughed. "I bet you'd like that. But you had your shot, Cowboy. It's somebody else's turn." He hopped off the couch. "C'mon, boys. Let's go get a beer. Let the bald man stew in his own juice."

"Where?" Hashtag said, reaching into a bag of Doritos.

"Anywhere but JP's. And put down that fucking feedbag. Don't you ever have eater's remorse?"

"What?" Hashtag said.

"Forget it," Bales said. He snatched the Doritos bag out of Hashtag's hand. "Let's go. I'm driving."

The idiots left the building and it was just me and the Artist. We watched a story on KCET about this seventy-four-year-old Japanese couple in Fukushima Prefecture who lost everything in the tsunami. For fifty years they'd made noodles in the community. Now they were homeless and broke. "We are too old to get jobs," they said. "And the politicians can't help us. We do not know what we are going to do."

Sad. The hits just kept on coming.

"I better go," I said, rising from the couch. "I need my beauty rest. I'm flying to Las Vegas tomorrow."

The Artist stood up. "But you're back on Friday?"

I dialed up the wattage on my smile. "Are you kiddin' me? I'd fly across the ends of the earth for finger foods and modern art. I'll be in constant communication."

He gave me an appreciative nod. "Thanks, dude."

We fist-bumped in the firelight.

"Later, man," I said.

"Later."

I talked with him a few more times after that night. But it would be the last time I ever saw him.

Splitting Atoms

I SAT ON Southwest Flight 009 staring out the window at the starless dark, my headphones blasting Pink Floyd's "Another Brick in the Wall." I'm not much of a gambler, but Las Vegas provides me with a much-needed change of scenery. I'm not talking about the Strip, that's for yokels. I'm talking about the beauty of hiking Red Rock Canyon, a full winter sun warming your face as you watch the red-and-white sandstone cliffs change color in the light. It truly is a magnificent trek, one that instills power and awe and rejuvenating energy. And one that always brings me closer to my mother.

I promised myself that I was going to get into the holiday spirit for the first time this season. No matter what the world threw at me. And while on the plane that night, I reread the day's events in my journal.

Los Angeles, December 19, 2012
10:45 a.m.

I walk out of CVS with cashews and toilet paper and see a defeated kid in a baseball hat slumped against the wall near my bike. He looks at it like he wants to steal it. I'm not talking about some old person down on their luck, or some blathering idiot, or some butt picker waiting on the lunch bell to ring. I'm talking about a young guy. Maybe twenty. And I think, I'm seeing a lot of street kids these days. He still has prospects. His bulb, however dim, still flickers. But it is definitely on the wane.

As I start to unlock my bike, the guy says, You know anyone that wants to buy a cruiser?

And I say, Do you have a lot of cruisers?

And he says, Naw. Just this one.

Well, it wasn't any better than mine. A black lowrider with bald tires and chipped paint. Silver duct tape on the seat. I slap the handlebars of my bike and say, I already got this one. But you won't have any problem selling it.

He's a polite kid, albeit strung out. Nervously tugging at the bill of his ball cap. He nods his head and says thank you. And I want to help him. I really do. You can see he is teetering on the edge of his future, and he seems like a decent guy. But at this point he needs saving. And that's something I can't do. I'm too busy saving myself. It is also quite possible that he's playing me. Knowing that CVS is how he eats. Ripe with old dudes and old women with bob haircuts exiting with their medication and feeling sorry for the street kid on the corner. It's tough. It really is. I know there are no jobs out there. I really want to help him.

But instead, I mount my bike and ride on.

3:15 p.m.

I walk to Sport Chalet. I need a new pair of running shoes. I try on a pair of Nikes and notice that I am wearing two different socks. I think about a guy I knew in school. Mismatched socks were his trademark. That and his genius IQ. I picture him splitting atoms somewhere. Me, I'm splitting socks. And beating the shit out of newspaper dispensers.

5:30 p.m.

The Artist calls and says that Hashtag told him they went drinking last night at the Kings Head in Santa Monica. And some forty-year-old chick came up to Homegrown and said, You're a very attractive man. I asked the Artist what Hashtag said she looked like. He said she was okay-looking but appar-

ently very rich. He also said she gave the impression that if you were locked in a room with her she'd eat you alive. He said she was skinny fat, probably a former 6 who was now a 5 but thought she was an 8. A poisonous combination.

Bales said her outfit cost seven thousand dollars. The shoes alone three. Bales said she came from a very prominent Los Angeles family but forgot the name. He did say that she started acting crazy and told Homegrown that she could buy this bar and everybody in it. And then Bales asked, How so? To which she replied, None of your fucking business, gray beard. Then Hashtag told the Artist it unraveled from there. Bales tried one of his shock techniques and said, I don't always like hookers, but when I do, I like to beat them. But that didn't faze her, and she said, Creepers like you belong east of the 405. To which Bales countered, East of the 405? Hell, I rarely go east of Lincoln! I'm AWOL, bitch!

She scoffed and left pissed off because Bales wanted to do her and Homegrown didn't. Then Bales asked Homegrown if the dispensary he gets his weed from makes a lot of dough. And Homegrown said, Yeah, thousands flow through every day. Bales then said, I got a gun. You get us inside and I'll take it from there. And Hashtag said Homegrown looked at him like he had two heads, but it still made them both uncomfortable.

I said, Do you think he meant that toy gun? And the Artist said, I don't know. Then Hashtag said Bales got really smashed and cozied up to a guy at the bar and started staring at him with a shit-eating grin on his face. Then before the guy could say anything he felt something and looked down, and realized Bales was pissing on his leg—his dick dangling out of his jeans. When the guy realized what was happening he said, What the fuck! Then Bales laughed and said, Why don't you go listen to some Petula Clark, sweet cheeks.

At the bar? I said.

Yes, at the bar. And then they got kicked out, and when they were leaving the parking structure, Bales gunned the Prius past the attendant and crashed through the wooden gate arm.

Wow. Did they catch him?

No.

That's unbelievable.

I know. He's one lucky dude.

5:53 p.m.

I take a short bike ride before my flight leaves for Las Vegas. I like to get the blood flowing before I sit

on a plane. I know it's a short flight, but the fear
of deep-vein thrombosis scares the hell out of me.

I ride east and when I get to the intersection of
Centinela and Washington I recall an epiphany I
had the other day. I was frantically swerving my
bicycle on Lincoln trying to avoid hitting all the
other bike riders, pedestrians, and bums. And it
reminded me of a trip to Tokyo that I'd taken with
my family back in '94. We were crossing the busiest
intersection in the world, the Shibuya crosswalk,
and a wall of humans rushed us like nothing you've
ever seen before. I was dodging people like a video
game, and then the calm voice of my mother said,
Richard, dear, you don't have to swerve. Just walk
straight ahead and the people will move around
you. And they did. And I realized it was the same
in L.A. I got it. There's a certain poetry about the
streets—an unwritten etiquette among bike riders
and pedestrians and shopping cart people. You yield
to moms and babies, stiffs and wheelchairs, crazies
and tennis ball sliders.

For the rest, you just move straight ahead.

That's the way it is on the street.

Small Dogs in
Sweaters

THE NEXT MORNING I woke up in Las Vegas on my mother's sofa with absurdly bright sunlight streaming in through large bay windows. Her black teacup poodle, Gigi, stood on my chest, head cocked, her twinkling black eyes staring into mine with both curiosity and affection.

"Good girl," I said, softly stroking her tiny head. "Did you miss me?"

She barked.

As I said before, Las Vegas is a welcome change of pace from Los Angeles. The sun is always shining. Never any June gloom or thick marine layers. While L.A. tries to quietly seduce you with her calculated siren song, Vegas grabs you by the dice and demands an answer to the question, "Are you in or out?"

Wiping sleep from my eyes and petting Gigi, I dwelled upon last night's dream. I was wandering the desert in Morocco smoking hash with Paul Bowles.

He says, *You are a mirage.*

I say, *You are a clone.*

He says, *Are you still dating that food blogger?*

No, I say. *It took her an hour to shoot a grape last night. A measly grape!*

What about that woman from Hollywood?

The chick who sells trucker hats on Etsy?

Yes.

No. Trucker hats? Really? That's so out of style.

He says, *Let me tell you something about me. I don't write fan fiction or steampunk, and I don't fucking Twitter. And I most certainly am not contemplating a travel blog.*

I sell real estate.

Ah. You did.

Yeah, I did.

And he says, *Maybe you should forget that.*

I was thinking, *Maybe I should*, when my mother emerged from her bedroom in her pink fleece bathrobe and said, smiling, "Good morning."

"Good morning," I said.

harlin hailey

"Did you sleep well?" she said, plugging in the lights to a beautiful Douglas fir Christmas tree.

"Like a log," I said.

"Why didn't you sleep in the guest bedroom?"

"I fell asleep watching Letterman."

"Well, I'll put some coffee on."

My mother's name is Grace. A proper, well-man-nered woman from a different time. She is elegant (even in jeans) and petite and thoughtful and in great shape for a lady of seventy-five. She carries with her the obligation (or burden) of the State Farm Insurance Corporation, whom she has proudly rep-resented for over thirty years. She is well loved in the community for her quirky sense of humor, blended with a practical perseverance that makes you feel special even in the most difficult of times.

And her parties are killer.

She said from the kitchen, "Have you thought about moving out of L.A.? I mean, you could live here for a while and save some money while looking for work. And you know I wouldn't mind if you came to work for me."

I stared at the blinking white lights on the Christ-mas tree.

"I don't know what I'm going to do yet, Mom."

I wasn't excited about writing auto policies during my golden years. But what choices did I have?

"Well, you think about it," she said, bringing me a fresh cup of coffee. "I'll probably think about retiring soon."

I took the mug from her hand.

"Thanks, Mom," I said. "What time's the party tonight?"

"Around seven. I want you to help me get ready today."

"Okay. Is that drunk lady going to show?"

"Which one?"

"The one that got blasted at Caesars Palace. Fell down in the parking lot and knocked her teeth out."

"Oh, New Teeth. She'll be here. Unless she gets totally polluted beforehand."

I sipped my coffee. It was strong and tasted of hazelnut.

"How's Jimmy?" she asked.

"Better. You remember I told you about his show tomorrow. He could finally make some serious money."

"His work is really good. I just hope he stays centered. He's jumpier than a long-tailed cat."

"He's a Sagittarius, Mom. That's how they operate. Always shooting arrows from the hip."

My mother rearranged the brightly wrapped presents under the tree.

"Well, if it works for him," she said, "that's all that matters."

"I'll be flying out tomorrow evening at five. Need to be at the airport at four."

"And when will you be coming back?"

"I told you, Christmas Eve."

"Is Rose coming?"

"No. She's spending it with her new boyfriend and his family in Aspen."

"That sounds lovely."

"And expensive."

"Now, Richard," she said, placing a candy cane on a rogue tree limb. "You're only in love once, son. What about your father?"

"He's going fishing with Alan down in Cabo San Lucas."

"Alan from Shreveport? His Tulane classmate?"

"Yes."

"Gosh," she said. She sat down on the opposite end of the couch, both hands cradling a mug of coffee. "I haven't seen him in *years*. I wonder how he's doing."

"Apparently okay. He's going to Cabo for Christmas. Swordfish ceviche and tequila. Things can't be all bad."

"No, I guess not."

I paused, staring at a pewter-framed black-and-white photo of me and my father on the mantel. It was Christmas 1974. Both of us stood proudly by the tree, me clutching a new pair of Rossignol skis—my long blond hair the same color as my Hang Ten shirt. And my beaming father in a blue silk bathrobe, his long arm draped paternally over my shoulder, tall, dark, and masculine like James Bond in *Diamonds Are Forever*.

"Speaking of Dad," I said, "have you talked to him recently?"

"A couple of weeks ago. Why?"

"Did you notice anything…anything funny, like he was forgetting stuff?"

My mother thought a moment, gently stroking the head of her poodle like a royal on the throne.

"No, our last conversation seemed as animated as ever. But at our age everyone forgets something."

I nodded.

"But I'll call him after the holiday," she said. "Check in on him. You want some eggs?"

"Yes, please."

She rose from the couch and walked toward the kitchen.

"I noticed you've put on a little weight."

"It's been a stressful few months. But I'm working on it."

Gigi, the teacup, was lying on her back, all sprawled out. I looked down into her little face. "You want me to rub your tummy?" I said. I tickled her soft pink underbelly with my forefinger and her legs wiggled. She was so small she looked like a black rat.

"I'm feeling better now, though," I said.

"That's good," she said. "Gigi and I are so glad to have you."

"I'm glad to see you guys, too."

Gigi looked at me with those big brown eyes that were too big for her head.

She knew she'd be the star of the show tonight.

Center stage.

I SPENT THE entire day helping Mom prepare for her Christmas party. So much for my hike. Most of it was spent driving around town looking for hard hats. My mother had the wacky idea to issue every guest a construction helmet just in case there was asteroid debris or any other end-of-the-world fallout.

On my quest, I saw a lot of tourists walking around town in shorts and T-shirts, freezing their asses off.

It always amazes me that people show up at Christmas in the desert wearing flip-flops.

It's forty degrees, moron!

But I accomplished my mission and brought home the goods.

My mother, who could give Martha Stewart a run for her money, had transformed her three-bedroom condo into a holiday wonderland. The living room was warm and rich, with stockings that hung just so from the mantel over a roaring fireplace. But not just any stockings—these were mini backpacks that displayed the words BUG-OUT BAG in silver glitter. Stuffed with bottled water, a pint of sour apple schnapps, and Hershey's chocolate bars, they packed just enough provisions to give any survivor of the apocalypse a fighting chance.

A jungle of poinsettias guarded the festive tree, competing with a variety of baubles and ornaments of great size and proportion. Everything including goldfish, pheasants, teddy bears, orbs, balls, bright lights, twinkling lights, and shiny gift-wrapped packages. And my personal favorite: a big green Martian blow-up doll wearing a Santa hat (which a drunk Marty Rosen would later punch out).

I drew double duty that night, DJ and bartender.

And when the first guest arrived, I had my hard hat in place and was ready to rock. Her name was Madeline and she was a sixty-nine-year-old New Age hippie from Topanga. Her long, silky black hair (wig) rode down her back like Cher's, and she wore a rainbow-colored "Shiva Rocks" T-shirt.

"Richard," said Mom, "this is Madeline, and she'd like one of your famous mango martinis."

"Nice to meet you, Madeline," I said. "How do you like it? Strong or mild?"

She turned to my mother. "If only I was twenty years younger."

"Well, you're not," Mom said and excused herself.

I poured vodka into the shaker. "Say when."

Madeline leaned over the bar and flashed a boozy smile. "So are you ready for the Rapture?"

Still pouring.

"I am," I said, slapping my hard hat.

Still pouring.

"Ooh. How are you going to celebrate?"

Still pouring.

"Ritual dancing, most likely."

"Me, too," she said. "And I took an extra OxyContin. Just in case."

"Just in case you miss the spaceship?"

She giggled and sliced the air with her hand. "Okay, that's good."

Maybe I'll just give you the friggin' bottle next time.

Gigi the teacup had yet to make an appearance. But several of the other guests had arrived with their precious dogs. Mostly small dogs: poodles, shih tzus, Pomeranians, feisty Chihuahuas, and a fussy fat cat appropriately named Chubby. Gabe Fackler was the only one who broke code, bringing his large neurotic Afghan Suzy, whom I later quieted with a kicker of vodka in her water bowl.

A short, stocky woman with battleship-gray hair holding two snorting pugs approached. "Can we lose the Christmas music, please?"

"Andy Williams got you down?"

"Oh, he has his place," she said, "but I feel the women would appreciate something more…"

"Celestial?"

Her pugs snorted.

"Why, yes," she said. "You read my mind."

I didn't know if it was her or the dogs, but something smelled of stale cigarettes and thrift-store dust.

"'Space Cowboy' coming right up," I said, thankful for these lighter moments.

She looked at me like I was a planet outside our solar system.

"Kidding," I said. "My exterior might be a little rough, but I can assure you I'm a soft touch inside."

The old woman shot me a searching glance. "You know who you look like?"

"Steve McQueen in *Bullitt*?"

She laughed. "No, that actor that played in *The World According to Garp*. What's his name?"

"Not Robin Williams."

"No, no. The man in the dress."

Twenty years ago I would not have been mistaken for a man in a dress. But time marches on.

"John Lithgow?"

"*Yes*," she said, "he's a wonderful actor."

"The evening's young," I said, "but I'll take it. This song's just for you. Enjoy."

I spun Blondie's "Rapture" and that got the ladies dancing, yellow hard hats bouncing and bobbing.

Leonard "Laconic" Robbins, my mom's eighty-year-old next-door neighbor, a retired Las Vegas show producer, sauntered over wearing his favorite hideous-green reindeer sweater. He looked like any number of the mature character actors you might've seen on any episode of *Perry Mason*.

"How you doin', Big Dog?" he said, draining his whiskey glass.

He liked to call me Big Dog. Which was fine with me. I'd been called a lot worse.

"Fine, Leonard," I said. "Can I get you another?"

"Please."

I took his glass and said, "Hey, Leonard. What actor would you say I look like?"

He thought a moment. "Maybe that shaggy-haired guy in *Wedding Crashers*. I mean…if you had hair."

"Fair enough," I said. "I'm getting better looking by the minute."

"Keep the punch bowl spiked," Leonard said, "and who knows what handsome fellow you might morph into tonight."

I smiled. "In my sweet dreams."

Leonard hitched up his slacks. "Let me ask you something, son. How does one connect the digital and physical worlds today?"

"I don't know," I said. "With dots?"

He scratched his chin.

"Coupons. That's what I was thinking."

"You keep racking that big brain, Leonard. Keep me posted on any major breakthroughs."

I handed him a whiskey.

"Will do," he said. He leered into his glass. "You know, the great thing about being at a party with people who can't hear is you can fart as loud as you want."

"You're all class, Leonard."

"Yeah, I know." He pointed at my mother's bedroom. "If the place is rockin' don't bother knockin'."

I laughed. "You wish, old man. 'Cause that really would be the end of the world."

He shrugged, licking spittle from the corner of his mouth. "Maybe so. Can I buy you something?"

"No, thanks, I'm the designated driver. Somebody's got to stay sober in case the aliens storm the Bastille."

At that moment, I got a call from the Artist. I excused myself and retreated to the quiet of the guest bedroom.

"The Artist surfaces. You good?"

"Good," he said. "How's the party?"

"A lot of old women with small dogs in sweaters. And a boatload of vodka."

He laughed. "Any hot GILFs?"

"I'm sorry to say *The Flying Nun* couldn't make it."

"Dang."

"In another lifetime, my boy. By the way, did Hector call you back?"

"Forget Hector!" he said, his voice rising with excitement. "I've got great news—*for once.*"

"Hit me."

"I finally won an immunity challenge, bro. I sold a painting! Twenty grand!"

"What?"

"Yeah, Beth called and said she showed this couple from San Francisco a picture of my work. They bought the red one. Said they were clients of hers from way back, and they liked to invest in emerging artists. Can you believe it? Off the picture! I get a sixteen-grand check on Monday. Plus anything else I sell at the show."

"Dude, that's awesome."

"I'm so relieved. You don't even know. It's been so long since I've had money."

"Since Billy Ocean had a hit?"

"Almost. Look, man, I haven't forgotten, either."

"What?"

"Everything you've done for me. Monday I'm taking you to the fish restaurant, and we're going to eat like kings. I'm talking sushi. Lobster. A seafood orgy. Whatever you want, man."

"Sounds good. Just promise me you won't go crazy with the money."

I heard laughter explode from the living room, clapping.

"Hey," I said. "Let's chat tomorrow. I've got beaucoup movement on the perimeter."

"All right. What time are you flying in?"

"Six. I'm going to cab it right from the airport. I'll be there by seven. Congrats again, man. You deserve it."

"Thanks, bro."

BACK IN THE living room, Gigi was busy holding court. She had just crossed over the proverbial galactic bridge and was now being celebrated for the best costume of the evening—a silver spacesuit complete with helmet and tiny antennae. The crowd parted as my mother paraded the teacup poodle around the room like a Westminster show dog, her pocket-sized legs high-stepping it across the Oriental rug.

I spotted New Teeth in the crowd, chugging something flammable from a green plastic tumbler. I gave her a half smile and a chin nod. She smiled back with those snow-white choppers. No doubt, already there.

You see, this was how I used to be—before everything went south. Gregarious and witty, the life of the party, moving about the world free of cynicism. In those first weeks of trying to heal, getting back to that old self struck me as insurmountable. But I promised myself I'd make it. Some days I think I have, others not so much.

Apocalypse Now

ON THE MORNING of December 21 I was up before the dawn. I was sprinting—not jogging—running full speed ahead through the dark abandoned streets of an affluent master-planned community.

If the world had ended, I wouldn't have known it.

The cold, dry desert air stung my face with each pump of the legs, each swing of the arms. I emptied my mind of all thought and just kept running. Running until I could run no more.

At 6:48 a.m. I arrived at the golf course clubhouse just as the sun was rising over Frenchman Mountain. I took a moment to catch my steaming breath, hands on my knees, as I heralded the dawn of a new era.

I wondered if New Zealand had survived. The first country to experience the shift. I knew one thing,

I was still here. Flesh and bone, all fifty-three years of me clinging to hope and life.

I observed the sun painting the sky, illuminating the lush, green grass of the country club golf course and rolling across the desert floor like a brilliant field of emeralds.

I was stretching when I heard his godly voice.

"It feels good to be alive, doesn't it?"

I turned and saw another jogger, a thin, sinewy man of perhaps sixty, with long silver hair and a deeply tanned face. He wore orange Dolphin shorts and black running shoes with no socks. The kind of guy who might have saved his Woodstock press pass.

"Yeah, it does," I said.

He breathed in deeply, admiring the brilliant sunrise. "It's beautiful."

I nodded. "Yep. Sure is."

"You know what this means, don't you?" he said.

"That I didn't get bailed out by the apocalypse? That I got to find a job?"

He smiled. "It's a new beginning. A chance to start over. An awakening of consciousness."

"Yeah?" I said. "I can use all the cosmic help I can get."

He tossed his long silver hair back and looked me straight in the eye, his life experience challenging mine. "Go forward, young man," he said, "with only good love in your heart. It is you who will lead us into the new world. Welcome it. Accept it. Take us home."

I looked away, and when I turned back he was gone.

. . . .

MY MOTHER'S HOUSE was like a warm cocoon—usually, anyway. But today the aftermath of last night's party was spread around the place like shrapnel. That included Leonard, fully clothed in his reindeer sweater and beige slacks and snoring away on the couch. I walked over and gently shook his shoulder.

"Wake up, Sunshine," I said. "This is your captain speaking. Your all-knowing seer."

He snorted and woke with a start, his sallow eyes focusing on the crouching pale shape before him. My bald head must have looked like a bright idea.

"Oh, Big Dog, Big Dog," he said, groaning.

"I only poured last night, Leonard. You're the one who drank."

I helped him to his feet, watched him struggle into his loafers, then walked him to the door. I could almost hear his teeth loosening.

"Your house is right there," I said, pointing out the window. "Right next door. Now go change out of those Christmas fatigues and get some sleep."

I nudged him forward, like a rusty old windup toy.

"Thanks, Big Dog." He touched his forehead with bony, trembling fingertips. "Oh, my. Oh, boy."

Hungover, slump-shouldered, his mouth wandering open, Leonard slowly shuffled out of the condo like he'd just had a hip replacement.

"Good morning."

I turned to see my mom striding out from her bedroom in her pink fleece bathrobe.

"Good morning," I said.

"How was your run?"

"Refreshing," I said. "The world still turns."

"Good. That means it's *Wheel of Fortune* tonight as scheduled."

"Love how you boil it down, Mom."

She stopped and placed her hands on her hips, her scientific eyes sweeping the living room. I knew what she was doing—she was taking in the spoils of war. My mother prided herself on messy parties, believing the harder the cleanup, the better the time. I could tell by the serene expression on her face that the end result was better than expected. The sea of red plastic cups, the small paper plates of marginally nibbled crudités, Ms. Anderson's ivory pump in the fireplace, and an empty magnum of Moët & Chandon champagne lying dead on the table, evidence of last night's steamy game of spin the bottle. Not pretty. Watching two old people chew tongue was like watching a bear eat salmon.

It was truly a messy sight to behold—one that would later send my mother gleefully scrambling for the vacuum attachments.

"Well," she said, checking off another successful Christmas party, "looks like everybody had a good time last night."

"Hard to call it a failure when New Teeth blacks out."

She laughed.

"I'll get some coffee on, then I want you to help clean up. What time does your flight leave again?"

"Five. We need to be at the airport about four. I'll guess we'll have to skip our hike."

"No problem," she said. "I have a little free play left at the Palms. I'll stop there on my way home."

We had the place spick-and-span by noon. My mom, bless her heart, was exhausted and retired for a nap. I checked my Yahoo horoscope:

Sun in Capricorn moving in today indicates the day to be lucky for you in all aspects of your life.

Sounds good, I thought. Maybe I'll pull a few slots at the airport. Or get lucky at the show. But does a fifty-three-year-old bald man ever get lucky?

I was just about to call the Artist when he beat me to it. I answered on the half ring.

"You alive?" I said. "The polar vortex suck you in?"

"These stupid people," he said.

"Who?"

"The NRA. These idiots are proposing an armed guard patrol in every school in the nation. They're insane. And then you got the government worried about raising taxes on the rich when you got kid killers. It's messed up."

"I didn't hear," I said. "I haven't watched TV in a couple of days."

Which was true. I had to check out for a while. Just be with my mom. I was aware they were burying children in Newtown. The entire nation was overwhelmed by great sadness. It was all just too much for me to handle right now.

"Did Beth call you?" I asked.

"Yeah, she just wanted to prep me for the show."

"What did she say?"

"She just said, don't let the gasbags occupy too much of my time. Don't be aloof. Smile, but don't be too engaging. And don't lean on my friends. Stuff like that."

"Good advice," I said. "Is Bales coming?"

"I haven't seen him yet, but he said he was. He was hanging out with Stoneface yesterday."

"The Russian?"

"Yeah, his new besticle."

"Where did he meet that guy again?"

"Work. I guess he was a security guard at the building."

I walked into the kitchen and opened the refrigerator door, searching for the strawberry jam for a PB&J.

"Well, maybe we'll get lucky and Bales won't show," I said. "But if he does, I'll be happy to give him the Heisman. What about Hashtag?"

"No. He flew out to Mexico a couple of days ago with a buddy of his. They're touring the Mayan temples."

"Must be nice," I said.

"Homegrown will be there."

"That lifts me up."

He paused, and I could hear the agitated shuffling of papers and the slamming of a desk drawer.

"Richard, do you really think I'm ready for this? What if people don't like my work? I mean, I'm starting to panic."

"Look, it's going to be great," I said. "You've already sold a painting. Just let the pieces do the talking."

"I know, but I don't know what to wear. My neighbor's putting pressure on me to move my Jeep. And I got this feeling."

"What feeling?"

He blew out a deep breath.

"That feeling like in *Deliverance*. You know? When they should have turned back when they saw that hillbilly kid on the banjo."

"Nobody's porking you in the ass," I said.

I heard him chewing on a towel, a low humming sound like whales mating. Something he did when he was extremely nervous.

"You know," he said, "I am so grateful for everything. I really am."

"Dude, focus. What are you going to wear?"

"I don't know, but I need a jacket. It's freezing here in L.A."

"I'd go all black again, maybe with a blazer. What about your Hugo Boss?"

"The moths ate it."

"No problem. Then go with your black leather motorcycle jacket over a white T-shirt. Dark Levi's. Black shoes. That make you comfortable?"

"Yeah, I guess that'd probably work."

I could hear the fear in his voice.

"Dude!" I said. "This is a joyous event. Smile. It's going to work out fine."

A long, profound silence.

"Richard?"

"Yeah."

He cleared his throat.

"We had fun, didn't we?"

"What are you talking about? Of course we had fun. More to come."

"Okay. But I need something from you."

"Anything," I said. "You name it."

I heard his voice catch, and we were quiet for what seemed like forever. Then he said at last, in a shaky whisper, "I might need to lean on you tonight."

"Lean all you want, bro. Lean all you want."

"Thanks, man," he said. "I'll see ya."

Easy with A Gun

MOM DROPPED ME off at McCarran International Airport shortly after four. I kissed her goodbye curbside, then stroked Gigi's muzzle for good luck. By the time I reached the gate, I had a full half hour before boarding. I took a seat in the waiting area and charged my phone. It gave me a moment to soak up the winter solstice. Inside the terminal the *bing bing bing* of slot machines occupied a few tourists, while I stared out the window. The shortest day of the year was fading away, and with it, the myth of the apocalypse.

Watching the twilight ooze colors, I recalled several nocturnal wanderings from last night's sleep. Dreams so intense, images so violent, I could only attribute it to the last bit of alcohol exiting my body. These weren't missing-tests-in-school dreams. They were more like mushroom clouds—Phuket bodies in the surf, school shootings, samurai warriors dis-emboweling themselves, guts dropping like cow placenta. Perhaps I had tapped into some psychic wasteland, hurtling through a universe of unwanted thoughts, discarded as so much space junk.

And then I remembered it—the potent moon-shine of my dreams distilled into one single poem. I quickly grabbed a pen and wrote it down on the back of my boarding pass. It was as if someone, or something, had guided my hand.

> easy with A gun
> i could pull the trigger
> you think it's so easy to intimidate.
> i'm a lover—not a fighter,
> only with injustice
> do i become Superman.
> i'm quick to the wit
> smart with A gun
> prefer laughter, having fun.
> go ahead—make your move...
> it's so easy with A gun.

I wasn't sure what it meant at the time, or how it had come to be. I had heard songwriters talk about their craft, about how words or phrases would come to them out of the blue, like at the market or in the middle of the night, or while driving or making love. But it had never happened to me before. Maybe I just hadn't been listening. Up until now, I'd just as soon have watched the season finale of *Swamp People*.

They called for the boarding of Flight 27 to Los Angeles and I got in line at the gate. That's when Beth phoned.

"Hey, stranger," I said.

"He's not here." Her tone was sharp, almost rude.

"Jimmy?"

"Yes. It's almost five. He was supposed to be here an hour ago to finish setting up. He's slotted for six paintings; we've only got three. And one is already sold."

"He's like that sometimes," I said. "You know… *late.*"

"That's unprofessional, Richard. You know I took him on as a courtesy to you."

"You took him on because he's talented."

"You're right. You're right."

"He's probably in the shower," I said.

She paused.

"You see, this is why I prefer to handle the work a few days prior. So we don't run into these problems. Artists are notoriously flighty."

"He's protective of his work."

"I understand that, but I've got seven other artists, seven other big egos I'm dealing with, and they're all here on time. It's unfair to them."

"Look, I'll call him. I'm in Vegas now, but I'll be back in town in an hour. I'll make it happen."

"I'd appreciate it. I've talked him up to several collectors." She sighed. "I'm sorry, I'm just stressed. If we can just have everything in place by six thirty, we should be fine."

"I understand. I'll call him. And I'll call you when I land."

"Thanks," she said. "Have a good flight."

Normally I would have been alarmed by a call like this, but this is how a creative town like L.A. operates. Nothing ever goes as planned. Artists flake. Actors OD. Directors, producers, and handlers enable. Yet somehow, at the very last minute, after an onslaught of immense pressure felt by all, the show magically comes together.

I was in the front of the line about to enter the walkway to the plane when I called the Artist. I got his voicemail.

"Hey, man," I said. "Just checking in to see how everything's going. You're probably on your way to the gallery. I'm at the airport now. I'll call you when I land. But do me a favor and call Beth when you can, just to let her know where you are. Thanks, bud."

I didn't think too much about it during my fifty-minute flight. Artists are artists, and if I had to go and track him down at his apartment or wherever he was holed up, that's what I was going to do. Something I'd done many times before.

The plane touched down at LAX at 5:54 p.m., and when the captain came over the loudspeaker and told us it was safe to use our mobile devices, I checked my voicemail. There were no messages. That's when I got concerned. I quickly dialed the Artist and got his voicemail again.

"Hey, man," I said. "I just landed. Where are you? Give me a call."

I hung up and hastily punched in Beth's number. She answered on the first ring, begging for answers. "Talk to me," she said.

"Did he show?"

"No."

"Shit."

It was then I got the feeling I needed to move, and move fast. I sprinted through LAX, dodging bodies and suitcases, my emotions clearly out of hiding. When I hailed a cab that night, I knew in my heart that something had happened.

Only this time I couldn't save the day. Couldn't fix the heater.

Colors of the Pier

IT WAS THE longest cab ride of my life. I didn't even recognize the city, just surreal frames of black and white whizzing by. I must have dialed the Artist a hundred times in that twenty-minute journey, my mind going places it didn't want to go.

When the cab driver finally turned into the alley behind his building, the acid in my stomach lurched up my esophagus and I regurgitated a portion of my dinner onto the backseat. Frozen, all I could do was stare out the car window at the flashing gumball lights, both hands pressed firmly against the glass.

The entire complex was blocked off by Santa Monica Police vehicles and yellow crime scene tape—a huge throng of onlookers corralled like cattle. The dark night thundered with helicopters, their searchlights knifing the sky with the same grandiosity of a movie premiere. And for some strange reason, at that moment I wanted to believe it was a movie premiere. That the red carpet had been rolled out and at any second one of the officers would be escorting the Artist to the show, his star finally burning bright in this light-polluted city.

But I was quickly jolted back to reality when a German shepherd jumped up and clawed at my window, snarling and showing its canines. I reeled back, and a police officer yanked the leash and the dog fell away.

What stands out most was the officer directing an ambulance as it slowly backed away from the parting mob, the sound of its tires crunching through alley gravel. The same gravel the Artist used to add texture to his artwork.

I vaguely remember stepping out of the cab, numb, and into the crowd of strangers. Some had cell phones raised high above their heads. Others were stunned into silence, hands covering their open mouths.

As I slowly pushed my way through the horrified crowd, I was looking for a familiar face, touching people, turning people, as if I were searching for some dead relative in a natural disaster.

My eyes captured only still images, fragments.

A CSI jacket.

A microphone on the mouth of a man with a black beard, his bright red lips dry and chapped.

A single palm tree, shimmying in the night wind like a hula skirt.

A pair of dirty blue mittens.

It must have been cold outside, but I hadn't noticed. And I'm not sure if I was shouting or not, or how fast I was moving, because my legs felt heavy and leaden.

The helicopter search beam moved away from the scene. It got dark. Then when the hard light arced across the crowd again, I saw her face flicker in the night sun. She wore a heavy overcoat with a Burberry checked scarf and a red wool beanie tight against her face.

It was Jae, the Korean woman I'd met in the alley. And later at the Halloween party. I quickly pushed my way through the bodies, stiff-arming everyone in front of me.

"Jae! Jae!" I shouted over heads and shoulders. "What happened?" But she couldn't hear me. My shouts lost to the deafening roar of helicopter blades. She never looked up, her aerodynamic eyes down-cast, crying into a pair of winter gloves. When I finally reached her, slightly out of breath, I said, "Jae, you remember me? The Artist's friend?"

She nodded, her round face pallid and translucent. She tried to speak and her body shuddered. "They say...they say..."

I grabbed her shoulders. "Tell me, Jae! Tell me!"

She choked back tears. She didn't say anything, or couldn't. And it was then I realized I was standing on the same alley ground where the Artist painted, his outdoor studio—his sanctuary. I looked down and saw a rainbow of dots, splatters, and spills of bright paint, aesthetic shades that had once created so much beauty. And when I looked up, I saw Jae's face, and I watched a lone teardrop fall, as if in slow motion, from the tip of her wide flat nose, float to the pavement, and splash upon impact, a thousand lakes and rivers washing away the colors of the pier.

"Please, Jae!" I said. "Please talk to me."

She swallowed. "They say...*him kill himself.*"

I shook her. "Who, Jae? Who!"

She hesitated, then looked down. "Ahh-tist."

My God.

I ran toward the ambulance as it rolled toward Wilshire Boulevard, my face bathing in the flashing red lights.

And I just kept screaming.

"That's my friend! That's my friend! That's my friend!"

. . . .

IT WAS HOMEGROWN who'd found him. Lying on his back in the living room with his jaw blown off, his left hand clutching a .45.

The bathroom faucet still running cold.

That's how the detective described it. Like some Hitchcock movie, except that it wasn't.

The Artist had been pronounced dead at the scene at 6:37 p.m. The same day the apocalypse died.

All this I learned while being questioned by the Santa Monica Police. I couldn't describe anything or anyone to you from that night. I was still in a state of shock when the questions hit me, seemingly out of thin air.

"Can you think of anyone that might want to kill him?"

"No," I said. "Wait. Yeah, this guy named Hector."

"This Hector, was he a friend?"

"No. A client…or was."

I might have given them another name, but I don't remember. And looking back on it, Bales should have been at the top of my list. But I wasn't thinking straight. My mind was operating somewhere between smudgy and hazy. Beige walls. Gray shapes. Steam rising from hot coffee.

"Uh-huh. What about you? Were you good friends with Mr. Miller?"

"The best."

"Did you know that he called a suicide hotline two days ago?"

"I was not aware of that."

"Huh. Did you ever hear him say that he thought about killing himself?"

"Never. We'd joked about it. How it'd make him famous. But that's all it was. A joke."

"Was he ever depressed?"

"Sure. Just like all of us. But I never once thought he was capable of that."

The detective with no face leaned back and said, "Evidence at the crime scene suggests homicide. Fragments of duct tape were entwined into the brain matter found on a painting. Normally, people who kill themselves don't duct-tape their mouths shut. And the angle of the bullet doesn't jive."

"I've given you a name," I said. "What are you waiting for?"

And then in this suspended moment, another voice dropped like a boulder from the sky.

"We got a match on that red Ford van. Stockton PD are in pursuit."

I was a complete blank, and I'm sure my catatonic state was something the detectives had witnessed many times before. That of a person who looked stoned or drunk.

"Mr. Jenkins?"

Vacant.

"Yes?"

"If you need to talk with someone, we have resources. Here's my card. Call me if you need me."

I don't remember taking his card. But I found it several days later behind my bedroom dresser.

"That's all for tonight," the detective said. "I'm sorry for your loss."

Sweet Dreams

I'M NOT SURE how I made it home. I think someone from the police department drove me. But if you would've pressed me on how I got from point A to point B, you would've received a bewildered "I don't know." I do remember walking into my apartment and thinking it was as dark and silent as a morgue.

What do you do after the death of a loved one? How do you occupy your time? Especially one such as me, a middle-aged bachelor, living alone, with only a handful of friends and family to call. One of whom you've just lost.

What was the shortest day of the year had turned into the longest night of my life. The clock on my microwave struck 11:03 p.m. I was tired, but I wasn't sleepy. So I told myself that in order to move forward, I would actually have to do something, no matter how mundane. Live in the moment. Find simplicity in the chaos. And then I recalled a Zen proverb from my high school philosophy class: "Before enlightenment, chop wood, carry water. After enlightenment, chop wood, carry water."

Do the work, stay present, heal.

I decided to make a hot cup of chamomile tea. Even the process of putting the tea kettle on the stove and boiling the water would require mindfulness. But in the middle of steeping the tea bag in the mug, I broke down. I cried and cried until I picked up the mug and smashed it against the wall. And then, not knowing what else to do, I turned on the eleven o'clock news. I sank back into my leather armchair and wrapped a gold afghan around my body.

On the TV, breaking news.

A high-speed chase with a red Ford van. The police were in hot pursuit and the helicopter spotlight was locked on the vehicle. Watching the van speed north on the 5 freeway, my first instinct was to call the Artist. He loved high-speed chases. We would often watch them together on the phone, discussing strategy and possible outcomes. I imagined how our conversation might have gone:

"What kind of move would you make if you were the cops?"

"That's a gnarly stretch of the Five near Stockton. I'd probably wait until March Lane to get aggressive."

"Are you thinking the pit maneuver or spike strips?"

"I'd probably tactical box awhile, see if he slows down."

"I doubt it. The guy looks mad as a hatter."

"You may have no choice other than a high-speed pit maneuver."

Our "conversation" was interrupted by the TV anchor. "What we know at this time is that the driver and the passenger of this red Ford van are suspects in a possible homicide in Santa Monica earlier this evening. The victim was an artist who was on his way to a show when he was found dead in his apartment from a single gunshot wound to the head around six in the evening. One of the neighbors' children reported seeing two men, one with a ponytail, and the other an older man with gray hair, loading two paintings into a red van. The child said that he'd often watched the artist paint near his home in the alley, and recognized one of the paintings being loaded into the vehicle."

I leaned forward and put on my reading glasses. The camera zoomed in on the driver, and there he was—Bales—his silver hair shining in the helicopter beam like a newly minted dime. Driving that van like he was ready for a wine country weekend. You might have thought I felt rage at the time. But I was still so numb, all I remember thinking was, *Kill him. Just kill the man. He wants it. I want it. And I can guarantee you the public wants it.*

They hadn't been fed in a while.

But I bet that poor sod Ivan the Russian didn't want it. All he could do now was hold on. I recalled what he'd said just before we went into Hector's restaurant that night: "*It is of no concern to me. I get paid either way.*"

Good luck cashing that check, Ivan. You stilted Russian fuck.

I knew this: Bales was going to go out in style. He said to me once, "I'll die just as I've lived, beyond my means."

After a few miles the van slowed down. The TV anchors surmised that it was running out of gas. The officers in pursuit seized the opportunity and quickly made a move, boxing the van in from all sides. Bales didn't hesitate; he swerved hard left and rammed a police vehicle. Then swerved right and rammed another. The third police car finally clipped his bumper and the van fishtailed sideways to a stop in the middle of the empty freeway. With guns drawn, the officers ordered surrender. But the van sat silent for several minutes, its shiny red paint job sparkling under the stars. Bales was no doubt trying to convince the Russian it was the only way out.

And for the first time, I was way ahead of him.

I pulled the blanket up under my chin and said out loud without remorse, "Do it, Bales."

And he did.

He jumped out of the vehicle with that toy gun drawn, and the cops riddled him with a volley of gunfire before the news could cut away. The bullets stood him straight up, arms outstretched like a cross, his body dancing grotesquely under the moonlight.

He's finally gotten someone to pull the trigger, I thought. The wait must have seemed like an eternity. He'd been walking dead for so long. It brought me back to that night when I had him in a chokehold in the Artist's apartment. I know now he wanted me to snap his neck, end it all. And I would have, had I known. But what sticks with me most is the song he was singing in bed that night. The Eurythmics' "Sweet Dreams." The haunting lyrics. Something about being abused.

His death didn't make me feel any better about things, but it was something the universe demanded. Bales knew that.

Looking back on it, maybe we *should've* called him Fucko. It's what he wanted. Nobody hated him more than he hated himself.

I clicked off the TV and cried in the dark. It was two thirty in the morning. And I guess I cried till I fell asleep.

Blinking Red Light

WHEN I WOKE the next morning, I noticed a blinking red light on my message machine. I hadn't thought to check it because it was my office line and it hadn't rung for so long it was the last thing on my mind. I was still operating somewhere between flash and thunder.

I also forgot to mention Ivan the Russian. He never made it out of the van alive, and we'll never know if he attempted to get out—he was killed where he sat. Which is what he deserved. Just sitting there, stone-faced, with that thick head, thick accent, and thick ponytail trying to form a complete greedy thought, before it was all snuffed out into the ether.

Sleep tight, comrade.

The tape I'm about to play for you now was later turned in to the police as evidence. Which enabled them to officially close the case. The message was from the Artist. More precisely, from the cell phone in his pocket. The detectives told me this was a common occurrence during a violent crime these days. The victim's ensuing struggle often resulted in an inadvertent dial—a butt dial, a pocket dial. Call it what you will, that dial was to my office line.

I warn you. It's hard to take. And the only thing worse than finding out a loved one has died is watching them die. In my case, hearing them die.

Beeeeeep...

Shh shh. It's okay, now, A. You're gonna be famous. Gonna meet the Rapture.

A whimper. Like a scared puppy.

Stop moving, bitch!

Voice cuts out. Garbled.

Ivan, more tape.

Duct tape unspooling, scratching. Rapid moans. Frantic, louder.

I said shut up! Shut up! Ivan, hit the bitch.

A slap, a low, guttural groan.

What are you doing?

Bump. I need a fucking bump.

Sniffing sounds. Hard sniffing sounds.

AAHHH! Shit! This fucking coke. The burn, OOOHHH!… fucking Homegrown. Steppin' on the shit. Steppin' on the shit.

Please, shut up. We haven't much time.

You shut the—

POP!

Silence, then—

You stupid Russian fuck! I told you not in the mouth.

He moved his head. How can I do?

SHIT! It's all over my shirt.

Silence.

Ah fuck! It's on the painting. FUCK! FUCK! FUCK! FUCK! FUCK!

Stop it. We must go.

Take off the tape. Take it off. Take it off. Set the gun down. Set the gun down.

Shuffling furniture, shoes scrambling on the hardwood floor.

The heartless, cold, amoral sound of a door closing.

And then,

silence…

Expanded Man

IT'S BEEN NEARLY two years since his death, but I still see that blinking red light every day. Even though I chucked that old machine into the Pacific Ocean months ago.

It was Einstein who once said, "The most beautiful thing we can experience is the mysterious. It is the source of all true art and all science. He to whom this emotion is a stranger, who can no longer pause to wonder and stand rapt in awe, is as good as dead: his eyes are closed." The Artist loved that quote. He had it scrawled on a Post-it note on his refrigerator door. Said it inspired him every morning before he went to work.

He was buried in his hometown of Natchez, Mississippi, on New Year's Day. More than eight hundred people attended the funeral. I didn't know any of them except his parents and his brother. I was surprised to see that many had come from California, most of them street people spending their last dime to get there. When I asked a few of them what they loved most about him, not one mentioned his paintings. But they all agreed that it was his ability to make you feel special. To just simply listen to what you had to say. One guy said he was the last true gentleman in a vulgar new world.

Hashtag no-showed. The lousy fat slob that he is. And word had it that Homegrown had suffered a breakdown after the death. Guilt-ridden for selling the drugs to Bales. He did, however, send a thoughtful note to the parents, saying that he loved their son very much, but being there in person was simply too much for him to bear.

After the service, a few of us were invited back to the historic Rosalie, a Federal-style mansion atop the bluff overlooking the Mississippi River. We dined on shrimp po'boys and crab-stuffed jalapeños. I don't remember what we had for dessert.

Most of the local dignitaries attended, and some of his high school friends. One of them was a tall, handsome guy in a flamboyant suit, a real Southern dandy. I remember thinking that if DiCaprio hadn't landed the role of Gatsby, this dude could've stepped in. Then someone pointed out a famous film director. I'd heard of some of his movies, but hadn't seen any of them. Which didn't mean a whole hell of a lot. I didn't get out much those days.

But what really sticks out about that afternoon was talking to Charles, the Artist's clean-cut older brother who now handles his estate. I was standing on the bluff with my hands in my pockets, staring out over the mighty Mississippi, when he approached me wearing a slim, dark suit and holding a painting, his thick chestnut hair slicked back collegiate style. When he got close, I could see the color blue in the artwork, the sun shining on its surface, its tinted layers reflecting brilliance in the harsh Southern light.

Charles stopped and held out the painting. "He wanted you to have this," he said. "He was going to give it to you."

It was the blue Mexican skull piece that I'd plucked off Hector's restaurant wall. The same piece I'd fought for.

My quivering hands took the canvas, and both of us tried to restrain our emotions. His eyes shiny and red, my Adam's apple bobbing.

"Thanks for being his good friend, Richard."

I lost it. "Goddammit, Charles, it's my fault. I'm sorry, man."

"Richard," he said, hugging me. "It's not your fault. Please, promise me you won't live the rest of your life blaming yourself."

I promised him I wouldn't, but blame stains.

I went home with that painting tucked proudly under my arm. I didn't even wrap it. Just carried it on the plane as though it were a small child.

Bales was right about one thing—the Artist was famous now. He was overwhelmingly the star of Beth's art show that night, his mysterious absence only fueling the ebullient praise. The *Los Angeles Times* art critic had this to say in his review:

"From the alley to the gallery, Mr. Miller's work wades into Basquiat's water, with two toes at first, then after much acclimation and contemplation jumps in with both feet. His sense of color and straight lines leaves us searching for a time when we wanted more, but knew we had to settle for less. The Colors of the Pier series is indeed a triumph. A true talent. Bravo."

I still keep in touch with Charles. He emailed me last week and said that a portion of the collection recently sold for $2.3 million at Christie's. He keeps me posted on what's happening with the Artist's work—who's buying and where. And I appreciate that.

I'M NOT GOING to say much about Bales, about how or why he broke bad, but there are some things you should know. The family granted only one interview, to the *San Francisco Chronicle*, and in that they stated that he had suffered from depression as a boy. And that they were deeply saddened for the loss of life, and were "shattered" over the deaths. That was all they revealed. And who could blame them? The loss of a child is devastating, but the loss of a child and others by his hand is unimaginable.

A psychologist said on record that his aggressive participation in sports most likely suppressed any desire toward predisposed violence during those early years, citing that famous NFL football player case.

There had been no mention of sexual assault. And why would there be? It would not be in any major corporation's best interest to disclose such savage acts, much less subject the victim to reliving the horror. Settlements had been agreed upon. Case closed. But I have no doubt that whatever went down in that dirty upscale Venice bathroom was just as Bales had described it to us on that night. An aggressive, brutal rape. Akin to something unleashed with such vicious, ungovernable force that it rattled even the most hardened of individuals.

The silence by all confirmed it.

As for the murder, I can't be certain when Bales decided to go through with it. The most logical guess would be the night Beth saw the paintings. I remember looking over my shoulder and seeing his black eyes peeking through the crack in the bedroom door. And just as I was surprised to find out how much the Artist's paintings were worth, so must Bales have been.

Author James Ellroy once wrote that murder stays true to its Motivational Trinity: dope, sex, and money. But he failed to mention the fourth. The loss of a job, the painful loss of identity. I realize now that I'd met Bales at his last party. A burning-down-the-house affair—his *Leaving Las Vegas* moment. He knew that a man of his age and past would never again achieve the money and status he'd once enjoyed. Not in this economy. There were no second acts.

Whatever monster had been bottled up inside him for the past thirty years had gotten the best of him in a sleek executive washroom by the sea. He was finished, and he knew it. The tech giants all talked, whispered at corporate retreats, and it was unanimous that his name would never be mentioned again—eternally stricken from the wired obelisk.

As he said, what was he going to do? Pick up dog shit for eight bucks an hour? So with no work in a crushing depression, and nothing else to live for, he was left solely with his pain—and his demons. A sadist free to roam the land like an animal, joining the ranks of the unwanted and the dispossessed.

It's difficult to believe that I had that many chances to stop him. But I'm not sure I would have done anything different. I'm just an ordinary man, not a hero. I like to think he'd taken all he could from this world, and maybe, just maybe, he thought he'd leave a little for someone else. That's what I like to think, anyway.

SO WHAT ABOUT me? I wish I could say, "Glad you asked." I wish I could show you a picture of me doing tai chi in a lotus garden. But that's a Hollywood ending, not real life. As I write the conclusion to my story, I am decidedly less angry, my grieving process complete. But frankly, the landscape remains the same. Black and white. Colors strained through gray. I now live in Van Nuys, in the same home and in the same room I grew up in. Angelenos will be happy to hear I'm back on the road again, driving Dad's late-model Ford Explorer, mostly to and from his doctor's appointments. But I still ride my bike every chance I get. I still like the rhythm of the street.

The economic recovery is not nearly as robust as hoped, the unemployment rate remains stubbornly high, and the President's approval rate is plummeting. He is speaking now from Galesburg, Illinois, telling the country how he's going to cut the deficit and strengthen the middle class. But none of us believe it.

I'm watching the "breaking news" speech with my father, but he doesn't understand it. He used to, of course. But he was diagnosed with Alzheimer's eight months ago, and I am now his primary caregiver. Every morning we watch *The Today Show* together. And every morning before he sits down to his breakfast of oatmeal and fruit, he walks up to the blue skull painting that I hung nicely above the fireplace. He stands there for a long moment in his gray sweatpants and dark blue cardigan, arms crossed, shaking his head in wonder. And he says the same thing every time: "Boy, that Jimmy sure is talented. How's he doing?"

And I always respond, "He's doing fine, Dad. Real fine."

"That's good. I sure hope he makes it one day."

"I hope so too, Dad," I say. "I really do."

Then he sits down at his TV dinner tray, the same tray I used to eat on while watching *Star Trek* back in 1968. And I watch him eat, the oatmeal sticking to the corners of his mouth, and I swell with pride. It's such a joy, and a pleasure, and an *honor* to be here for him.

Sometimes I take him down to the Fraternal Order of the Eagles and show him his picture as past president. "Hey, Dad," I say, "do you remember this handsome guy?" And you can see the lights are off, but I swear to God he never fails to crack a smile. Then his pal Bernie—who's afflicted with the same horrible disease and now thinks he's a ball boy for the Dodgers—saunters over to my father, and they meet again for the very first time.

And I told myself I'm not going to lecture. Not going to preach or be that guy. But goddamn. We can do better. Because my story is your story. You're not a brand, you're a flawed human. Not a commodity, or a machine to be used and discarded. Help each other.

Chop wood, carry water.

What else is there?

I RETURNED TO the Wilshire Arms only once. I stood in the alley for what seemed like an eternity, toeing pebbles and staring at the paint flecks in the concrete. The neighbors must have thought I was just another bum looking for a fix.

I studied the building's expanse of beige stucco, feeling distant and remote, as if I'd never stepped foot in the neighborhood before. I remember I wanted to see inside the Artist's apartment, I don't know why. But when I knocked on the front door, a young blond woman with a UCLA sweatshirt answered. I told her what I wanted and she politely declined and shut the door. Who could blame her? After all, I was the same crazy old bald guy who'd beat the shit out of a news rack. But I did catch a glimpse of the inside. It had been stripped down, remodeled, modernized, and sanitized into some chic, sparse, Ikea-like box—airy and unrecognizable in every way. I felt nothing. No character.

That's what the Artist used to say. How he couldn't believe they were tearing down the old post office, or some other historic building. "*Community over commodity!*" That was his rallying cry. Then I'd quietly remind him that Los Angeles doesn't care who you are, what you are, or how long you've lived here. She will always sell you out to the highest bidder. That's just the way it is.

One thing is for certain, my selfish nostalgia trips are over. I no longer pine for the life I used to have. When somebody asks me, "Do you remember when?" I say, "No, no, I don't." Because there is only what we hold dear today. There is no time for sloppy thinking. And when people try to tell me how to live my life, or ask me, "Don't you want it all?" again I say, "No, I don't." I don't have to play that game anymore. I've earned the right to live on less. It took me a while to get here, but I've finally arrived at who I want to be.

Who I am.

An expanded man.

THE OTHER DAY I had a meeting down by LAX. I was cruising north on Sepulveda listening to John Lennon's "Watching the Wheels" when I decided to take the coastal route home, catch the sunset up on the bluffs of Palisades Park.

Our old stomping ground.

Not a day goes by that I don't think about the Artist. About all the great conversations we had. It's not easy finding someone to talk to, much less someone who'll listen to what you have to say. And if you do find someone like that, hang on to him. Because it's easy to take friends for granted.

As if by magic, I found a parking spot on Ocean that day. I strolled across the wide seaside avenue and entered the park, a warm Santa Ana breeze ruffling the back of my denim shirt. The evening was glorious, the twilight a tourist's dream. I leaned forward on the concrete railing and stared out at the bright and shining sea. I heard seagulls crying, and palm trees clacking, and then I thought I heard his voice in the wind.

If you'd been an outsider looking at me, you would've seen a contemplative, unremarkable middle-aged man looking at the ocean and talking to himself. But oh, inside my head!

"What do you think about the Dodgers this year? You think that new kid can save them?"

"He's looking pretty good. Kind of a prima donna, though. But it's still early in the season."

"Prima donna? Who cares! The guy runs like Mantle and hits like Sasquatch!"

I chuckled out loud. Just two dudes shooting the bull. I miss him every day.

I inhaled a deep breath of salt air and looked off into the pink sunset. I thought back to when the Artist tried to show me Sagittarius in the clouds.

I wondered if I could find it now, my eyes circling the sky. For a long while I studied cloud shapes, formations and conglomerations, searching through endless piles of salmon-and-orange-hued cotton balls. I saw everything but the Archer.

The scales of Libra.

A snow angel with a broken wing.

Polar bears and alligator lizards.

But I still couldn't find it. So I put a hand up to my ear and listened to the wind.

"You have to look for the arrow first."

"I can't see it."

"It's right there."

"Where?"

"There."

And this time I saw it—Sagittarius the Archer, half man, half horse, rising up through a pale red sky. Its bow and arrow outstretched across its majestic body, shooting from the hip.

Just like the Artist, I thought.

For a long moment I stared at its splendid form. Then the wind shifted, and the sky moved, and I realized the arrow was now aimed at me. Before I could blink, it struck me. Somewhere deep, close to the bone.

I shoved my hands into my pants pockets and shivered in the late-evening light. In the distance, the Ferris wheel spun by the sea, and the sounds of construction vibrated between the surf and the city.

ACKNOWLEDGEMENTS

LET ME START by saying that no cats were harmed in the writing of this story. I'm not sure how cats entered into my creative process, but they did. Maybe I'm a cat person and don't know it.

Anyway, I couldn't have done this book alone. I had a team of outstanding publishing professionals to help bring it out into the world.

I believe the reader deserves the very best from an author, so I aim for as high a quality a publication as possible.

With that being said, finding a good team is never easy. It reminds me of a song by Three 6 Mafia, "It's Hard Out Here for a Pimp."

But I got lucky. From editorial to design, these are the kind folks who made it all happen. Thanks to my early readers, especially Danelle McCafferty and NY Book Editors. Your professionalism and invaluable insight was much appreciated.

To my developmental and line editor, James Morgan, the guy who did all the heavy lifting, thanks for working your magic and shaping this book. A hearty thanks to Kira Rubenthaler at Bookfly Design for her outstanding copyediting and on point suggestions. It's always a pleasure working with you. Thanks to my highly skilled and enthusiastic copyeditor and proofreader, Eliza Dee. I appreciate your honest feedback. And as always, a big thank you to my proofreader Donna Rich for her final manuscript polish.

My father was fond of saying, "first impressions count." Thanks to David Gee for his brilliant cover design, and for showing the world my best impression. To Colleen at Ampersand Book Interiors, thanks for your formatting expertise, your attention to detail, and making the interior of the novel shine. More to come.

And finally, thanks to all my friends who had to endure the countless questions on cover images, titles, and bits of dialogue.

Your help was money.

About the Author

HARLIN HAILEY WAS born in New Orleans and educated at the University of Southern California. Free of vampires, shapeshifters, and werewolves, he writes contemporary adult fiction set in the modern world. Dark humor, a strong social undercurrent, and music and pop culture references often characterize his work. In another life, he has pounded the pavement for corporate America, guest DJ'd on the "World Famous" KROQ radio station, and dabbled in the exciting field of no-money-down real estate. He is the author of the award-winning novel, The Downsizing of Hudson Foster. He lives in Los Angeles.

IF YOU ENJOYED the book, please consider leaving a positive review. It is the fuel that keeps all indie authors running.

. . . . • • •

THE AUTHOR WELCOMES all comments, rants, typo sightings, suggestions, and queries from rabid fans who want the skinny on his upcoming releases. He can be reached at:

HARLINHAILEY@GMAIL.COM

Made in United States
North Haven, CT
10 March 2024

49787299R00268